THE CHOICE

By Kathleen Sprout

PROVERB PRESS

The Choice

ISBN-13 978-0-9833964-1-3
ISBN-10 0983396418

Cover Image ©Saimnadir / Dreamstime.com

DEDICATION

This story would not have been possible without the help and encouragement of author Bonnie Blythe. Thank you, Bonnie for prodding me all the way to publication. Also a special thank you goes to my special friend, Kathy Kramer who so patiently answered my questions about diabetes. Thank you also, to those who critiqued this manuscript along the way. Your advice only made this story better. A special thanks to Mom who is not anything like Maude. Last, but not least, thank you, Lord, for sending me encouragers and prayer partners for this writing journey.

Chapter One

Maude's Journal
August 15th 2009

    After all these years, I'm homeless. I have to get far away from here. There's no choice. I'm going to go live with Sandra and her daughter. The least she can do after I raised her is take me in.

***

I couldn't help but grin as I stood on the porch watching the real estate agent pound the stake of the for-sale sign into my manicured lawn. After eighteen years of living in neighborhoods full of traditional families and raising Cammie on my own, freedom loomed just around the corner.

The Realtor, Mort, practically guaranteed the house would sell within a month. And why wouldn't it? I'd broken every fingernail on both hands just keeping up with the yard work till I was forced to get the glue-on nails for going out in public. Now it was time for me. Seattle waited only sixty-five miles away along with a brand new job, a significant pay raise, good benefits, and three weeks paid vacation. Once I passed a routine background check, I would be an official employee of the Federal Bureau of Investigation.

"That's it for the day, Sandy." Mort waggled his hammer in the air. "The ad with photos will be on the Internet by tomorrow morning, and I'll be bringing potential buyers around by the end of this week."

I closed the door. Closed it on life in the suburbs, and closed it on a life of telling half-truths regarding Cammie's father. Thanks to the small savings I'd managed to accumulate and Cammie's college scholarship, she'd be off to the university soon to pursue a degree in marine biology. I'll be free. On my own, for the first time in my life.

My arms tingled, sending cool shivers along their length, in contrast with the August mugginess. My new place would have air-conditioning. And maybe a pool and clubhouse to relax in after a hard day at my new job.

The doorbell rang. Had the Realtor forgotten something? Opening the front door, I almost didn't recognize the skinny woman standing on the step surrounded by suitcases. This woman with the thinning gray hair sticking out every which-way looked three steps away from the homeless shelter. In the edge of my vision, a yellow cab pulled away from the curb.

My throat tightened, nearly choking me. "Mother? What are you doing here?"

My mother picked up one of the smaller bags and pushed past me into the living room. "I've left your father, the old coot. I'm going to live with you and Camellia."

I caught my breath. How could I get my mother out of there before Cammie saw her? There was no way I would ever allow her to get her hooks into my daughter. Or for that matter, me again.

I grabbed my purse and car keys. "I'm taking you to a hotel."

"Mom? Who's here?" My daughter's voice came from deep in another part of the house. "Is it Teddy?"

"It's nobody you know, Cammie," I called over my shoulder. "I've got to go out for a while. You can reach me on my cell if you need me." Grasping my mother's elbow, I steered her back toward the front door.

"Stop pushing me around, Sandra." She yanked her arm away, with surprising strength for a woman her age.

"Who are you talking to?" Cammie's voice neared.

Too late to give in to an urge to push my mother out onto the porch, I turned to see my daughter enter the room.

2

My mother advanced on her and enveloped her in a huge bear hug. My mouth fell open as I observed this uncharacteristic behavior unfold before me. She had never hugged me. Ever. No, she was more likely to lie in wait and pounce on me like a venomous rattler.

Cammie's widened eyes peered over my mother's shoulder as she moved to release herself from this total stranger's arms.

"Camellia. My granddaughter. I would have known you anywhere. I'm Maude, your grandmother." My mother made it sound as if she'd been searching for Cammie forever. Feelings I hadn't acknowledged since I was a teenager coursed through me like the stench of week-old cooked cabbage. Musty, heavy, and unpleasant. A stark contrast to the sunny, airy home I'd made for my daughter.

"Mother." I tried to keep from gritting my teeth. "You can't just barge in here, unannounced, and uninvited, expecting we'll be able to entertain guests."

My mother paid little attention to me, but instead seized Cammie by the shoulders, twirling her around as if she had every right to touch my child. "I see myself in you."

"Not a fat chance," I muttered under my breath.

"You're my grandmother?" Cammie's face didn't quite break into a welcoming smile, but threatened to unless I quickly intervened.

"Cammie," I said in what I hoped would be a firm enough tone. "There seems to be some kind of family emergency. Why don't you go finish what you were doing while I get this sorted out?"

"Emergency nothing." My mother predictably turned and pierced my self worth with a simple stare. "I'm here for a visit. A nice long visit, while I get my career as a best-selling author off the ground."

Cammie fixed her gaze on me. "Why didn't you tell me my grandmother was coming to visit? We could have gotten the spare room ready for her."

"The spare room is full of boxes from the attic."

3

My mother made an offhand waving motion in the air. "I don't need anything fancy. Just a bed and a desk where I can put a typewriter."

"Grandma, nobody uses a typewriter anymore. But you can use my computer when I'm not using it." My daughter's face lit up at the prospect of teaching someone how to use her computer.

"Cammie!" The situation was fast getting out of hand. "She can go to a hotel. We're in the middle of packing and moving. Or did you forget?"

"How could I forget? I'm about to be ripped away from all my friends and now you're trying to deny me the chance to get to know my grandmother." Cammie's eyes welled up with tears.

"Sandra, I'm shocked you'd abuse my only granddaughter this way." Even though I towered over my mother by at least four inches, she managed to look down her nose at me. That was the proverbial last straw.

"You're a fine one to speak of abuse." I couldn't hold it in any longer.

Cammie flinched. She'd never heard me use that tone of voice. A new awareness entered my daughter's eyes. A watchfulness, as if I might go berserk and suddenly start tossing furniture around the room. Before Cammie's fears of my head spinning around like a possessed person became a reality, she grabbed her grandmother's suitcase and marched down the hall toward her room.

"Come on, Grandma, you can have my room and I'll sleep on the couch."

Without even looking at me, my mother followed her out of the room. My face burned. How could Cammie be so dense? Didn't she realize there was a good reason she hadn't seen her grandmother before? Couldn't she figure out what an inconvenience company would be right now? Not to mention the fact everything could be ruined. All my plans for the future as well as the carefully constructed stories of my life before Cammie.

Cammie's chatter drifted down the hall. My hands clenched into fists and pounded against my thighs. What kind of demented thinking caused my mother to travel clear across the country to stay with a daughter she'd clearly written off eighteen years ago? And to leave behind her marriage of nearly fifty years?

What could Daddy have done to cause this? All he'd ever done was sit in his worn-out recliner hiding behind his paper, never daring to lift his voice to my mother. Still . . . he might be able to shed some light on the situation.

Determined to head off a disaster, I pulled my address book out of the drawer of the phone stand and flipped through till I found my parents' number. Punching in the nearly forgotten area code and other digits, I listened to the repeated rings on the other end. No answer. Of course my mother wouldn't have dreamed of investing in an answering machine. I placed the receiver back in its cradle.

Who could help me out of this mess? My mind raced through the list of my few friends and acquaintances. Not one of them would understand the seriousness of my problem. If they knew all there was to know about me, they'd immediately grasp why I didn't need this complication in my life right now. And face it. My mother was decidedly more than a little complication. She was probably bent on destroying Cammie's life the same way she nearly had mine. Instead, it looked as if I was the one who would be cast as the villainess.

The more I thought about it, the more I feared I wouldn't be able to force my mother out. She and Cammie would fight me all the way. The key would be to somehow keep them apart.

Cammie reappeared. "Mom? Could you bring in Grandma's other baggage? I'm going to change the sheets on my bed and move some of my things out of the closet."

"Sure." My legs felt like fifty-pound sandbags were attached to them as I walked to the front porch to get the suitcases. Now I was becoming an accomplice to my own destruction. Maybe I should throw a huge Welcome to My Home party . . . invite the neighborhood in. That should make both of them happy.

I bent to pick up the largest bag and the handle came off in my hand. Since to my knowledge, my parents never vacationed, I could only assume the old, ratty hard-sided bag had come from a thrift store. Whatever she had brought with her weighed enough to give a grown man a hernia. How was I supposed to bring it in the house? For sure, my mother hadn't carried it to the porch. The cab driver must have unloaded it for her. I squatted down and pushed it across the threshold of the front door. Just one more delight I could record in my memory.

"Be careful with that." Her irritating voice cut through my grunts and groans as I heaved the second bag next to the first one. "You never did show respect for my possessions."

"Would that be the pot calling . . . ?"

Cammie appeared again just as I was ready to invite my mother to take her bags and herself back outside again. "Let me help. Gran brought all her diaries with her and they're probably too heavy for you."

"I'm not some over-the-hill weakling who can't do a simple job. And since when do you address someone you've just met as *'Gran?'* She is your grandmother, not one of your girlfriends." I glared at my mother who stood behind Cammie with a satisfied smirk on her face. She wasn't going to be content until she drove a wedge between us. Just the way she had with Daddy and me.

"No need to get snippy." My mother sniffed, "I invited Camelia to call me Gran. It's a term of affection, you know. And that seems to be in short supply around here."

Oh gag me with a ladle. What my mother knew about affection could fit in a gnat's ear with room left over for her to flap her bat wings around. And my daughter was falling for her rhetoric, all because she wanted a big family. Maybe I should have given into Cammie's wishes, and married

6

Charlie years ago. The only problem with that scenario was I didn't love him. Not the way I had loved Cammie's father. Charlie loved me, though. But would that be enough to build a marriage on? Not. Not even to give my daughter a family. Why couldn't she be satisfied with the life she and I had?

"Cammie, take the smaller bag to your room. Mother, you stay here. We need to talk." Cammie did as she was told, but I could see by the look on her face she didn't want to be left out of the conversation. She probably didn't trust me alone with her grandmother.

"What do you wish to speak to me about, Sandra?" My mother made herself comfortable on my chintz easy chair.

I sat across from her and steeled for what was to come. I'd only stood up to her one other time, but when she tried to make me back down, I'd run away instead of holding my ground. Was I finally adult enough to assert myself? After all, this was my home, my daughter, and my future.

"Since you're already here, I guess you can stay for a couple of days. However, there are a few rules you need to be familiar with." I hoped my mother would balk and leave.

"Rules? Come now, Sandra. Remember whom you're addressing." She sat a little taller in the chair, her gaze never wavering from mine.

I ignored her posturing. "First of all, I don't know what happened between you and Daddy, but I will not have you criticize him in front of Cammie."

"Oh bother. The girl is old enough to hear the truth. He's a spineless-"

"Mother, let me finish, please. Secondly, I will not allow you to undermine my role as Cammie's mother. You are a visitor here. I insist you to respect that in my home."

"I can't imagine what you're talking about." Her lips tightened into a thin line.

"Thirdly, you need to understand that this will be a short visit. I'm in the process of selling our home and there will be potential buyers coming in and out. Cammie and I have a lot of packing to do. We can't be distracted by the need to entertain anyone. I'm sorry if this sounds harsh, but you couldn't have come at a worse time. Do you understand?"

My mother stood and looked around my living room. "I understand perfectly. Although I can't imagine what my granddaughter will think if you push a helpless old woman out on the street."

Helpless as a pack of wolves. As if I didn't have enough to worry about with Cammie and Teddy getting so serious, now I'd have to continually monitor what went on in my own home.

"Nobody's pushing you into the street. When your little visit is over, I'll do whatever I can to assist you in returning home to Daddy." *I'll buy her a first class plane ticket if that's what it takes.*

She took a step toward me, freezing me with the full force of her glare. "I will not be going back there, so you can forget that notion."

My face grew hotter. "What exactly happened between you and Daddy?"

"I don't intend on discussing it with you, young lady. Perhaps when my book is published you can read all about it."

Had my mother totally gone nutso? "You don't know anything about writing a book. You can't even type, can you?"

"My granddaughter will teach me. And writing a book will be easy. I've always planned to do it someday. All I have to do is organize my journals and cut out the boring parts."

My mother looked at me as if I were the dense one.

"And, I plan on making enough money so I won't have to be put in the position of staying where I'm not welcome."

"That could be never. I'm sure writing a novel is not all that easy."

8

"Disparage me all you want. I've seen lots of authors on Oprah and other programs. All I'll have to do is get somebody important to read it, and it'll become a best seller. You'll see."

In view of her big plans, I had visions of my mother living with me forever. Leaving her home all those years ago had been easy. How easy would it be to get her to leave mine? "Let's just call Daddy and see if we can smooth over whatever fight you've had." I reached for the phone.

My mother postured like a cougar ready to pounce. "I forbid you to call your father. He has no say in this."

I sucked in my breath. Clearly, this had been more than a little spat. I backed away from the phone before she exploded all over my cozy little living room. There was clearly no choice but to call him after everyone had gone to bed.

I didn't have long to wait. My mother pleaded travel fatigue, went to Cammie's room and closed the door right after the dinner I hastily threw together. I escaped to my bedroom and dialed the number I'd looked up earlier. Ten rings later, I hung up. Where could he be? It had to be at least 9 PM in Detroit.

I killed time for the next hour, buffing out the skid marks in the hall left by Cammie when she scooted the heaviest suitcase to her room. She had settled onto the couch studying what I assumed was her Sunday school lesson plan for the first through third graders she taught every week. No doubt that was another indication of how she missed having other children around.

After brewing myself a cup of chamomile tea, which was advertised as guaranteed to relax me, I called my parents' number again. Still no answer. Something was really wrong. Daddy had always been a homebody. He couldn't have changed that much over the years. Why wasn't he answering the phone? Disappointment and concern offset any soothing effects of the tea. Too many changes threatened to upset my orderly existence. I didn't like it. Not one bit.

Chapter Two

Maude's Journal
June 1958

> *Tonight is my high-school graduation. I'll be joining my classmates on stage wearing the cap and gown I rented with my babysitting money. Mom and Aunt Louise will be there. Dad won't. Big surprise. He wouldn't dream of tearing himself away from his buddies at the racetrack or tavern long enough to attend the ceremony. Everything always seems to come ahead of me where he's concerned. Unless Mom's not around to be his punching bag. Then he actually looks at me long enough to call me names. I have a job lined up now that I'm graduating, and as soon as I get my first paycheck, I'm gone. Mom can come with me or not. It's her choice. She'll choose him though, like always. She tells me all the time that her Bible says it's the wife's responsibility to be submissive. I guess that means the church wants women to be doormats or even get beat up on occasion. That's why I'll never go to church or marry a man who believes that way.*

***

Breakfast on Saturday mornings had always been special for Cammie and me. It was our chance to catch up on all the previous week's happenings. We usually cooked together, taking turns with whatever main dish we'd decided on. Cammie's specialty was a cheese omelet with lots of salsa on the side, and mine was homemade cinnamon rolls.

With the unexpected arrival of my mother, I didn't get a chance to set the dough out to rise the night before so we'd have to make do with toast. Cammie was usually in the kitchen by the time I had the coffee brewing. In fact,

Cammie trying to beat me to the stove was kind of a running joke between us. However, Cammie's voice drifting down the hall let me know she'd chosen to go in to visit with her grandmother instead. My stomach knotted, sending a wave of resentment through me. My mother had managed to ruin my weekend. I had hoped to drive Cammie to Seattle so I could show her the condo I wanted. Somehow, I didn't see my mother's presence as helpful. I didn't trust her in my home without me there, either, so we would stay home.

I opened the refrigerator, hoping to spot something easy to fix without resorting to frozen waffles. Cammie's laughter set my teeth on edge. This was no time to be laughing. Didn't she know my entire schedule was being thrown off? I shoved the door closed. They could just subsist on dry cereal and a banana for all I cared.

I pulled some bowls out of the cupboard and set the table. The brightly colored breakfast place mats and matching napkins would be wasted on my mother but habit dictated I use them. Still no sign of Cammie, even with all the clattering around I did.

One more time, I went to the phone to call my dad. Once again the phone rang repeatedly.

"Mother!" I hollered down the hall. "Did you even *tell* Daddy you were leaving?" I pictured my dad out looking for her . . . checking the hospitals, scouring the neighborhood. Worrying.

Two pairs of footsteps echoed down the hall. My mother came into view first. "There's no need to shout."

My jaw tightened of its own volition. I hoped I never used that condescending tone of voice with *my* daughter. Thankfully Cammie was not one of those teenagers who delighted in seeing her mother disrespected. However, if she kept hanging around the wrong kind of people, namely my mother, some of the attitude was bound to rub off on her.

12

"I was just telling Gran about our special Saturday morning breakfasts." Cammie's voice trailed off as she surveyed the table with the cardboard boxes of wheat and bran cereals displayed prominently in the middle.

I suppressed the explanation that there was no sense making our guest feel too special. If we did, she might decide to move in with us permanently. A shiver raced down my spine at the very thought.

"Why Sandra, you remembered my favorite bran cereal. How thoughtful."

Was there a tinge of sarcasm in my mother's voice? It certainly wasn't like her to dish out a compliment.

They seated themselves at the table, leaving me to get out the two-percent. I then busied myself at the sink to avoid sitting with them. The bananas skins were dotted with dark brown bruises but I silently dared anyone to complain.

Cammie bowed her head as she usually did and whispered a short blessing over the food. I wondered what my mother thought about that. She never had put much stock in religion. I always tried my best to support Cammie's beliefs, grateful she had chosen to run with the church crowd rather than any of the gang of kids who drank and partied every weekend.

I stole a glance at my mother who stared at Cammie like she'd just announced aliens were in the backyard. Yep. Nothing had changed. Her facial expression matched her outfit, a gray cardigan over a plain dress, which hung on her as if it were two sizes too large. The entire ugly outfit looked out of place in my colorful breakfast nook. When she reached for the milk, I could see a hole in the sleeve of her sweater. Had my parents fallen on hard times? Is this why my mother left?

"Mother, you never answered my question."

She answered without looking at me. "What question?"

"Does Daddy know you're here? Why don't you call him and let him know you arrived safely?"

13

"I'll thank you to mind your own business, Sandra." Once again her voice held more than a suggestion that she was speaking to an errant child.

I glanced at Cammie to see what she thought about her grandmother's rudeness, but she seemed busy studying the wheat flakes in her cereal bowl. I didn't want to launch a full-scale war in front of my daughter. But how was I going to avoid it? I needed to figure out a way to get them apart and keep them apart.

The phone rang and my hope soared, thinking it would be my dad. When I was a girl he was always able to give me good advice so we could both keep the peace with my mother. How long had it been since I'd even heard the sound of his voice? The few times I'd used the poor judgment to call, my mother had inevitably answered the phone and I was lucky if she passed the phone to him when I asked.

I banged my hip on the corner of the kitchen counter in my haste to pick up the call. "Hello?"

"Good morning! Morty here. I have good news!" The real estate agent's voice was not what I wanted to hear. However, any good news would have been very welcome about then.

"What is it?"

"We've already got some bites from the Internet ad I put up last night. I'm bringing a young couple around this morning who are looking for a starter home."

Starter home? He didn't need to remind me I didn't exactly live on the Street of Dreams. Was it his way to get back at me for snubbing his dinner invitations? The tract home was the best I could do, raising Cammie alone. And it was nearly the nicest kept house in the neighborhood. As anxious as I was to leave, I felt defensive about what he said. As if he were describing my home the way my mother probably viewed it.

"I guess that would be okay." Maybe my mother would be forced to see what an inopportune time it was to visit. "What time will you be here?"

"We'll be there in about twenty minutes. We're just now leaving the office. I ordinarily wouldn't bring them when you were home, but they are from out-of-state, anxious to buy, and have cash. And I don't have to remind you . . . no dishes in the sink, newspapers lying around, no clutter."

"I think I can figure out what to do." The man was really beginning to annoy me. I hung up and took a good look around. "We have potential buyers coming to look at the house this morning. Cammie, as soon as you finish your breakfast, please put away the blanket and pillow you left on the sofa. And mother, would you put your suitcases out of sight in Cammie's closet?"

Cammie finally looked up from her cereal. "We took care of that this morning. I cleared out a couple of dresser drawers and half the closet in my room so Gran would have a place to put away her things."

I rubbed the place on my hip where I'd banged it on the counter. It felt like a bruise had already formed. Just like the bruise spreading on my agenda. What would be next? Would Cammie paint my mother's name on the mailbox? What was happening to my life? My mother had been here less than twenty-four hours and already I was starting to view Cammie as the enemy too.

"Fine. I'll clean up the kitchen and refresh the potpourri."

"Is that what I smell?" My mother wrinkled her nose. "Have you forgotten that I hate flowery smells? People die from allergies, you know! I guess I'll just stay in my room—"

"Cammie's room," I interrupted.

"And work on my novel. I've already found my starting place."

"People expect a home that smells nice, Mother. Can you take a Benadryl or something? There's some in the

15

bathroom medicine cabinet. And I'll keep the potpourri at this end of the house."

My mother didn't sound all that excited about her new book writing project. Not when she could stay in the kitchen and torture me. She sniffed and gave me that look, which let me know how I was inconveniencing her. However, having her behind closed doors and out of sight was not such a bad idea.

"I'll make sure these people only take a quick look into Cammie's room so we won't disturb you." I'm sure my voice projected annoyance.

"Thank you." She stood and stomped off, leaving half of her cereal and the week old banana untouched.

I gave Cammie a slight smile and shrugged my shoulders but only met with her accusing stare. That look made me ache. Never before had I felt so separated from my daughter. Yet here we were, on opposite sides of the issue of her grandmother's visit. We might as well have been on opposite sides of the country. And there was no way I could explain away the force of my feelings toward my mother to her. It would require the revelation of too many things. Painful things.

I turned away so I'd no longer have to look into her eyes. Once my mother was gone, I was sure life would go back to normal. But how long would that take?

Cammie rinsed out her bowl and put it in the dishwasher. Without uttering a word, she left the room.

I slumped down into one of my highly polished oak kitchen chairs. My mother had already put her stamp of doom on it. Cammie was all I had, and a rift had formed between us. What would our lives be like in another week? Scalding tears tried to force their way to the surface, but I fought them back. At least I could control them.

Looking around the cozy country kitchen I'd worked so hard to decorate, the colorful curtains and matching cushions on the chairs . . . they all mocked me. Would I ever be able to define my life away from the misery I'd grown up with? The last eighteen years might as well have not happened. I was right back under my mother's influence. All I had to do was recall some of the horrible thoughts I'd been having since the evening before, to prove myself correct.

If only I had someone to confide in. Someone who wouldn't judge me or turn away. But I had no one like that. How could I? I'd held myself apart from close relationships all these years. In some part to protect Cammie, and if the truth were known, partly to protect my own reputation.

The doorbell jerked me from my thoughts. I stood and arranged the chairs around the table, then hurried to the front door.

The young couple with Mort seemed pleasant enough. They followed him around while he pointed out various features of the house. I tried to stay out of their way as much as possible, even though our small three-bedroom place didn't allow much room for keeping out of sight.

The phone rang and I picked it up, grateful for the distraction. "Hello?"

"Sandy? Charlie here. Is everything all right? You sound funny." My friend's familiar voice calmed me somewhat.

"I'm fine. The Realtor is here with someone looking at the house is all."

"Boy, lady, you aren't wasting any time are you?" His voice was laced with disappointment.

"Charlie, I've been telling you for over a year now that I'd be moving away. That I've accepted a new job already. I'm only waiting for the background check to be completed and I'll know the starting date and can give notice here."

"I know. I just keep hoping you'll change your mind and stay."

"I won't be more than an hour away. Two hours at most depending on where I live."

"You can't deny we won't be seeing nearly as much of each other. My offer still stands, you know."

17

I tried to silence my sigh of guilt mixed with exasperation. If there had been the tiniest spark between us, I might have considered his marriage proposal for Cammie's sake. Instead, Charlie settled for being a frequent companion and friend. I, on the other hand, was perfectly content without an extra person around to try and please.

"I have company here now. Is there something special you called me about?"

"I'd hoped I could come around and take my two best girls out to breakfast."

"We've already eaten." The memory of the farce of a family meal stabbed at my growling stomach.

"Oh." He paused, obviously waiting for an invite over anyway.

I wondered if I could possibly find an ally in Charlie. Without giving him a detailed explanation of my history with my parents? It was worth a shot. "Why don't you drop by a little later?"

A commotion in the hallway drowned out his answer. I turned to see the young couple making a beeline for my front door with Mort huffing and puffing behind them. He shot me a dirty look before closing the door behind him.

Forgetting about Charlie, I dropped the phone in its cradle and charged down the hall to my daughter's room. "What on earth happened in here?"

My mother looked at me with a satisfied half-smirk on her face.

"Answer me! And where's Cammie?"

"Sandra, you're shrieking again."

"I am not shrieking!" I could feel my eyes bulge out with the force of my anger behind them.

"My granddaughter excused herself to go to the bathroom. Is there a problem?"

"What do you mean, *is there a problem*? Those people stormed out of the house like they'd seen a rat. What did you say to them?"

I watched her draw herself up into what normally would be an intimidating pose. However, she misjudged the strength of my temper.

"Well?" My hands curled into tight fists and perched on my hips. I waited to hear what she'd said to blow the potential sale of my house.

"I merely answered their questions. And I'd appreciate it if you didn't take that tone with me. I'd hoped you'd matured over the years and would know how to speak like a lady."

I thought of all kinds of unladylike things to say to her, but my jaws were clenched so tight I couldn't manage to spit anything out. She continued to look down her imperious nose at me and didn't offer any further explanation.

I left Cammie's room, slamming the door behind me. That's when I remembered I'd hung up on Charlie. I quickly called his number but got his machine. He'd either already left for my place or he was nursing hurt feelings and screening his calls.

I tossed a load of clothes in the washer while I waited for the next irksome event to happen. I didn't have to wait long.

"Sandra, I'd like a word with you, please." My mother had evidently grown weary of writing her 'great American novel' and had discovered some new way to get my blood boiling.

"Spit it out, Mother."

"I couldn't help noticing you've allowed Cammie to flaunt her misguided beliefs around. I can only hope she doesn't act like a fanatic outside of this house."

"What on earth are you referring to?" If I'd wondered how long it would take my mother to find something wrong with Cammie, I no longer had to guess.

"I think you know. The praying. The religious books all over her room. She even has a picture on her wall with some kind of verse on it." She pressed her lips together. "I taught you better than to believe all that nonsense. It's nothing but superstition and an excuse for men to dominate women. I'd hoped you'd pass the same wisdom on to your child."

"I fail to see how Cammie's faith in God affects you. Are you afraid you won't be able to sleep with all those things in the room? Perhaps you should rethink your decision to stay here."

As I waited for her to respond, I was struck by the incongruity of my mother standing there all pious looking and complaining about Cammie's choices.

"Well, if you won't guide her properly, I'll just have to."

"You won't do anything of the kind." I deliberately kept my voice to a loud whisper in order to keep from screaming. "She has a right to believe whatever she likes."

My mother's eyes changed from a squinty glare to opening wide in mock horror. "Don't tell me you're into that junk too." She nodded her head from side to side. "That's why you're defending her." She shook her finger at me. "You're one of those Jesus freaks. No wonder you've been hiding out here, a thousand miles from home."

"Mother!" I strained to keep my anger under control. "I left home because you gave me no other choice. It had nothing to do with church and you know it."

"You'll be sorry. You should never leave some church in charge of instilling their dangerous ideas in your daughter. You're shirking your responsibilities as a parent."

I couldn't believe we were having that conversation. My mother, of all people giving me a lecture on raising my daughter? And most ludicrous of all, speaking of values? The only values my mother had were a huge long list of everything and everybody she disapproved of.

My mother snorted. "I'm right, aren't I?"

Suddenly everything seemed turned on its head. Here I was, defending church when the most I'd ever attended was Christmas, Easter, and any special programs Cammie was

20

involved in. It wasn't as though I was against religion. I merely didn't see its relevance in my life. Now, the entire subject was becoming another source of conflict in my home.

"No, you are not right. And I remind you again, you are a guest here, and if you don't wish to pack up right now, you will start butting out of our lives."

She moved a step closer and shook her index finger in my face. "Don't blame me if your daughter ruins her life just like you did."

"My life is just fine. Cammie is fine." It occurred to me that I'd stumbled upon one of my mother's hot buttons and if I pushed it hard enough, she'd go home where she belonged.

"Cammie's future is only beginning. If you don't control her she will make the wrong decisions."

"Stop wagging your finger at me. Cammie is nearly a grown woman. I wouldn't dream of trying to control her. Isn't that what you're trying to do to me? Control? It's not working. Now if you'll excuse me, I need to see if my clothes are ready for church tomorrow. Perhaps you'd like to go with us?"

While I watched my mother sputter I wondered what I'd gotten myself into. Cammie and whoever the current pastor was would surely die of shock if I showed up. However, I couldn't think of a better way to put Cammie and me on the same side of the growing contention between her grandmother and me.

Chapter Three

Maude's Journal
January 1959

I'm finally in my very own apartment. It's so cool! I thought this day would never come. I wanted to move out months ago but Mom got sick with cancer, I couldn't very well leave her. I'm glad I stayed. Now she's gone and at least I had those last few months with her. I hate to think of her trying to cope with Dad's drinking and temper by herself. He even showed up drunk at the funeral. There's no reason to stay anymore. I hope I never see him again. If I ever marry, it won't be to a drunkard and wife beater. How sad to come to the end of your life and there's nobody left who cares about you. Now that I'm on my own and I don't have my dad looking over my shoulder, I'll start dating. I know exactly who I'll get to ask me out. Of course he's too shy, so I'll do the asking. That way I can pick the time and place.

***

It was a relief when my mother stomped back down the hall to Cammie's room. I hated fighting. Almost as much as I hated unplanned events.

A sigh escaped me as I considered all the chores I needed to attend to. For starters, I needed to call Mort and smooth things over with him. He probably would be out all morning though, taking his clients around to see other places. I wanted a fast sale on my place. I planned to send earnest money to the Realtor who listed the condo I had my heart set on, just as soon as I knew I had a firm offer on my house. Even if my house didn't close right away, I could afford to make double mortgage payments for a couple of months.

Then I wanted to come up with a logical explanation for attending church the next day with Cammie. She'd given up asking me long ago and would probably fall over in a dead faint. But I almost desperately looked forward to the opportunity to get some alone time with her. On the other hand, I wondered what would happen if I insisted my mother come with us. Would she run for the hills? Better yet, would she go home?

In the meantime, I still had gobs of packing to attend to. Cammie stayed out of sight the rest of the morning. I could only assume she was avoiding me. My pride wouldn't allow me to beg her to come out and spend Saturday morning with me. I could only imagine what kind of garbage my mother was filling her head with.

Charlie arrived a little before noon with a bag full of deli sandwiches and chips. As soon as I saw him, I could feel tears well up in my eyes. Even though there wasn't a spark of electricity between us, he was still the kindest person I knew. He had been there for me many times over the years of our friendship.

The sound of his baritone voice cheered me. "I thought you could use a break from your packing. I know I haven't been very supportive of your decision to move, and I'd like to make it up to you somehow."

"Oh, Charlie," I sighed. "If you only knew how welcome you are. Let's put these goodies in the kitchen, and I'll catch you up on the latest news."

"You sounded a little strained on the phone. I hope your news isn't bad." He plopped the bag on the kitchen table and removed the individually wrapped subs. He'd even included a half dozen huge macadamia nut cookies I loved.

"It's bad all right." I pulled some glasses from the cupboard and set them around the table. "It seems I have an uninvited houseguest, just when I'm trying to put everything in order around here."

23

"Cammie didn't say a word to me at work about you having company. Who is it?"

Concern filled his blue eyes, making me want to unload everything. How tempting it was to lean on such a good man when my life seemed to be falling apart. Still, I didn't want to draw him too close. It wouldn't be fair to give him false hope of there ever being a future for us.

Maybe I was demented for still carrying a torch for Cammie's father, but I couldn't help it. I still thought of Brian as my life partner. We'd even written and signed a covenant when I was still in high school . . . that we'd never love anyone else. Every time I looked at Cammie I was reminded how much I loved him then. How much I'd always love him.

"Sit and talk to me, Sandy," Charlie said.

I took the chair next to him. Would he really be able to offer any sound advice? Every solution that came to my mind involved mayhem.

"Did I hear the doorbell ring?" My mother's voice blew into the kitchen like an unwelcome gale. "Oh. I see we have company. Are you another looky-loo come to see this house?"

Charlie stood up while I rested my red face in my hands.

"I'm Charlie Dalan, a friend of the family." He stuck out his hand and smiled. "And you are . . .?"

"Oh my. A true gentleman. I guess I spoke too soon. Are you and my daughter dating?"

I jerked my head up. My mother had literally simpered. "No, Mother, we're only friends," I snapped.

A brief look of hurt crossed Charlie's face. I probably shouldn't have been so abrupt, but I knew where she was going with her ridiculous grin. Charlie was exactly like the boys she always tried to push me into dating when I was a senior in high school. The ones voted most likely to fade into the woodwork. Not that I had anything against men with manners, but I had always preferred a more take-charge sort of guy over the quiet type. Someone like Brian, whom my mother had always loathed.

"Oh, what a shame. I've always thought Sandra has been alone far too long. And it's obvious that Cammie could use a male influence in her life."

Oh man, leave it to her to get in that little dig.

My mother took a step closer and held onto Charlie's hand just a little too long for my comfort. Was I going to have to put up with her pathetic matchmaking along with her interference in everything else? And if she was so dazzled by Charlie, she was going to love Cammie's boyfriend, Teddy, who didn't have an assertive bone in his body.

Charlie extricated his hand from my mother's grip. "So you're Sandy's mother?"

"Yes. I'm Maude Hughes. Please sit down so we can visit. Oh. I see we're having lunch. It looks very substantial. I'm afraid I'm starving. I didn't get very much for breakfast." She shot me a meaningful glance.

Charlie held a chair out for her and again seated himself. Turning to me he said, "Then you must have reverted back to your maiden name when you lost your husband?"

"Harrumph!" My mother snorted, making me want to give her a good kick under the table.

Instead I jumped up and got out some plates and napkins and placed them on the table. "I'll go get Cammie." I escaped the kitchen before Charlie could ask me any more questions.

Cammie's bedroom door stood ajar so I lightly tapped on it and stepped in. Cammie was on her knees at her bedside with her Bible open in front of her. I slipped back out, wondering what she was praying for. Probably for peace in our home. I knew she saw me as the guilty one for keeping the tension going. Hospitality was important to Cammie. I'd always been content with only Cammie for company, while Cammie loved having a lot of people

25

around. She was no doubt ecstatic over the chance to get to know her grandmother. We would never agree on that issue.

The faint sound of rustling and soft footsteps coming toward the door let me know Cammie had finished her prayer. Then we stood face to face, neither one knowing what to say to quell the uneasiness between us. "Cammie—"

"Mom." To give my wonderful daughter credit, she reached out first and nearly crushed me in a hug. "I don't want you to be mad at me."

"Oh, honey. I'm not mad at you. It's just that the atmosphere has gotten a little strained with a third person in the house." I stepped back from the hug and tilted up her chin with my index finger. "This move we're making has been hard for you to accept. I know that."

"It's not just that, Mom. I don't understand why you don't like Gran."

"There are reasons going back many years, Cammie. There's no sense dredging everything up again. I can only say we parted ways years ago by mutual agreement."

"How can you part ways with your own family? If it was so long ago, why can't you forgive each other so we can be a family? So I can have a grandmother?"

"We're very different people with different values. You're nearly an adult. You should understand not every family is perfect."

"What values? God wants us to forgive one another. His values are the important ones. If you would only attend church with me, you'd come to understand."

Cammie gave me the perfect opening. A way to get back into her good graces. "I've been thinking about doing just that. How 'bout if I go with you tomorrow, Sweetie?"

"That would be wonderful!" She hugged me again. "And Gran too?"

"I doubt she'll say yes, but you can ask her." I was reluctant to break off the hug, but the thought of my mother and Charlie alone together made my hair stand on end. "Come on, Cammie. Let's have some lunch."

"Hi Charlie. I didn't know you were here." Cammie pulled up a kitchen chair next to my mother. Gran, you'll come to church with us in the morning won't you?"

The expression on my mother's face was priceless, as if someone announced there were slugs in her sandwich. I could see her struggling not to alienate Cammie, but her lifelong prejudices were not going to be overcome that easily.

"I'm not much for church goin'." She turned to Charlie. "Do you go along with all this foolishness?"

Poor Charlie. Caught between my mother and the proverbial hard place. "I have a golf game in the morning." He shot me a quizzical look, knowing full well I usually had plenty around the house to keep me busy most Sunday mornings and even had joined him for golf on occasion. But not church.

My mother let out a sigh of what appeared to be relief. I couldn't imagine why it mattered to her what Charlie did with his weekends. However, Cammie and I were back in sync. That's all that counted.

Cammie and Charlie turned the conversation to some humorous goings-on at their office for the remainder of our lunchtime. My mother's occasional glare in my direction didn't bother me at all. She could go back to picking at her food. I'd gained control again.

Later, I walked Charlie to his car. "Thank you again for bringing lunch."

He leaned against the fender, one hand on the hood and the other in his pocket. A slight breeze ruffled his sandy hair. The picture of a man totally at home with himself. "Any time. I was glad to have a chance to meet your mother. I don't think you've ever talked about her. Is your Dad still alive?"

27

"Uh. Dad stayed home. She decided to take a little vacation. I'm not sure why she came here. We've never been all that close."

"She seems nice enough."

I could see Charlie was puzzled, but I decided not to confide in him. At least for now. "It's only going to be a short stay, and then I'll be able to get back on schedule."

"Oh? I got the impression from her that she planned on staying indefinitely."

"We haven't actually worked the details out yet." I took a couple of steps back, signaling my return to the house. It was time for another talk with my mother. The talks to set her straight seemed to be an hourly occurrence.

"Telephone!" Cammie's call saved me from further explanation.

"I've got to run. Thanks again, Charlie." I headed for the house.

A glance at my watch confirmed I'd wasted most of the day. Knowing most of it was on non-essentials didn't brighten my mood any. I picked up the phone.

"Hello?"

"My dear Ms. Hughes, do you or don't you want to sell your house?" Gone was the Realtor's former friendliness. His tone of voice made me feel like I'd been called into the vice-principal's office for shooting spitballs at the history teacher.

"Of course I do. Whatever gave you the idea I didn't?"

"Well for one thing, you swore to me you had the house checked over for termites and such. I trusted your word. I guess I should have demanded the inspection report before I listed your property."

"I most certainly did. I have the report right here."

"Then why did your mother tell us about a severe cockroach problem you were having?"

That old witch! "Morty." I adjusted my voice to a sickly sweet tone. "Please don't pay any attention to the ramblings of that demented old woman. She's known for

28

making things up. I should have warned you, but I had no idea she'd butt in to your potential sale."

"Demented or not, those folks made it abundantly clear they no longer trusted me to accurately represent any home I showed them. We both lost."

"I am so sorry. What can I do to make things right. I'm really anxious to sell."

"For starters, you can arrange to vacate your home when I'm showing it to clients. That includes any crazies you have living with you."

"Just give me a little more notice next time, and I'll take care of it."

"I'll be talking to you. So long."

I set the phone down with a lot more gentleness than I felt right then. Flogging my mother would be a little extreme, but that's exactly what I felt like doing. However, the next day's headlines would scream out elder abuse, I'd go to jail, and Cammie would be left without a mother. I'd have to think of something else.

Taking several deep breaths, I tried to calm down. Cammie most likely had her weekly Saturday night date with Teddy, so I planned on waiting till she was out of the house before I confronted my mother again.

The long minutes ticked by like an ant trudging through honey. Teddy finally arrived, and I let him in. My mother stayed in the bedroom so we were spared further embarrassment when he met her for the first time.

Teddy wore pressed khaki slacks and a shirt and tie. I'd never seen him look sloppy, even when he was a little boy. I liked Teddy . . . just not as much as Cammie did. She needed to meet exciting new people. She was far too good for small town life and small town people.

I watched through the window while the kids walked to Teddy's car and drove away. The house seemed too quiet like it always did when I was alone. The silence was something I'd have to get used to now that Cammie was nearly an adult.

Another unsuccessful effort to reach my dad didn't improve my mood any. I needed his input. Somehow he'd managed to live with her for years and years without committing any crimes against her person. My way of dealing with her was to put as much distance as possible between us. It never occurred to me to move to a different continent but that idea appealed to me as I contemplated confronting her about her behavior with the Realtor.

I put off the coming fight as long as possible but there was no delaying it. Besides, I had to feed her dinner, so some conversation would be inevitable. Neither of us excelled at small talk.

I decided to fix something I figured she'd approve of and lead into the subject gradually. That was it! I'd try to butter her up . . . ask her what she would like for supper. Certainly taking the direct approach hadn't worked with her so far.

I tiptoed down the hall just in case she was sleeping. Delaying our talk would give me more time to prepare. I imagined it would take several days for her to get used to the time change and she would be going to bed early in the meantime.

As luck would have it, she was awake and fiddling around with Cammie's computer. She pressed the power switch when she saw me.

"Did Cammie show you how to shut the computer down properly? You need to exit from Windows first."

"I didn't have time to go through all that rigmarole. I didn't want you snooping over my shoulder at my book."

"I have no intention of peeking at your book. I'd rather wait till it's published and be surprised." *Yeah, right.*

"Well an author can't be too careful, you know. There are all kinds of people who would dearly love to steal other people's ideas."

I made an effort not to roll my eyes. Since she'd already announced she was writing her life's story, and I'd

30

had more than my fill of her life, poking around her so-called book fell way down on my list of priorities.

"Actually, I came in to see what you would like for supper." I waited expectantly for her to conjure up a complicated menu to test my sincerity.

"Something light would be fine. Maybe some chicken noodle soup?"

I squinted at her, trying to figure out what she was up to, being so compliant and all. Her wary stare back indicated she wondered the same thing about me. Maybe hope for an uneasy truce wasn't so far fetched after all.

"I'll call you when it's ready." I escaped down the hall before the spell broke.

She came into the kitchen as soon as I announced the food was ready. I'd taken care to use my nicer place mats and napkins. A pot of steaming tea sat in the middle of the table along with a basket of hot buttered biscuits. I waited for her reaction. Anything. A nod of approval, perhaps. Certainly nothing as extravagant as a compliment.

I could feel her stare as I ladled the soup into our bowls. She passed when I offered her a hot biscuit. "But this is very nice, Sandra."

The veins on the back of her hands were way more pronounced than when I'd still lived in her home. The joints of her fingers were slightly swollen and the tips bent sideways at odd angles. I glanced at my own manicured hands, fully expecting to see the first signs of age, but so far they still were mine, not a clone of my mother's.

Angry lines etched the skin around her mouth and eyes, giving me a glimpse of my future if I continued the bitterness I felt. I wouldn't have to feel this way if she'd only stayed home. Still, I needed to at least try and temper my responses to her. As the saying went, "If you aren't getting the results you want, change your tactics."

"How's your soup?"

"It's okay."

"Now that we're alone, I'm wondering if you could tell me exactly what Daddy did that caused you to leave."

"I don't want to go into that."

"I'd like to help if I could."

"Then start by minding your own beeswax!"

"I don't understand why you're being so defensive and secretive. After all, this is affecting me and Cammie too."

She slammed her spoon down with all the force of a woodsman swinging a hatchet. "Why? Why should I confide in you? You'd only take your father's side just like you always did!"

"I don't know what you mea--"

"You know very well what I mean!" My mother jumped up from the table, knocking over her cup of tea. "I devoted years trying to raise you right. And what did I ever get in return? Nothing! That's what!" She turned and stalked into the living room.

"What is it you want from me?"

"Respect! You owe me that much!"

Each decibel her voice rose, the more frustrated and angry I got. I followed her into the living room, ready to do battle . . . all my earlier good intentions forgotten.

"I owe you nothing! And all your yelling at me isn't going to convince me otherwise."

"Go ahead and say it! You hate me!" Her voice reached magnum proportions, her face nearly purple with rage. I feared she'd have a stroke any second.

"Shut up and calm down!" I was nearly screaming just to be heard over her hysterics.

The incessant ringing of the doorbell broke through, stopping us both in mid-sentence. I took a deep breath and went to open the door. A man in a dark suit, and close-cut hair, stood on my front porch.

"Ms. Hughes?"

"Yes?"

He peered past me into the living room where my mother still stood. Then he pulled a leather badge case and

ID from his inside jacket pocket. "I'm Special Agent Matt Boyce with the FBI. I'm here to get the names of your neighbors and friends so I can interview them for your background check. Perhaps I should begin with this lady behind you."

Chapter Four

Maude's Journal
July 1960

> *I visited Mama's grave today. I wanted to tell her I'm getting married. Not that I need her blessing. I only wanted to reassure her I picked out a man who treats me like a queen. Not a no-good drunk like Dad. I haven't even seen or spoken to him since the funeral. James is just the opposite of Dad. He agrees with me on everything. Just last night, while we were looking at apartments, he signed a lease on the one I wanted; even though at first he said it was way too expensive. He knows how important it is to me to have an attractive home where I won't be ashamed to invite my friends. It has two large bedrooms.*
>
> *James said the second bedroom would be perfect for when we start a family. However, I pointed out to him we should be in our very own house in the country before even thinking of having a family. He looked disappointed, but knows I'm right. Besides, now he'll work all the harder to scrape up a down payment on a house of our own. I only have a couple of months to plan my wedding. Then my married friends won't keep saying that I'm so picky I'm destined to be a spinster.*

***

There I stood in the middle of my living room with my mouth open, staring at the FBI guy. He stood tall, rugged looking, feet apart, a notebook and pen in his hands. No nerdy pocket protector in sight. Nope. This buff guy exuded authority and he knew it. Of course I'd known there would be a background investigation. I never expected it to go much beyond checking my job references. I certainly never expected an intimidating stranger to be standing in my home scowling at me.

While I examined him, he recorded statements from my mother. She did her best to make me look like a candidate to arrest for elder abuse.

"Now how long did you say you've lived here?"

"She doesn't live here," I said, trying to set things straight right from the beginning. "She's only visiting. A short visit."

Special Agent Unfriendly made a point of ignoring me. He tipped his head down toward my mother who looked on the verge of collapsing.

"Why don't you sit down, Ma'am? You look a little stressed."

My mother dropped onto the sofa. "Thank you. I am a little upset. It's not a pleasant thing to have your only daughter tell you that you're not wanted. And this, after I did my best to raise her to be a decent human being. What will I do now? I have no place else to go."

"Mother! That is a bald-faced lie." Did she have any idea what kind of trouble she was making for me?

The FBI guy whirled to face me. "I'm going to have to ask you to leave the room if we have any more outbursts like this."

"Wait a minute." I paused only long enough to take a deep cleansing breath. "This is my living room. Where do you get off ordering me around?"

"And *this* is my job. You-" He thrust his index finger right at me, "are dangerously close to interfering with a government investigation."

I felt every last drop of blood leave my face. He made it sound so serious. It was one thing to blame my mother for wrecking my chances at a dream job. What was I doing taking the weapon out of her hands? Why, if I would only let her babble on, he would see how deranged she was. Wouldn't he?

35

Time to regroup. "Of course you're right. I'm sorry my impatience showed."

"And are you usually this *impatient*, lady?" He left no doubt that he would have chosen a more condemning description and sounded as irritated as I felt.

"No, of course not. It's just been a long and vexing day. Why don't I go put a pot of coffee on?"

"Sounds like a good idea. Take your time." He helped himself to my most comfy chair, his knees inches from my mother's.

"Dear, would you mind bringing me a little cup of tea while you're at it?"

My jaw stiffened. Only she could whine like a three-year old when it suited her. I'd seen her do it with Daddy plenty of times. Always working on an unseen agenda. This time she was trying to portray the victim. She'd probably keep it up until I was hauled away in handcuffs.

At least she wouldn't try to play matchmaker. This guy was much too old for Cammie and probably too young for me. No, she had tagged this guy as an ally all for herself.

I headed to the kitchen and the coffee pot. Once I'd measured out the coffee and filled the water reservoir, I tiptoed across the floor to see if I could hear what they were saying. My mother was probably painting me as some kind of serial killer. A frustratingly low mumble of voices was all I heard.

Why hadn't anyone warned me about this background check procedure? Not that I could have done anything about it, but at least I would have been a little more prepared. Surely all the stellar references on my job application would outweigh any garbage my mother would feed him. But what if they took her claims of me throwing her out in the street seriously? Everything hinged on getting this job. My move to the city, Cammie's education . . . all of it.

I put the teakettle on for my mother. Picking up the kitchen phone, I dialed my parents' home again. *Oh please,*

Daddy, be home this time. Again, my efforts resulted in a dozen unanswered rings. My shoulders slumped as I replaced the receiver.

"I'm ready for you now." The agent's voice reached me from the kitchen doorway. "Were you calling your attorney? It hasn't come to that yet, but I'll be sure and let you know when it does."

Straightening up again I treated him to the most innocent expression I could muster up. "Surely, the FBI wouldn't be involved in a little disagreement among family members."

He stared me down like a hornet contemplating a target. I couldn't help but notice his eye color was identical to his gold-flecked brown hair. "I figured I'd better make sure that's all it was."

"And are you satisfied? Even you probably have differing opinions on things with your own family."

"True. But we seldom raise our voices to the point they can be heard all over the neighborhood."

There was no point in trying to convince the agent it was my mother who started the yelling match. The fact was, we'd both been yelling. All I could do now was nod my head and try to smooth things over.

"You said you were ready for me. Why don't we sit at the kitchen table? The coffee is nearly done." I didn't wait for his answer, but got out a couple of cups and set them out. Too bad there weren't any homemade chocolate cookies in the jar to soften him up. But then, he could accuse me of offering a bribe.

He pulled up a chair, and sat back with one ankle perched on his opposite knee. Clasping his hands behind his head, he stared directly at me, a move clearly designed to intimidate.

I glanced toward the living room, fully expecting my mother to make an appearance for her tea any minute.

As if he could read my mind, he nodded slightly toward the door. "She told me she needed to go lie down.

37

Why don't we begin by you telling me your side of the story?"

"S-story?" I stammered like an idiot. He made it sound like he expected me to spin a fable. "There's really not much to tell."

Suddenly leaning forward, he pulled his notebook toward him. "Have it your way. Sit down. I have a few questions."

After turning the heat under the teakettle down, I slid into the space across the table from him and folded my hands demurely next to my empty cup. Sounds of brewing coffee gurgled in the background. Taking a deep breath, I prepared myself to give him whatever information he needed.

"It says here on your application you have one daughter. Cammie is it? Where is she?"

"She's out for the evening. With a friend."

"And the friend's name?" His poised his pen in the air.

"Teddy. Teddy Anderson."

"His address?"

"I'm not sure. About four streets over. On Highland. He lives with his parents."

"And their names?"

I racked my brain but for the life of me, couldn't come up with their first names.

"How long have your daughter and Teddy been friends?"

That was easy. "Since first grade." I hoped the rest of the questions would be as simple.

"Yet you don't know the Anderson's first names?"

"Actually, I don't think their last name is Anderson. I think it's something else." I continued on, sure that Agent Boyce thought I was dumber than dirt. "You see, I think they are divorced. I mean Teddy's mom and real dad. And she must have remarried. I'm positive they have a different last name than Teddy."

I watched as he scratched out something in his notebook.

"Do you consider yourself a good mother?"

"Of course I do! I've dedicated my entire life to raising her." I felt my hackles rising and hoped he didn't notice.

"Kind of like your mother did for you?"

"Now just a minute! There's no resemblance whatsoever between me and my mother." My hands, no longer deliberately relaxed on the table, clenched in my lap.

He stopped his writing and rested his piercing gaze on me. "You always have such a short fuse?"

"What do you mean?"

He lifted an eyebrow. "Let's go another direction. Tell me the names of three of your neighbors."

What was he doing changing gears like that? Was he trying to confuse me? Trip me up? I searched my memory bank for three neighbors I knew. Was knowing one's neighbors a requirement for working for the government? I met his gaze which hadn't wavered.

"I'm waiting." His lips barely moved when he spoke.

"Well, there's Mrs. Connely. She lives in the house next door."

"Would that be on the right or the left?"

"Left. Right! Her house is on the right when you leave my house." Which would be soon, I hoped.

"And how long have you known her?"

"Since Cammie started first grade. That's when we moved here." I hoped he wouldn't ask me anything about her. We'd never exchanged more than a few words.

"Good."

Oh yay. I'd finally given him a correct answer. However I knew he wouldn't be pleased with the rest.

"Another name?"

"I really don't know any other neighbors."

He looked at me as if either he didn't believe me, or that I was the very first genuine hermit he'd ever met.

39

"I work full time." I knew this sounded like a lame excuse to him but I felt the need to explain. "I really don't have time to do the coffee klatch thing with my neighbors."

He wrote more in his notebook. And wrote. And wrote. Did he think I was unsocial? Worse yet, hiding something?

Finally his note taking ceased. His eyes met mine. They told me nothing about his thoughts but I was again mesmerized by the warm color nearly hidden by thick eyelashes.

"I think the coffee's done." I jumped up, making a scraping sound with my chair as I escaped his gaze. At least pouring coffee gave me something to do with my hands. I grabbed the carafe and poured his out first, hoping he didn't see my hands shaking. Avoiding his stare, I poured mine and returned the carafe to the coffee maker.

"Do you take cream or sugar?"

"Black is fine."

I turned back to the table, nearly tangling my feet in the process.

"Relax." The corner of his mouth rose in a half smile. "What are you afraid I'll find out?"

"Nothing. I have nothing to hide. It's just that I'm afraid I started out making a bad impression, that's all. I'm not used to being interrogated. I'm not a terrorist, you know." Why did he have to bore holes through me with those eyes of his?

"This is hardly an interrogation. And if I even suspected you were a terrorist, I would have questioned all of your neighbors before this."

I looked for the half-smile again, but his mouth remained stubbornly unexpressive. "Are you always this serious?"

"Only when I'm having problems getting information." He tapped the edge of his coffee mug. "Is this job so important to you?"

"Yes. It is."

"Tell me why." His voice imparted warmth I hadn't noticed before. Ah, a new tactic on his part.

"It represents a reward for the hard work I've put in all these years. A large raise in pay. Responsibility." I took a deep breath. "And mostly, the opportunity to be part of something important."

"Tell me about Cammie's father." He hoisted the mug to his lips, taking a small sip of the steaming coffee.

"That was a long time ago. I was a teenager."

"About the age Cammie is now, right?"

He didn't need to remind me my daughter was at a vulnerable age where boys were concerned. Old enough to have all those romantic feelings, but too young to make wise choices.

"Yes."

"And are you saying he's no longer in your life?"

"Yes. That's what I'm saying."

"Does Cammie have regular contact with her father?

"She never knew him."

"Because?"

"Why do we have to dredge up something way in the past?" I didn't want to open those old wounds again by talking about him. My feelings were already too close to the surface where Cammie's dad was concerned.

"We want to make sure someone, or something in your past doesn't rear its ugly head and put your security clearance in jeopardy. We'll need to contact him."

"Oh. I guess that makes sense."

"His name?"

"What?"

He exhaled loudly. I guessed he wanted to get the interview over as much as I did.

"Brian. Brian Chapman."

"And where does he live?"

"I don't know. He sort of disappeared before Cammie was born."

"Did you look for him?"

41

"A pregnant teenager doesn't exactly have the resources to launch a missing person's search. His family moved away and the letters I sent him came back marked no forwarding address."

"Have you considered how easy it would be to locate him now with the Internet?"

I'd been examining my nails as I spoke. When I looked up, he looked nearly sympathetic. I moved both hands around my coffee mug. I'd probably misinterpreted his understanding. "He never once tried to get in touch with me. After all this time, I'm not about to track him down and interfere with whatever life he's made for himself."

"Don't you think you owe it to Cammie?"

"There you go again. Implying I'm not a good mother. Don't you think I've considered it? I decided it's not worth the risk of him rejecting Cammie too. She doesn't deserve that kind of pain."

He frowned and I watched with a heavy heart as he scratched out more notes. There was no reason at all for Brian to appear in my life. Cammie had all the male influence in her life she needed with Charlie and her pastor at church.

"Just so you know, we'll be contacting him."

My heart pounded at the thought. "Do you have to tell him about Cammie?"

"I won't be doing the interview. Someone from our Midwest office will. Probably the same person who'll be interviewing your father. We're in the business of gathering information, not disseminating it. But I'd advise you to contact him and tell him yourself." He made it sound as if that too, would be a requirement.

"Could you have whoever talks to my Dad ask him to contact me? Tell him it's important?"

"I can't promise anything."

Agent Boyce asked a few more family history questions that thankfully didn't tear open any more wounds. Then he tossed back the last of his coffee and stood.

"I think I have enough to get me started." He held out his hand for a handshake. "It was nice meeting you."

I stood, wiped my hand down my thigh before offering it to him. A jolt of electricity spiked through me at the contact. The shock increased, going down to my toes, when he actually smiled at me. His eyes crinkled and he had deep dimples on each side of his mouth. I suddenly found myself wondering if I'd be working with this man in Seattle. Seeing him nearly every day. *Assuming I passed all his tests, that is.*

Slightly shaken, I walked him to the door. My mother still hadn't made another appearance so at least there wasn't that to worry about. Watching him walk down the sidewalk to his nondescript late model sedan, I couldn't help notice the broadness of his shoulders.

As he drove away, my gaze switched to the sight of two people in a heavy embrace and lip lock in the front seat of a car I identified immediately as Teddy's. They didn't even notice me until I reached the passenger side window.

Chapter Five

Maude's Journal
August 1971

We're moving into our brand new home today! Life couldn't be more perfect. James has been a wonderful husband - treats me like a queen. He buys me whatever I want and takes me out to dinner at least once a week. The only cloud in our otherwise idyllic life is our lack of children. James has wanted to be a father ever since our wedding. I wanted to wait till I knew for sure James wouldn't sour on marriage and me. I hope we haven't waited too long. I didn't tell him, but I'm a few days late. It could be the excitement of moving. I don't want to get his hopes up.

***

I don't know if Agent Boyce saw what was going on. His car disappeared down the street. Evidently he was saving scouring my neighborhood for a different day.

I waited back in the house for Cammie to come in. Even though she and Teddy jumped apart when I tapped on the window, she didn't seem to be in much of a hurry to leave him. Patience had never been one of my virtues and I paced back and forth from the kitchen to the living room. I was already revved up from the FBI interview. Cammie's indiscreet behavior only added to my anxiety.

When she finally came in, she defiantly lifted her chin and looked me straight in the eye.

"I suppose I'm in for a big lecture."

"Cammie! Where did you get this attitude?"

"Mom! I'm out of high school now. All we were doing is kissing, for crying out loud."

Cammie's lipstick, which she had so carefully applied before leaving on her date, was nearly nonexistent. Her lips were swollen. I wanted to get Teddy by the throat and shake the living daylights out of him.

"What would your grandmother think if she'd seen you?"

"I got the impression you didn't care much for what she thought."

"Cammie, I don't like your tone of voice at all. What is happening to you?"

"If you'd only listen to me once in a while, you'd know. Instead, you're bent on your own agenda, never considering what I might want or feel."

"That's not true! Everything I've done is with you in mind."

"Whatever."

My head pounded and I knew no amount of massaging was going to help. Still, I rubbed my temples in an attempt to make the pain go away.

"See? The minute I say something you disagree with, you have one of your migraines. I feel like I can't even talk to you anymore."

My head snapped up. Did she really think I tried to manipulate her by purposely bringing on a headache? "I'm not feigning it if that's what you're insinuating and I don't care much for the implication."

"Mom, you keep avoiding the real subject. I'm sorry you have a headache. I have to go review tomorrow's Sunday school lesson."

Cammie turned her back on me and walked away. She was right about one thing. I hadn't had a chance to get down to the issue of her and Teddy. If I had, the gap between us would have widened even further. I hoped fervently that going to church with her the next day would bring us closer again.

Back in the kitchen, I mulled over our situation as I cleaned up from my visitor from the FBI. Even as I looked

45

forward to seeing him again, I dreaded the thought of him possibly bringing me bad news regarding my job application.

***

The next morning I made a heroic attempt to be pleasant to my mother . . . with *attempt* being the operative word. She entered the kitchen complaining about the noise I made as I started breakfast. Did I really need to get up so early on a Sunday? Then she protested about the shower running in the bathroom next to Cammie's room.

"We are getting ready for church," I said, all pious and superior. She didn't need to know it would only be my second time attending that year. "Perhaps you'd like to join us?"

I knew full well what her answer would be and didn't care. Leaving her alone in my house was a lesser evil than her ruining my morning with Cammie. I waited for her sharp criticism of anything smacking of religion when Cammie bounced into the room.

"Good morning Mom. Good morning Gran." She planted a kiss on each of our cheeks before heading to the fridge to pull out a carton of orange juice.

"Good morning, dear." My mother's sour disposition took a sudden turn for the better.

"Mom, Gran's coming to church with us this morning. Won't that be fun?"

About as much fun as setting fire to my hair and putting it out with a tack hammer. "Are you sure you're up to it, Mother? You're still not used to the time change. Jet lag, you know."

"I came by bus. And it's nearly noon at home."

"That's funny. A moment ago you were complaining because you wanted to sleep longer." It wasn't easy to sound sweet with my jaw clenched, but I did it for Cammie who had her back turned and couldn't see my disappointment.

Cammie seemed determined to put the previous evening's argument behind us. She pitched in and helped

46

make breakfast, giving me the sense that things were back to normal between us. My mother slipped into uncharacteristic silence. Whatever the reason, the harmony in my kitchen, false or not, filled me with relief.

After finishing breakfast, I left Cammie with the job of loading the dishwasher while I escaped to my room to find something suitable to wear for church. Growing up, my church-going friends told me they dressed up for services. Dressing in your "Sunday best" was more than a figure of speech back then. The last time I'd attended Cammie's church, I noticed everyone there dressed in casual clothes.

Before pinning my hair back with the silver and turquoise barrette Charlie had given me for my last birthday, I slipped on a simple cotton skirt and matching blouse. One last check of my makeup and I shoved my feet into a pair of sandals and grabbed my purse off the dresser. The weatherman had predicted a scorcher so there was no reason for a sweater even for the early service.

Cammie, her Bible in hand, and my mother waited for me in the living room. We all piled into my car and were nearly to the church when Cammie mentioned I'd taken the wrong turn.

"If you don't know how to get there, why didn't you let Cammie drive?"

My knuckles turned white on the steering wheel. Had my mother guessed this was a rarity for me?

Cammie saved me from further embarrassment. "There's a shortcut to the over-flow parking lot you probably forgot about, Mom."

"Uh, right." I circled the block and pulled into the entrance marked "Parking lot B." An attendant directed us to a vacant space. Less than five minutes passed before a shuttle bus came by to pick us up and deliver us to the front of the church.

Finding seats in the large sanctuary proved to be a challenge. Summer vacation apparently didn't stop people from flocking to Sunday service. I wondered if there was a

47

special event going on I hadn't heard about. Cammie led us to three seats together near the front.

Several people stopped and hugged Cammie who made introductions to my mother and me. You would have thought the place was full of felons, the way my mother snatched her hand back from all the greeters. Granted, the effusive welcomes made me a little uncomfortable, but there was no reason to be rude. The music started and we found seats, putting an end to all the banter.

Cammie's pride in bringing visitors showed all over her face and demeanor. Did she get extra points for bringing in the unchurched when it obviously wasn't Christmas or Easter? I couldn't help feeling a little resentment. Just like the time I caught her praying for me. I did not need religion to make me a better person. I'd done pretty well on my own.

The music started before anyone else had an opportunity to come over and check us out. Teddy arrived and slipped into the seat next to Cammie. I glanced at my mother, who remained seated when everyone else stood and clapped to the beat of the music. Her pinched expression shouted disapproval. I didn't know if it was the guitars and drums she hated or just the fact she was in church.

Cammie's gaze met mine and she grinned happily before facing the stage and singing again with renewed vigor. Shame fell over me like a blanket to see how little it took to bring joy to my daughter's face. Religion was one of the few things we hadn't shared. Would it have been so hard for me to go with her a little more often?

After twenty minutes or so, everyone sat down and the pastor began his sermon. Like the other times I'd attended, he started with a few jokes, presumably to get people's attention. I had to admit, he had a knack for drawing in my attention. His style reminded me of a relaxing chat at a casual gathering of friends.

Soon, however, he got down to the business of preaching. Everyone around us opened their Bibles and

48

followed along as he spoke. If I'd had a Bible, I wouldn't have known where to find the passage he referred to. Cammie tried to share her Bible with Mother, but her gesture met with indifference.

I turned my attention to the pastor, who cautioned everyone to extend the forgiveness to others in order to reap the full blessings of Christ's forgiveness of us. Apparently, according to his take on things, everyone needed God's forgiveness. By his definition of God's perfection, that statement included me as well. In fact, the pastor continued, the entire Bible was filled with stories of forgiveness and reconciliation. This is why Jesus went to the Cross.

Forgiveness was the exact subject Cammie and I had discussed the evening before. Had she somehow clued the pastor in that I would be there?

Then a shard of fear pricked my heart. If God couldn't accept me based on my efforts to do good in the world, what chance did I have of gaining admittance to heaven when I died? Even a fool had to believe in a life hereafter. Didn't Jesus die for everyone?

Peeking at my mother out of the corner of my eye, I wondered what she thought about what we were hearing. Forgiveness had never been in her vocabulary. Then it hit me. It hadn't been in mine either. At least as far as my mother was concerned. True, what she'd demanded from me as a teenager seemed unforgivable. However, was I willing to take my anger with me to the grave? Was God going to accept my excuses and blame her for my shortcomings, letting me off the hook?

The pastor made point after point, each one emphasizing that unforgiveness was not an option, even if the guilty party showed no remorse. As hard to swallow as his sermon was, my heart knew he was speaking the truth. From now on, I'd try to make peace with my mother. No matter how hard it was. I'd always been able to do anything I'd set my mind to. This shouldn't be any different.

The service ended with an invitation for anyone needing to make amends to come to the front and someone would pray with them. If the person, who we were on the outs with, was present, we were encouraged to approach that person and bring them with us. My pride wouldn't let me do either one. What would people think if Cammie's mother admitted publicly to a hard and bitter heart? My feet stayed glued to the floor.

Dozens of people streamed to the front of the church. Cammie, my mother, and I stood and moved into the aisle. Moving toward the back of the church proved difficult due to the human traffic pouring in the opposite direction. Were there really that many people who had my problem? How could that be?

We finally emerged into the spacious foyer where the welcome smell of coffee wafted through the air. I needed a good dose of caffeine to clear my head by then. Somehow, I got separated from Cammie and Mother, so I just followed the crowd into a large gymnasium sized room. Ah. Just as I'd hoped. Several large silver urns and paper cups were placed strategically on tables around the room.

I reached the nearest table and reached for a cup, then felt a hand on my elbow. Turning to see who it was, I felt my jaw drop. "You followed me to church?"

Special Agent Boyce didn't even have the good sense to look embarrassed. Amused was more like it. "It occurred to me I might find you here since you listed this church on your info sheet."

I gulped. If I'd had an Adam's apple, it would have bobbed up and down like a yo-yo. I wondered how far he would take this investigation. "I'm not an official member here. I only attend once in a while. Being a single mom doesn't leave a lot of my weekends free."

"So you said when I asked you about your neighbors."

"Well, perhaps shadowing me will give you the information you want." I turned and filled my cup from the nearest urn. Instead of the dark pungent liquid, I hoped for,

50

all I got was hot water. In my haste to find something to do with my hands, I failed to notice the hand-lettered signs on the table stating the contents. You would have thought the brightly colored tea packets identical to the ones I had at home had tipped me off.

I reached for the nearest one and managed to tip over my cup, leaving a large wet spot on the white tablecloth.

"Nervous?"

"You'd make anyone nervous," I snapped.

"Here, let me—" He plucked a cup from the stack, and filled it with water with one smooth movement. "I'll hold it while you dunk."

"Dunk?"

"Your tea bag. I don't see any doughnuts around."

Oh my, didn't I sound like the intelligent one? One more strike against me.

"Sugar?"

"I can get it myself, thank you." I took the cup from him, balancing it in one hand while getting the sugar and simultaneously managing to keep my purse's shoulder strap from slipping down, dropping it and its contents all over the floor.

In the meantime, he got another cup and poured himself a steaming cup of coffee. I noticed again that he took it black . . . the way I would have if I'd only been paying attention.

"Why don't we sit over there by the window?"

I looked around, hoping to see Cammie, my mother, or anyone else I might recognize. As flattering as it was to have a good-looking, okay, gorgeous man attach himself to me, I wasn't under the mistaken impression his interest was anything but professional. Somehow, a church didn't seem like a good place to further our interview.

"I'm sure your family is fine. They aren't going to leave without you. You did drive here in your car didn't you?"

What? Had he followed me from my house?

"Do you usually stalk the people you're investigating?"

51

"*Stalking* is hardly the term I'd use. Come sit down with me. It will only take a moment, I promise."

"What term would you use, then?" I managed to get my question out as he again grasped my elbow and moved me to the side of the room. "I can't imagine why the FBI sees my personal life so important that you're out working on a weekend."

"Actually, I didn't come here specifically to see you. My sister and her family attend this church. I'm watching my nephews while they're taking a much needed weekend away."

He let loose of my arm and gestured to an empty chair. Seating himself in the chair next to mine, he sent me a smile I was sure was designed to put me at ease. It didn't.

We sat side by side in silence, sipping our drinks till I thought I would scream from tension. This guy was good at his job. He managed to keep me off-balance nearly all the time. No doubt he had crooks lining up and begging to confess to him. Compared to the people he normally must deal with, I shouldn't have posed a challenge to him at all.

He finished his coffee while I was still taking tiny sips of tea to keep from burning my tongue. He set his empty cup on the floor, sat up and turned toward me.

"I haven't been able to ascertain the whereabouts of your daughter's father."

"I told you. His family moved away before Cammie was born."

"Are you sure you've never heard from him in all this time?"

"Of course not. He's not in my life."

"You wondered why I've gone to all this trouble to complete your background investigation."

I looked around to make sure we weren't being overheard. What would people think?

"Our current office manager is in the reserves and has been called up for active duty. It's critical we fill that position while she's gone. If we were to hire you, you'd be

52

privy to some highly sensitive and classified information. We can't take a chance on anything in your background that could become a problem. Understand?"

I nodded my head, not quite knowing how to respond.

"I suggest you do your part and try to reach your ex boyfriend. It could make a difference whether you get this job or not. It would be a shame if you didn't. Your other qualifications are exactly what we're looking for."

So he knew I'd never been married. I guessed it wouldn't have taken a mental giant to figure that out when I hadn't checked either *divorced* or *widowed* on my original application.

This guy was not making things easy for me. "If the FBI can't find him, how am I supposed to find him? Are you sure it's important? What if he finds out about Cammie? What if he wants to be part of her life?" *And would he ever forgive me for not finding him years earlier?*

"I guess you'll have to get your priorities in order. Do you want the job badly enough? If not, say so right now and save me a lot of trouble. How you handle telling him about Cammie is up to you. We're not going to tell him. However, if there's anything in his background to concern us, you won't get the job.

"I can't imagine there being anything about him the FBI would object to."

"Let's hope not."

I stood, anxious to get away and think about what I'd learned . . . both from the morning's message and from the man who stood with me.

Before you go, there's one more thing."

"Yes?" *What now?*

"Our man back East can't seem to locate your father. There's nobody at home. Would you happen to know where he is?"

53

Chapter Six

Maude's Journal
March 1973

My daughter is nearly a year old now. I never would have believed how much a baby could change my life. Everything seems to revolve around her. My husband hasn't taken me out to dinner since before she was born. He says she's too young to leave with a sitter, and he doesn't want her exposed to germs out in public. It's like I don't even exist. As soon as he gets home from work, he makes a beeline for her crib. I've tried keeping her up during the day so she'd be asleep when he gets home, but he only wakes her up to play. I'm beginning to wonder if having her was a mistake. He's spoiling her rotten and worse, he's neglecting our marriage.

***

Cammie and Mother kept a steady stream of conversation going on the drive home from church. Cammie tried to draw me into whatever they seemed to be talking about, but I was too distracted by my conversation with Agent Boyce. Not only that, but the memory of his spicy aftershave still lingered. The contrast between his attractiveness and the fact he held my future in his hands had my stomach tied in knots. I'd never been a gloom and doom sort of person, but it looked more and more like my dream job was only that . . . a dream.

To top things off, fear for my dad escalated every time I thought about his absence from my parents' home. An out of order telephone was no longer a possibility. It would have been fixed by now. He was gone. If he was out looking for Mother, why hadn't he called me? What if he'd had an accident? What if he was sick and couldn't make it to the door or phone?

I nearly missed the turn into our cul-de-sac. When we entered the house, I saw the blinking light on my answering machine. Daddy? I punched the play button only to hear Mort's voice telling me he had more prospects to buy the house and would I kindly leave the premises between five and six in the evening?

Oh well, I would take Mother out to dinner, since as usual, Cammie probably had plans with Teddy. Spending some so-called quality time with Mother would be an opportunity to try out the forgiveness and reconciliation thing from that morning's sermon.

Mother disappeared into Cammie's room to "work on her novel." I sent Cammie to the spare room to go through her winter clothes and discard anything she wouldn't be taking to college.

I fixed a light lunch of pasta salad and tuna sandwiches and stuck them in the refrigerator for later. Going to my own room to seek some privacy, I pulled my laptop from the closet and hooked it up to the telephone wall jack. My dialup Internet connection wasn't the fastest, but it would have to do. I typed the name of my hometown, Detroit, into the search engine and waited for the information I sought to come up. There it was. Hospitals. There were several, and even more in nearby communities. I scribbled the names and phone numbers on a scratch pad.

I started to disconnect, then remembered my conversation with Agent Boyce. I wasn't crazy about finding Brian, but I figured I might as well start looking in case I changed my mind. I surfed to a people finder location and typed in Brian W. Chapman. There were dozens listed. I narrowed it down to Michigan, and then nearby states. No likely hits. I tried deleting the middle initial with the same results.

Leaning back in my Chintz bedside chair, I wondered what I'd do or say if I actually did find him. Heard his voice.

Shivers danced down my arms. Surely he wouldn't want to hear from me after all these years. And if I did manage to locate him, what would his reaction be to finding out he had a daughter? A daughter I'd kept from him. Would he believe I thought he'd abandoned me? That I was devastated after I'd given myself to him, and then he merely left and never looked back?

If I'd only known where he was then, I'd have followed him to the end of the earth. Surely he would have married me if he'd known. Even a shotgun wedding would have been preferable to what Mother tried to make me do.

Forgiveness. Did I have it in me to forgive my mother? Really? Wouldn't that be the same as saying her actions didn't matter?

I shut down my laptop and put it back in the closet. After reconnecting my telephone, I called the hospitals on my list. One by one, strangers on the other end of the line stated there was no James Hughes listed as a patient. I hung up, relieved and disappointed at the same time. *Think. What are their neighbors' names? I could call them. What about Daddy's friends from work? Did he stay in touch with them after he retired?*

I pondered calling Agent Boyce at the number he'd written on the back of his business card. Had the investigator who'd gone to Daddy's house noticed anything unusual? Mail and papers stacked up on the porch? I wasn't exactly in a position to fly back there and check myself. On the other hand, Mother had only been at my home for three days. Even figuring in the trip out here, it was hardly enough time for the place to look abandoned.

I rubbed my temples, trying to work out the tightness in my upper facial muscles. Then I left my room, calling out to Cammie and Mother on the way to the kitchen. Getting myself a glass of water, I took a couple of pain relievers before setting the food out.

Lunch was uneventful. Cammie had enough tact not to press us for our opinions of her church. Neither Mother nor I volunteered our views, either. The epiphany I'd experienced was something I wanted to keep to myself. I didn't need Mother to articulate her views. I'd grown up with them.

Cammie filled us in on her evening plans and seemed pleased when I told her Mother and I were going out for a nice dinner. She pitched in and helped me spiff up the house for the Realtor and his clients.

I'd made dinner reservations at a good steak and seafood place. Living in the Midwest, I'm sure Mother seldom had a chance to enjoy fresh shellfish. In fact, I don't remember my parents going out much at all. We either went places as a family, or we stayed home.

Later on when we arrived, Mother raised her eyebrows as we entered the restaurant lobby. "Kind of a showy place isn't it? I don't have money to throw around on fancy meals."

"This is my treat, Mother. And it's not as expensive as you would think."

"Humph." She squinted into the darker interior as if she were looking for something, anything, to criticize.

I will not let her ruin the evening. I will not let her ruin the evening.

A young man dressed in black pants and vest and a white shirt arrived to take us to our table. He handed us each a menu and asked if we'd like to order something to drink.

"I'll have an iced tea with no lemon, please."

"Just plain water for me, sonny," my mother announced. "I'm not much for drinking alcohol."

He didn't as much as pause at my mother's gaffe. "I'll be right back with your drinks and to answer any questions you may have about our specials."

We fell silent as we studied our menus and waited for him to return.

"I've decided to forgive you." My mother's shrill pronouncement broke into my attempt to decide between the seafood fettuccini and the crab stuffed red snapper.

"What?"

"You heard me. I'm going to forgive you."

"May I ask what for?" My snapping turtle gene threatened an appearance but I pushed it back.

"For all the mean, rotten things you've said and done since I've arrived here, that's what."

I glanced around to see if anyone at the nearby tables had heard her accusation. Everyone seemed to be studying their plates. However, their sudden lack of conversation told me they'd not only heard, but were poised to hear the next utterance from our table.

"Mother," I hissed. "Could you keep your voice down? We don't want to disturb the other diners."

"Well, excuse me. I thought you'd be pleased."

That she'd beat me to the punch? Hardly. "Of course, I'm pleased. You must have taken this morning's sermon to heart." I knew the church service had nothing to do with her declaration, but thought I'd get that jab in.

"I did nothing of the sort. I just figured it's time to let bygones be bygones. Especially since we're going to be living together."

Oh groan. She certainly wasn't making things easy on me.

Our waiter returned to take our order. "We need a little more time."

"Could I bring you a starter while you decide? We have a nice sampler plate with fried calamari, stuffed mushrooms, and grilled tiger prawns. Or perhaps you'd like the hot artichoke crab dip. It comes in a bread bowl."

"Mother?"

"Order whatever you want. She wrinkled her nose in distaste."

I forced back a retort. Here I was, trying to show a little kindness and she wanted to rob me of it. Was it so she could play the martyr later? Obviously we weren't using the same script.

58

Turning to the waiter, I indicated the sampler plate would do fine.

"I'll be right back with it and two plates, ma'am." He backed away, leaving us to our "mother-daughter" festivities.

Glancing around, I noticed the other diners had turned their attention back to their own tables, picking up their conversations. I wondered how long it would be before we grabbed their notice again.

Living in constant turmoil drained my energy and distracted me from the things I really needed to concentrate on—namely selling the house, moving, and starting my new job. I had to think of a way to smooth things over with Mother. I didn't believe for a moment she had *absolved* me from any imagined past grievances. However, she seemed almost desperate to stay with us. Considering how she really felt about me, her desire to live with us made no sense whatsoever. Until I knew what her motives were, I had no chance at all of changing our current situation. Somehow, I had to draw her out.

We sipped our drinks in silence. Mother twisted her head around, this way and that, gawking at the people at nearby table. Then she turned her attention to the beach decor hanging on the walls. In fact, she looked everywhere but at me. Since I had been pronounced *forgiven*, was it up to me to keep the conversation going? If I could only get her talking. About anything significant. Especially anything I wanted to know. If only I knew how.

The appetizers arrived. I saw she wasn't going to help herself, so I selected two of each item for her plate, and passed it across the table to her. She looked at her portion, then at me, as if she were waiting for me take the first taste.

"I guarantee the food isn't poisoned here, Mother."

She snatched up her fork as if she'd like to use it as a weapon. Then she sort of moved her stuffed mushroom over to the side of the plate. She stabbed one of the prawns, lifting it up as if to get a better view of it. I tired of waiting for her to inspect her food, and turned my attention to eating mine.

Think. How can I draw her out? Everyone likes to talk about themselves, don't they? "Ummm. The calamari has such a light batter." I looked up in time to see Mother wrapping her mushrooms in a napkin. "If you'd like to take those home for later, I'm sure the waiter will bring us a box."

"No thanks." She stuffed the bundle into her purse and went back to examining her prawns.

"Have you decided yet?" The waiter was back.

"I think I'll have the crab stuffed sole. Mother?"

Mother looked up, giving the waiter her sad stare. "Do you have any tomato soup? I don't want to take advantage of my daughter's generosity."

"Oh, for crying out loud. It would serve you right if I let you order soup and then have to watch me eat my sumptuous meal."

My mother turned her *oh-so-innocent* eyes toward me. "I told you earlier, we would be starting fresh again. I'm trying to do my part by not letting you foolishly spend your money on me."

Both my fists lay clenched in my lap. "Knock it off, Ma. Either order a meal from the menu or I'll order for you." *Preferably something with a strong sleeping pill in it. One that will last till you're ready to go home.*

"OK. If you insist," she said, hanging her head.

I thought she wanted to be a writer, not an actress. Had Daddy actually fallen for this baloney all these years?

Mother handed her menu to the waiter. "I'll have the surf and turf. I'd like my filet well-done. And could you put my lobster tail on a separate plate? I think a Caesar salad would go nicely with that. Baked potato with sour cream, chives, and bacon bits. Don't forget the butter. Do you have any cheesecake?"

"Yes, ma'am. Lemon or chocolate?" The waiter waited, pen poised in the air.

"On second thought, I think I'd rather have the key lime pie. And could you bring some more napkins?"

"OK. I'll be right back with your salads." He turned and left.

I watched Mother place a tiger prawn in her mouth. She chewed it as if the act required all of her attention. *Why is it so difficult for her to carry on a normal conversation with me? Instead she sends me these little obtuse messages while speaking to a third party.*

The waiter returned with a breadbasket and our entrees before my mother spoke again.

"How long have you and Cammie been involved in all that church stuff?"

My participation had never been what I'd call "involved." But keeping up the illusion that Cammie and I shared that bond overrode any squeamishness I had at telling a white lie. "Cammie expressed an interest in church when she entered her teens. I thought her association with the other young people there would be a good alternative to the kind of friends she'd meet at public school."

"And were you right?"

"Of course. You can't deny my daughter is a wonderful young woman."

"With the exception of her religious fanaticism, I'd have to agree. She's certainly a loving granddaughter, despite your attempts at filling her with lies about me."

"What lies, Mother? Your behavior speaks for itself. In fact, I've never told Cammie *anything* about you."

"Except that I was dead." My mother's pale gray eyes stared at me with a coldness that chilled me to the bone.

"I never told her you were dead!"

"Hmpf." She stabbed at her lobster and with the other hand, took her steak knife and sawed off pieces big enough to make a sandwich. After laying her butcher implements aside, she picked up the container of melted butter, pouring it over her baked potato till the entire mess pooled onto her plate.

I wondered if she'd ever had a lobster on her plate before. Rather than tutoring her on the fine art of restaurant dining, I wisely kept my mouth shut and let her make the mess. A three-year-old would do better.

She took a bite of her potato and scrunched up her mouth. I expected her to spit it out at any moment. Instead, she gave me a triumphant look and swallowed after chewing it at least twenty times. "They certainly believe in lots of garlic," she said, wiping her mouth with her napkin.

In order to avoid answering, I reached for my water, taking a long slow drink. I averted my gaze from her plate, wondering how anyone could keep from losing their appetite looking at the jumbled up mess. My own plate still looked like the photo in the menu. Each item lay in its own place. The vegetables did not touch my fish, and my dinner roll sat on the pristine bread plate. I never could stand any kind of disorder. Perhaps that explained why my mother's presence upset me so much. Everything she did, every word out of her mouth, skewed my perfect life out of whack. Still, for the time being, I remained stuck with her.

"Tell me about your book."

Mother narrowed her eyes. "Are you really interested?"

"Of course I am." Another white lie.

"I haven't really begun the actual writing part. I'm still going through my journals to decide what to include."

"Do I understand correctly that you're writing an auto-biography?"

"Something like that."

"I suppose Daddy and I will be in it then?"

"I would hardly leave out the man who abused me for so many years."

I felt my blood heat up to the boiling point. "Daddy was *not* an abuser!"

"Oh, yes he was. And he deserved what he got."

Chapter Seven

Maude's Journal
April 1977

I thought those little brats would never leave. James had to go and rent a pony for Sandra's fifth birthday party. As if that wasn't enough, he hired a couple of clowns to come over and entertain all her friends from kindergarten. I've never heard so much squealing as those girls did. You'd think James was a little kid himself, the way he carried on, laughing like a fool at all their ridiculous antics. He never once acknowledged I was even there! Except of course, when it was time to bring out the cake and ice-cream which he also ordered from the most expensive place in the mall. I'm going to have to put my foot down. If he doesn't start paying more attention to me and less to that spoiled daughter of ours, he's going to be very sorry.

***

My heart nearly stopped at my mother's words. "What did you mean, *he got what he deserved?* What exactly did he get?" *Besides some peace and quiet.*

Mother sat across from me calmly chewing her food as if her tongue hadn't been dripping with venom only a moment before.

"Are you going to answer me?"

"I meant," she said, pointing her fork at me, "he's all alone now."

My eyes welled up with tears at the thought of my father sitting by himself in that empty house, with no one to care for him. But then, he wasn't there, was he?

"Is that what your leaving was about? A ploy to make him so lonesome he'd come after you?" As soon as the words left my mouth, I realized he hadn't even called once to see if she was with me. Why?

"Of course not. Besides, what went on between us is not your concern. It's private. What goes on in a marriage should be between two people—not anyone else."

"Aren't you violating that privacy by writing this book of yours? Besides, you're only telling the story from your perspective. What about Daddy's side?"

"By the time my book hits the best seller list, it won't matter anymore."

Before I had a chance to digest this last remark, the waiter appeared again to check our progress. "Are you ready for your desserts? May I clear your plates?"

I had lost my appetite by then and motioned him to take my half-eaten dinner away. Mother sent her plate back as well, except for what she wrapped in a napkin and stuffed in her purse. I'd never been able to figure out why she treated Daddy so shabbily. I never saw or heard him do or say anything remotely objectionable. I'd long ago come to the conclusion she was mean to the bone. She would never change, despite her statement of beginning anew with me.

Glancing at my watch, I saw that Mort would have had plenty of time to show the house and be gone by now. I made a big production of finishing my after-dinner coffee and calling for the check, hoping she'd get the hint and hurry and clean off her plate. For all I cared at that point, she could smash her dessert in her purse along with her mushrooms.

At last we left the restaurant and got in my car for the long silent ride home. Renewed concern for my dad dominated my thoughts as I drove. Mother acted as if she were glad Daddy was alone. Did she realize he was probably relieved nobody was around to harp on him every day?

When we got home, my mother took her purse full of leftovers into Cammie's bedroom and shut the door. I hoped the things she took had been paid for. I hadn't thought of counting the silverware before we left. I sat in the quietness of the living room, wondering why I'd been selected to have my life turned upside down.

Normally, when I had to wrestle with a problem or decision, I started a project like cleaning out the refrigerator, or putting new shelf paper in the pantry. Just the act of organizing something seemed to help order my thoughts. Not this time, though. Fatigue had completely taken over my mind. Besides, I'd already spiffed up every square inch of the house in preparation for selling it.

Darkness fell, turning my living room into a gloomy cave. The lone streetlight on our street, threw weak rays of light onto driveway. I don't know how long I sat there, but finally I saw headlights flash across the window, signaling Cammie's arrival. My mood immediately perked up.

Cammie flipped on the hall light when she came in. "Mom? What are you doing, sitting here in the dark?"

"Just thinking."

Cammie flopped down next to me on the couch. "I'm glad you're still up. I wanted to tell you something."

Oh please don't let it be bad news.

I reached for her hand. "What is it?"

"I wanted to thank you for taking Gran in. I love getting a chance to get to know her. I've always wanted a grandmother around. This is like a dream come true."

Oh Cammie. If you only knew. "I thought you were happy with our lives. Haven't I given you every opportunity a girl could want?"

"It's not the same thing. Don't get the idea I don't appreciate everything you've done. You're a great mom. Having Gran here is just sooo icing on the cake."

"You realize she won't be here long. Besides, you'll be going away to school soon."

"But if she comes to Seattle with us, I'll be able to see her all the time. She can tell me all about when you were a little girl. I wonder if she brought any photos. I've never seen pictures of you when you were young."

65

"I didn't bring any with me when I moved out here."
Take my mother to Seattle with me? Had Cammie lost her mind?

"You've never told me why you moved here."

A sigh escaped my lips. I'd kept the whole truth from Cammie long enough. Between the FBI background investigation, and my mother's presence, I'd be foolish to think I could hide my past from my daughter any longer. "I'm sure you've probably guessed I was never married to your father." I waited for her reaction. Her disappointment in me.

Cammie's gaze was steady, holding no judgment. "I've always wondered. But you never seemed to want to talk about it, so I didn't ask. I was even afraid you'd been a victim of rape or something."

"It was nothing like that. I was very young. Your age, actually. I thought I was in love and we foolishly let things get out of hand one night. We were both sorry afterwards, because we'd promised each other we'd wait till we were married. We vowed never to do it again. And we didn't. But after several weeks went by, I discovered I was pregnant. Actually my mother suspected it first, because I had severe morning sickness. She forced me to go to the doctor and then we knew for sure."

"What did your boyfrie—my dad say?"

"I never knew. My mother dragged me home and locked me in my room. Then she went over to his house to confront him and speak to his parents. She came back and said none of them wanted anything to do with me."

"But you said you were planning to marry someday."

"I thought so. Oh, honey, I never wanted you to feel your father didn't want you, and I didn't know how to tell you he ran out on me."

"But didn't you talk to him?"

"I never got the chance. He left on vacation with his family, and when they came back, he wasn't with them. I called them several times, trying to find out where he'd gone and they told me he'd met someone else in another

66

town." I rubbed a tiny escaped tear off my cheek. Even there in my comfortable living room with Cammie, the memory still hurt.

"That still doesn't explain why you moved here."

"My mother felt it would be best if I put you up for adoption. I couldn't do that. I refused to give you to strangers. You were mine. It would have been impossible to raise you in my hometown without causing my parents, and eventually you, a great deal of embarrassment, so I left." I waited for her reaction. The fact that my mother had told me to *get rid of the baby* would remain a secret.

"But you could have gone back later."

"No. It wouldn't have worked. My mother made it plain I wasn't welcome."

"What about my Grandpa?"

"He never stood up to her in his life. He was the best dad ever. But he would never go against her. I'm not even sure she told him I was pregnant until after I left home. He never said anything at all about it to me."

"I don't get it. Why did she come here then?"

"I don't know. It makes no sense."

"I bet she wants to make amends. Look how happy she was to see me."

Cammie always wanted to believe the best of anyone. I was the cautious one. "It would be wonderful if that were true, but I imagine she has another agenda."

"Mom, you're too suspicious. I think she must be sorry. She's been wonderful to me."

"I hope she continues to be nice to you, honey." Cammie's attitude was a tribute to the fine young woman she'd become. For years I'd feared her reaction to my unwed status. That she'd think less of me. Yet she sat, holding my hand, without a judgmental bone in her body.

"Do you think—I mean, would you be upset if someday I tried to find my father?"

"Give yourself some time to let this sink in first. Besides, I wouldn't know where to begin looking for him."

67

"I'd like to try someday."

"Do you think you'd be prepared for the possibility he may not be happy to see you?"

Cammie held herself very still. "I hadn't thought about that."

The sadness in her voice broke my heart. How I wish I had measured the consequences of my actions when I was her age. But I wouldn't trade having Cammie for anything.

"You know, the FBI is doing a background check because of the job I've applied for. They are already looking for him."

"I don't understand. Why?"

"It's only a precaution. In case he's a criminal or something."

"Of course he's not." Her eyes widened. "Is he?"

"I doubt if he's anything except an upstanding citizen. He was a wonderful person. I'd be surprised if he's changed much."

"But he left you in the lurch. I don't think I want to know him."

"He was young, honey."

"So when they find him, they'll let us know?"

"I think so. At least that's what agent Boyce told me."

By finally getting the facts of Cammie's birth out in the open, I realized I no longer had to worry about my mother spilling the beans. I should have trusted in the relationship I'd built with my daughter. If I'd been truthful with myself, I also feared the knowledge would give Cammie license to take things too far with Teddy.

I had worked my rear off to provide a good home for my daughter. It hadn't been easy. In the beginning, I went without things to provide her with formula and diapers. I never once asked anyone for help. Cammie and I always had a wonderful relationship. She could tell me anything. I was the one who held back. She was always a good child, even as a baby. Yes I spoiled her, but it never affected the goodness inside her. She's been the one thing I've cared about. Like a mother bear, I'd sacrifice anything for her. Now my mother's presence might ruin everything. She wants to come between my daughter and me. Why? She never wanted me, why would she want my daughter?

"Did you enjoy church this morning?"

Cammie's question reminded me of my resolve to forgive my mother for her transgressions. To be the kind of mom my daughter would always look up to. "Yes, I did. In fact I'll be attending again, if you like."

Cammie turned and pulled me into a hug. "Of course I'd like! I've always regretted we didn't share such an important part of my life."

I squeezed her, and then broke off the embrace. "I've always supported your wish to attend church haven't I?"

"It's not the same thing, Mom. Letting me believe what I want, and sharing those beliefs are two different things. And it's much more than merely going to church."

What does Cammie want from me? "I'm aware of that. I just don't want you to build your expectations of me too high. After all, it's not like I'm going to jump in and start teaching a Sunday school class, or sing in the choir."

"We don't even have a choir. We have a worship team."

I shrugged. Had Cammie completely missed my point? I wanted to dabble my toes in the water, not swim the English Channel.

"You know what would be great?"

"What?" *Here comes the challenge.*

"If we could participate in the upcoming street ministry together."

"I don't think you've told me about that."

"There's a man coming to visit our church who works with the homeless. He's going to organize a group of us to go to Portland and work with the Union Gospel Mission."

"I don't know how we could take the time to do that, with all we have to do to get ready to move."

"It would only be a few days. It would be so much fun to go. Kind of a last outing together before I go off to school."

"It doesn't sound like fun to me. What would we be doing exactly?"

"I don't know for sure. But when I know the date the man is coming, I'll let you know. He's going to explain everything."

The thought had some appeal to me. Cammie and I needed some time away from my mother. I didn't mind working in a soup kitchen if that's what we'd be doing.

"Let me think about it. It will depend on how quickly we can get everything done. Remember, we've planned a garage sale for next weekend. And there will probably be last minute shopping we need to do for your dorm room."

"Think hard, Mom. I think it would be a blast. And I know they need more adults along since it's mostly high school kids going."

There go my hopes for spending alone time with Cammie. Still, we'd be away from my mother. I stood. "Tomorrow's a work day. We need to turn in. We'll talk about it again, I promise."

Cammie rose from the couch and kissed my cheek. "Good night, Mom."

I went down the hall to my room, satisfied things were beginning to look up.

***

The next morning, I rose early and made French toast for all of us. Mother came to the table and never once wrinkled her nose, but only took half a slice. I held my tongue and didn't ask her what she did with her mushrooms from dinner the night before. I would merely make sure all the wastebaskets were emptied so there wouldn't be anything in there to attract mice or bugs.

I was putting the last plate in the dishwasher, when Mother finally spoke up. "I'd like to make a couple of long distance calls while you're gone. I'll pay for the charges of course."

"Mother, you don't have to pay me if you're calling Daddy."

"I didn't say anything about calling *him*."

I caught Cammie's look of surprise. Maybe her rosy glasses had faded a little.

"Of course you can make your calls." Evidently she didn't want to share who she wanted to call. A friend? Neighbor? Why not Daddy? My mind again went back to the strange things she'd said the night before.

"Thank you. I'm going to go work on my novel now." She shuffled out of the room without a backward glance.

Later in the day I sat at my desk at work trying to figure out why the feeling of foreboding surrounded me. My office, while small, had a large window. The desk was polished and free of clutter. I tried to keep both my work space and responsibilities as supervisor for a group of accounting clerks as organized as my home.

My intercom buzzed. It was one of the receptionists telling me I had a call on line three. I picked up the receiver and punched the button.

"Sandra?"

"Mother?" The identity of the caller explained why I'd felt dread swishing around in my stomach.

"Why can't you at least answer your own phone? That snotty girl who answered wanted to know my name. I told her it was none of her beeswax."

I clamped my teeth together, biting my lip in the process. "Ow!"

"What?"

"Nothing. Why did you call?"

"I just thought you'd like to know . . . that FBI guy is here again and he wants to talk to me. I told him he couldn't come in without a warrant."

Chapter Eight

Maude's journal
April 1982

Today is Sandra's tenth birthday. I took her and two of her friends to the skating rink. Afterwards we stopped at that new ice cream parlor in the mall. The girls each gave my daughter a nice present, and I drove them home. James was sitting in his chair by the window, reading the paper when we got home. For once, he hadn't butted in where he didn't belong. I'm glad I finally had it out with him. When given the choice of showing me the respect a wife deserved, or me taking Sandra and leaving, he made the wise decision. Tonight he's taking me to the movies. The neighbor woman is coming over to babysit Sandra.

***

I must have set a record making it home. Special Agent Boyce hadn't even moved from my front porch. I pulled into the driveway. Next door, Mrs. Connely knelt in the flowerbed bordering our properties. She often worked in her garden, as the blaze of color everywhere attested to. But I didn't take time to wave or otherwise acknowledge her presence. My future depended on smoothing over whatever damage Mother had done this time.

"Looks like you got off work a little early." He leaned against the doorframe, casually, as if waiting for a bus.

I nearly tripped in my haste to get to my front door. "I got a call and figured I'd better get home."

He abandoned his relaxed stance and met me at the steps. His eyes spoke silently of concern. "Tell me. Is your mother hiding something?"

"Why would you think that?" I knew full well how he'd gotten that impression. Why in the world had she refused to let him in? Didn't she know how that would look? I knew what her bizarre behavior might do to my chances for successfully passing the background investigation.

"You've answered my question with another question. Do you want to try again?"

I was painfully aware of my neighbor only a few yards away. Discussing Mother in public wasn't high on my list of desired activities. "Let's go inside. I'll make some coffee and we can talk."

He gestured toward the door. "After you."

I tried to turn the door handle, only to discover it was locked. I punched the doorbell and then gave the door several hard raps. I was fumbling for my key, when Mother opened the door. I pushed past her, barely reigning in my desire to chew her out. All I needed was another family fight in front of Agent Boyce.

"I'll be in my room."

"I have a few questions for you first." Agent Boyce followed me inside.

"Sandra's job has nothing to do with me."

"Mother! Would you please cooperate? What's the matter with you, anyway?"

He glanced back at me. "How about that coffee you promised?"

I could take a hint. I needed a few moments to compose myself anyway, so I went to the kitchen. With any luck, he'd have her in handcuffs by the time I got back with his coffee. I didn't know what the penalty would be for not cooperating with the FBI, but throwing her in the slammer for a while might teach her some manners.

Agent Boyce appeared in the kitchen before the coffee finished brewing. "Do you mind if we sit down?" He pulled out a kitchen chair.

I sat across from him like I had before. Uncertainty had replaced hopefulness this time though.

"I'd hoped your mother could shed some light on your father's whereabouts. I don't know if she's deliberately playing dumb, or if she really doesn't know where he is."

I nodded. "I've tried talking to her about him too, with the same lack of success."

"How do your parents get along?"

"I think they may have been having some problems. The day she arrived here, she told me she'd left him."

"My problem is this . . . he is nowhere to be found. One of their neighbors found a note on her door, asking that the mail be picked up, but it was unsigned. She didn't know if your mother or father wrote it. Unfortunately she'd tossed it in the garbage, so there's no way to check the handwriting."

I could feel my throat tighten. The room tipped, making me dizzy. I took a couple of deep breaths. Maintaining control took all my strength.

He reached across the table and touched my hand. "Are you OK?"

I took another breath, letting it out with a long shudder.

"There's no reason to be alarmed. At least not yet."

Not be alarmed? Too late. That ship had already sailed. I searched his face for some kind of clue to his truthfulness.

"We'll keep investigating till we find your father. He probably went off on a fishing trip or something."

"Daddy doesn't fish," I whispered.

"There *is* one thing you should know."

"Go ahead. It can't get any worse."

"The police in your hometown tell us they'd once been called to your parents' home to settle a domestic dispute. A neighbor had reported some yelling and screaming."

"That's not true! It's a lie my mother made up. Daddy is the gentlest man I know."

"Actually, they thought your mother had punched him in the eye. There was no arrest though, because your father claimed he ran into a cupboard door. His injuries didn't warrant any medical attention, so the officers left and only filed a report as a simple disturbance."

At that moment I wanted my mother punished for every bit of harm she'd ever caused anyone. Her treatment of my dad was unforgivable. It didn't matter what I'd promised God on Sunday. If He really existed, the world wouldn't be so insane. "Can't you arrest her or something? To make her tell you where my father is? What if she's hurt him? What if she locked him away in the basement? He could be starving to death while we sit here talking."

"There's no evidence anything like that has happened. But we'll continue looking." He reached toward me again. "I think you know, this has to be cleared up before I can sign off on your pre-employment investigation."

My head throbbed. "It isn't fair. She shouldn't be able to mess up everybody's lives like this. I want her gone. Out of my house."

"That might be a mistake. I don't think she presents any threat to you or your daughter. She may come around and give us some answers if we take the pressure off a little bit."

"You mean I should let her stay here? And pretend to like it?"

"That shouldn't be so hard. You can get some wise counsel at your church. Do you belong to a small group? I'm sure you know the value of prayer with your brothers and sisters in Christ."

Church speak. He might as well be conversing in Swahili. Yet I couldn't dispute his sincerity, or his kindness.

His eyes reminded me of a warm velvet blanket. I needed that kind of warmth around me, shutting out the cold fear in my heart.

"You look as if you want to tell me something." Matt's voice matched the softness of his eyes.

"I was just remembering something my mother said. She said my dad deserved what he got."

75

"Don't get yourself worked up. We're not ready to start digging up your parents' backyard yet," he said with a smile and a twinkle in his eye.

"I suppose your think that's funny, *Agent Boyce*!" How could he jest when my father remained unaccounted for?

"I'm merely trying to get you to look at things a little more objectively. And since I think we'll be meeting several more times, I'd prefer it if you'd call me Matt."

I was still mulling over the possibility of something buried in my mother's flower garden. Something or someone.

"Have you considered having your mother checked out by a doctor?"

A new threat to my sanity? "She doesn't seem to be sick. Her appetite is good. Besides, at her age, a few aches and pains are probably normal."

"I think you know I'm not referring to a strictly physical thing. Although she is pretty thin. But sometimes certain illnesses will cause personality changes or erratic behavior."

I got up from the table and poured our coffee. My mind swirled with all the possibilities my imagination could dream up. I barely had time to digest one thought before another threat reared its hideous head.

I replaced the coffee carafe and glanced at the clock. Dinnertime. How long was Matt planning to stay?

"Normally I start dinner as soon as I get home from work. Would you like to stay and eat with us?" I fully expected him to say no. After all, wouldn't it be a conflict of interest or something if he accepted a meal from me? However, I didn't want to be alone in the house with my mother. I knew I couldn't control what I said to her. I needed him to stay so I could concentrate on anything but what she'd said at the restaurant.

He looked at his watch. "I'm off the clock now." Then he surprised me by saying yes. "On one condition."

There's always a catch. Did he have more ugly possibilities to discuss with me?

"What?"

"You let me help."

That was unexpected. A man who cooks? Why hadn't anyone scooped him up and carried him to the altar? I pulled some hamburger patties out of the refrigerator. "How are you at working a grill?"

"That's my specialty. Is it in the backyard?"

"Right through that door. I just filled the propane tank so it should be ready to go."

"Leave everything to me." He winked and gifted me with a dazzling smile before he ambled out the back door. He removed his jacket and tie and placed them over one of the patio chairs, before he began preparing for the meal.

I found a can of baked beans and emptied it into a pan with a little brown sugar and chopped sweet onion. Matt stuck his head back in the door long enough to ask if Cammie would be coming home to eat with us.

"I can't think of any reason why not." I looked at my watch. "She'll be home in about twenty minutes."

I got out a bright colored tablecloth, the buns and condiments and carried them to the picnic table outside. I couldn't help admiring him as he puttered around the grill, getting everything ready. He moved as if he'd been cooking all his life. As if it were the most natural thing in the world to him.

I made a second trip into the house for the plates and silverware, but not before I took notice again of the handsome picture he made standing in my back yard. This was the kind of thing I had missed out on for all these years without Brian.

I was digging through one of my drawers looking for something to flip the burgers with, when my mother entered the kitchen. My body immediately stiffened as I turned and faced her.

She glanced out the window. "Why is he still here?"

77

"He's having dinner with us."

"He's using it as an excuse to pry information out of us."

"That shouldn't be a problem. We have nothing to hide," I said pointedly.

She continued watching him. Glaring at him would be a more accurate description.

"Well, wait till he finds out you had Cammie out of wedlock. He won't be so friendly then."

"He already knows. And Cammie does too." It felt good to say that to her. She could no longer hold that piece of news over my head.

"You tell people? No wonder you've never been able to land a husband."

"I'm not married, because I've never found anyone I loved as much as Brian."

"You call what you did with that boy love?"

"What do you call love, mother? Do you love Daddy? Did you ever love me?" I escaped into the backyard with the beans and salad, before I had to hear her answer.

"Hey, what's wrong?" Matt reached my side in three huge steps. "You look as if you're about to cry."

I shook my head, not trusting my voice.

"Never mind." He placed his hand on my shoulder. "I can see your mother shooting daggers out the window at us. Don't let her get to you."

"I can't help it. She's always known how to push all the right buttons."

Matt chuckled. "Stay out here with me then. I don't think she'll misbehave as long as I'm here."

Matt couldn't have known how protected he made me feel. My dad had been the only other man who'd ever made me feel that way. Yet in the end, he hadn't been able to protect me from *her*.

"I'm home!" Cammie's voice projected all the way through the house and outside. I turned and saw her kiss

78

my mother on the cheek before she came outside. She gave Matt a puzzled look. A look that turned hopeful.

"Cammie, I don't think you've met Special Agent Boyce from the FBI. He's been doing my background investigation for the job in Seattle."

He stuck out his hand. "Call me Matt. It's nice to meet you. I've heard all about you."

Cammie's shoulders slumped a little. Had she thought I'd found her father in less than twenty-four hours? Guilt stabbed at me like a double-edged blade. I suddenly had a clear picture of what I had cheated her of while she was growing up.

"Well, if you want my opinion, she's the best mom in the whole world. The FBI would be lucky to get her, too."

A guttural sound came from my mother's direction, but I managed to ignore it.

Matt put the meat on the grill, and he and Cammie chatted about her summer job till the wonderful odor of barbequed burgers let us know it was time to eat.

Cammie called my mother out of the house, and we all seated ourselves around the table. I expected Cammie to ask the blessing as she usually did, but Matt asked if he could.

I peeked at my mother. She ignored our bowed heads and reached for the baked beans.

"So you're a Christian," Cammie said, obviously pleased, after Matt finished.

He smiled. "Yes I am. In fact, I sometimes attend the church you and your mother go to."

"Really? I don't recall seeing you there."

"I only attend when I'm in town visiting my sister."

Really? What's her name? Maybe I know her."

"Patty Browning"

"I *do* know her. She teaches Sunday school. Where do you live?"

"Seattle."

Cammie glanced at me than back at Matt. "I guess that makes sense since you work for the FBI. Do you have any children?"

"Cammie, maybe you should give him a chance to eat his dinner." I gave her the look most kids know so well. Perhaps she didn't realize she was interrogating a master at the third degree.

"That's OK." He tilted his head toward my daughter, as if she were the only one present. "I've never married. I always figured my job would intrude on my family life. I have a couple of swell nephews, though, and I do fun things with them whenever I get the chance."

The wistful look on Cammie's face punched yet another hole in my heart. Anyone could see, Cammie included, what a great father Matt would make. Renewed anger toward my mother raised its ugly head again. If I'd been allowed to stay with them and keep Cammie, my father could have helped fill the void left by Brian when he'd taken off.

"I'd love to meet them sometime." Cammie's sincerity came through, reminding me how much she liked kids.

My daughter warmed up to Matt like she never had to Charlie. But then the same thing could be said for me. It had been a long time since someone new and exciting had come into my life.

Matt answered her, "I think we can arrange that."

We ate in silence for several minutes.

"Mom and I might go on a missions trip." Cammie's excitement permeated her statement.

"That's great! Where?" Matt grinned at her, giving her his full attention.

"It's not overseas or anything. It's aimed at the street people in downtown Portland."

"Sounds fine. I've done that myself, a time or two."

"Maybe you'd like to go with us."

I choked on my burger. Every eye turned toward me. Cammie jumped up and whacked me on the back a couple of times.

"I'm alright. I'm alright." I waved her away.

"That wouldn't happen if you'd chew your food the way you were taught." My mother uttered her first words since she sat down with us.

Matt's watchful gaze spoke of his concern. At least two people at the table cared whether I choked to death or not.

I took a sip of coffee and drew several deep breaths. "How does ice cream sound for dessert?"

My mother spoke again. "None for me. I might be getting lactose intolerant. And you know what that does."

Whatever the symptoms were, I figured I didn't want to hear about it. Especially while we were eating. And . . . she'd never been sick a day in her life as far as I knew. I shot her a glance. But she did seem a bit pale. In fact her color bordered on ashen. I looked at Matt, whose questioning gaze told me he'd noticed too.

"Mother, are you feeling alright?"

"I'm a little woozy, that's all." The words were barely out of her mouth when her eyes rolled back and she slumped in her chair. Cammie and I jumped up at the same time, each grasping an arm to gently guide her to the ground.

Chapter Nine

Maude's journal
April 1988

> Sandra turned sixteen today. I gave her money to take some of her friends to the movies and then out for pizza later. This was her first girl-boy party. I detest that boy Brian. He's always trying to get Sandra to go to church with him. Of course I told her she couldn't go. Nobody has to tell me what Sandra would be in for if she got hooked up with his kind. James is taking me to dinner again tonight. I picked a place our newspaper rated with four stars. Not that James would even notice. But I figure if I have to sit across the table from a man who hardly talks to me, I might as well enjoy the meal. My life with James has not turned out how I'd hoped. Sometimes I don't think he loves me any more than my father did.

***

"Her breathing's funny," I said to Matt who had come around the table to assist. I gave her arm a little shake. "Mother, wake up. You've fainted."

She didn't answer. I shook her again.

"Why won't she talk to us?" Cammie wailed.

Matt took over, positioning her straight out on the ground. "I think you should call 911. She's out cold, and I don't like her color."

"I'll do it." I ran to the kitchen. The sound of Cammie's sobs followed me.

The dispatcher tried to get me to stay on the line, but my anxiety overrode her request. I rushed back outside.

"They're coming right away. How is she?"

Matt's placed his thumb and forefinger on my mother's wrist. "She's breathing, but her pulse is a little weak."

"So you don't think she's faking, then?" I whispered.

Cammie heard and sobbed louder. Cammie couldn't have known about the conversation Matt and I had earlier, but my mother might have been eavesdropping. I wouldn't put it past her.

Matt looked up at me. "No. She's not faking."

When I heard sirens approaching, I ran to the front of my house to guide them to the patio. The medics motioned the three of us to stand back. One of them called out questions about Mother's health and any medications she had been taking. The only question I knew the answer to, was her name and age. I felt my face heat up. My lack of knowledge about my own mother must have seemed awful to Matt.

Someone rolled one of those folding gurneys up to where my mother lay. "We're going to transport your mother to the hospital."

"I want to stay with her," Cammie choked out.

"Sorry. There's not enough room to take any family members." The medic looked at me. "Have your husband take you directly to the emergency room. You can be with her there as soon as she's stabilized."

They loaded her on the gurney and wheeled it around the house to the front where the medic van waited. Mrs. Connely abandoned her garden and ran up to ask what had happened.

"Something wrong with Gran." Cammie accepted the hug offered by our neighbor.

I watched them load my mother in the ambulance and then ran in the house for my purse and keys. The medics were pulling away from the curb, lights and sirens going, when I got back. I turned to Matt.

"I'm sorry there wasn't time to correct the medic who thought you were my husband. I need to drive Cammie to the hospital now. I'm sure we'll be talking—"

"Wait a minute," Matt interjected. I don't think either of you should be driving as upset as you are. I'll take you."

"Thank you, but that won't be necessary."

"I insist."

"Mom! Let's just go!" Cammie ran toward Matt's sedan.

I didn't have the strength to argue with either of them. Matt led me to his car, and buckled me in the front seat. On the way to the hospital, he tried to fill the silence with encouraging words, but my ability to concentrate on what he said fell short. I glanced at Cammie in the back seat. Her head was bowed and I could see her lips moving. She had bonded with my mother in such a short time.

Matt dropped us off at the emergency room entrance. Cammie and I hurried inside while he parked his car. The woman at the counter handed me a clipboard with all kinds of papers to fill out. When I came to the "next of kin" space, I wrote in my dad's name. *Somebody needs to notify him. But how?* I filled out the forms as best as I could, but again was struck with how little I knew about my mother.

Cammie and I waited in a room evidently set aside for agitated family members. Matt joined us, and offered what comfort he could to my daughter. I found it difficult to believe he had no children of his own. He was a natural comforter. I mentioned my concern about contacting my dad.

Matt excused himself to make a phone call to his Midwest contact. "Would you like me to give your pastor a call too?"

"Yes, please." Cammie answered before I had a chance to reject his offer. My mother certainly didn't want a pastoral visit. I saw no need, at least at that point, for a busy pastor to come to the hospital when we all might be going home before he arrived.

I watched Matt make his way out of the waiting room.

Cammie touched my arm. "How long do you think we'll have to sit here before they'll let us see Gran?"

"I have no idea. Probably not long, though." I rubbed the back of her hand.

"I thought I'd run down to the chapel and say a prayer for her."

"Just hurry back. Once your grandmother gets checked out, I'm sure she'll want to go right home." I watched Cammie leave. How like her to think of praying for her grandmother.

A nurse appeared from behind the double doors of the patient area. "Ms. Hughes?"

I jumped up. "Yes?"

"Could you follow me please?" She turned and pushed open the door she'd entered through.

I barely made it through the door before it shut. She walked ahead of me at a brisk pace, her rubber-soled shoes making soft swishing noises on the floor. We rounded a corner and entered an area bustling with activity. A nurse's station stood in the middle of the large room. Tiny curtained cubicles circled the perimeter of the room, each only a few steps away from the hub of the room where nurses, doctors, and some people I couldn't identify, went about their business. Nobody looked up when we walked past.

The nurse stopped in front of me, nearly causing a collision. Evidently those white shoes of hers had superior braking power as well as built in speed.

"Wait here." She pointed to the floor where I stood, then disappeared behind a curtain.

A groan came from one of the cubicles somewhere off to my right. Low murmurs of conversation came from every corner of the room and from the nurse's station in the middle. The smell of disinfectant assaulted my nose. I strained to hear what was going on behind the curtain where my mother lay.

After what seemed like an hour, the nurse reappeared. "The doctor will speak to you in a moment."

I looked over her shoulder and through the space in the curtain she'd left open. Two people hovered over the bed, fiddling with lines and tubes and knobs. I got a glimpse of an IV in my mother's arm.

"Excuse me." A husky young man approached wheeling a gurney. He pulled back the curtain and pushed the gurney to the side of my mother's bed.

"What's going on? Are you taking my mother somewhere?"

The man, who I assumed was the doctor, turned and spoke. "We're sending her upstairs for an MRI."

He turned back, and they lifted her onto the gurney. They covered her with a light blanket and the younger man wheeled her out. I caught the look on her face. It was pure, unadulterated fear.

The doctor motioned me into the cubicle. My mother's clothing lay in a heap on one of the chairs. The nurse picked them up and put them in a bag, motioning me to sit down. I sat, and then stood again. *Had they noticed me wringing my hands? Is that why they asked me to sit down? Did I look so distraught that I might faint?* I shoved my hands into the pockets of my slacks.

The doctor looked up from whatever he was writing. "Your mother is very sick. I see from her chart she's married. Have you notified her husband?"

Very sick? "Uh, someone is trying to reach him. She's visiting here and he stayed back home in Detroit."

"I haven't been able to get very much information out of her. She's a little disoriented."

"What's wrong with her?"

"You know she's diabetic."

No, I didn't know.

He continued, "Evidently she hasn't been paying much attention to her insulin levels. In fact I gather she hasn't been taking care of herself at all."

"That can be treated, can't it?"

"In most cases, yes. But I suspect she's lost a great deal of kidney function. That's what we're trying to determine now."

"But she's going to be all right, isn't she?"

The doctor shook his head. "I can't tell you anything for sure right now. We need to keep her here at least overnight. Longer, if we can't get her stabilized."

"When is she coming back here?"

"It depends on how many patients are ahead of her in radiology. You can wait here, if you like."

"Can my daughter come back here too?"

"It wouldn't be a good idea. Any kind of commotion or stress would only aggravate her condition."

I dropped onto the chair. I knew very little about diabetes. Or kidney problems. Would she need dialysis? Would she need round-the-clock care? Was her condition terminal? I'd have to get some education on the subjects immediately.

I couldn't sit still. I stood and paced back and forth in the tiny cubicle. While I wanted her out of my life, I certainly didn't want her to die. If she did, I'd go to my grave knowing our relationship never worked. As toxic as her personality was, should I have made more of an effort to get along with her? I didn't even know why she hated me. That was evident long before I got pregnant. Was it that she'd never wanted children? Was I so unlovable as a child?

I'd spent the years of Cammie's life trying to ensure we had the kind of relationship I'd always wanted to have with my own mother. I'd spent the same years, wondering what I'd done to make my mother dislike me so. If something happened to my mother now, there would never be a chance to resolve our differences. Was I prepared for that?

I sat again, and closing my eyes, leaned my head on the wall behind me. Visions of my mother as a younger woman flashed before me. She'd been pretty. Energetic. Remote,

87

and sometimes snappy, but not the same bitter old woman who'd arrived on my doorstep.

Nearly a half hour later, the nurse returned. "We just got a call from the doctor. He's read the results of the MRI and has admitted your mother to a room upstairs. If you would return to the waiting room, someone will tell you when you can see her."

I felt numb. I rose and found my way back to where Cammie was probably waiting and fretting. When I entered the waiting area, I saw Matt still there, holding Cammie's hand and speaking intently to her. They both looked up as I neared.

"Your grandmother will be staying here overnight." I plopped down in an empty chair across from them.

"What's wrong with her? Is it serious?" Cammie's red eyes told me she'd been crying hard.

"It could be serious. She's a diabetic and is having some complications. The good news is, they are doing tests and treating her."

My brief explanation mollified her for the moment.

Matt left and came back with a cup of coffee for me, and a soft drink for Cammie.

"You remembered how I take my coffee."

"It's my job to remember things."

So his acts of friendship were his duty? How easily I'd fallen for his kind words, thinking maybe he actually cared. I'd gone my entire adult life not being gullible as far as men were concerned. I'd always been able to discern their motives. *Oh, Matt you're very good at what you do.*

Our glances met. Mine deliberately cool, and his all warm and fuzzy. "I didn't mean that the way it sounded."

My spine stiffened. "I don't know what you mean."

Matt grinned, exposing the dimples on each side of his mouth. "Sure you do. Do you always have your guard up?"

Until recently. "Do you always read imaginary motives into what people say?"

88

"What they say, their facial expressions, body language . . . yes, I'm told I'm good at it, too."

"There's a fine line between confidence and arrogance."

Cammie shifted position in her chair. "How long do we have to wait here, anyway?"

Matt jumped up. "I'll go see what the holdup is."

Despite whatever his agenda was, his presence reassured me. I watched him stride to the information desk. The woman there listened to whatever he said to her, and picked up the phone. I couldn't hear what was being said, but Matt nodded his head and came back to us.

"Your mother's in room 904. You can go up now."

I looked at my watch. "There's no need for you to hang around here. Why don't you go on? Cammie and I can take a cab home."

"I wouldn't dream of leaving you ladies here alone. I've got nothing better to do anyway." He gestured. "Follow me. I'll take you to the elevators."

"How do you know so much about this hospital?"

"My sister's boys were born upstairs in the maternity ward. Here we are at the elevators." Matt punched the call button. "I managed to get in touch with our Midwest office. They're going to send someone around to talk to your parents' neighbors. Also, your pastor isn't available this evening, but one of his associates can come by and pay your mother a visit if you like. I told him you'd let him know if anyone was needed."

How easy it seemed to sit back and let Matt handle everything. As a single mom, I'd had to take charge all the time. What would working in the same office with him be like? If our friendship were to grow, would I increasingly lean on him? Be tempted to give up my independence?

The "ding" sounded, signaling we'd arrived at our floor. Cammie rushed ahead and found Mother's room first. By the time Matt and I caught up, she'd already stationed herself next to the head of the bed.

Mother seemed alert but tired. She reached toward Cammie and clutched her arm. Cammie patted her hand, and then leaned down to kiss her cheek. When she stood again, I saw tears streaming down my mother's cheeks.

Chapter Ten

Maude's Journal
June 1990

> *Sandra graduated from high school tonight. Unlike me, she had the benefit of having both parents at her ceremony. James went behind my back and bought her a car. It's nicer than the car he got me three years ago. And how did she show her appreciation? She got herself knocked up. By Brian, the so-called Christian. He's gonna regret he ever met her. I'll see to it.*
> ***

My mother's cold, steely persona disintegrated right in front of me. Seeing her reduced to a quivering old woman, unexpectedly brought tears to my eyes. I swiped at them before anyone saw. I needn't have worried. My mother never loosened her grip on Cammie, nor did she take her eyes off her.

Matt stepped into the room next to me. "Mrs. Hughes, we are doing everything we can to contact your husband so he can be here with you."

My mother finally turned her gaze from Cammie. "He won't be coming." Then she broke down into choking sobs.

Fear washed over me like a tidal wave. What did she mean? She made it sound so final. Like he'd died. Didn't Matt wonder about her statement?

Matt stepped to her bedside and laid his palm on her shoulder. "You don't know that for sure."

Mother rolled away from him, pulling loose one of the lines, which were attached to her. An alarm sounded and two nurses rushed in. One nurse said, "You people need to leave the room so we can do our jobs." They went straight to her side and began checking her over and fussing with tubes and other gadgets. I didn't even know the function of most of the equipment, but they must have been important to bring everyone running like that.

Cammie stroked her grandmother's head. "I'm staying."

Nobody objected.

"We'll be right outside." Matt took my arm and led me to the hall.

Right across the hall from my mother's room, was an alcove with several comfortable looking chairs. I took the one closest to the hall, and Matt sat next to me.

"Your mother and Cammie have gotten pretty close."

I nodded my head, not trusting my voice. I closed my eyes, but I couldn't erase the image of her lying so helpless and distraught. In the past, I'd only seen her react to stress with anger. Lashing out. What made her that way? I could only speculate. But she'd definitely lost her usual edge since she'd collapsed.

Matt reached for his cell phone, looking at the caller ID. "I need to find a pay phone. They don't allow cells in here. I'll be right back."

After Matt left, I really felt alone. What was I supposed to do? I clearly wasn't needed in Mother's room. Not having some kind of action plan disquieted me. I busied myself with stacking the magazines in straight, even piles on the tables. As I gathered them, I noticed their titles. *Who reads golfing, hunting, and bride magazines while they're sitting around here?*

I envisioned someone planning a wedding while a loved one lay terminally ill in one of the rooms. *Surely the magazine was placed in there by mistake. Should I sort these by title? Date?*

I soon got bored, and stepped out to look up and down the hall. How long before someone would come to explain Mother's condition? The doctor downstairs barely scratched the surface of all my questions.

I sat down again and absently thumbed through a year old copy of a popular women's magazine. My eyes wouldn't even focus long enough to read an article. I slammed it down on the table. The only break in my monotony was an occasional announcement over a speaker hanging in the corner of the alcove. It provided little real diversion, since most of the messages were in code, or named people who were total strangers.

Footsteps came down the hall toward me. I stood, hoping I'd be able to speak to a doctor or nurse. A face peered around the corner. No such luck. "Charlie." I hadn't expected him at all.

He advanced toward me, enveloping me in a stifling hug. "Why didn't you call me? I haven't heard from you all day, and then I found out you were here."

I extricated myself from his grasp and took a step back. I was in no mood for our lopsided friendship. There were enough complications in my life right across the hall. "How did you know I was here?"

"Cammie called to let me know she might not be coming to work tomorrow. Naturally, when I heard your mother had been hospitalized, I came right over."

"There was no need for you to do that." My jaw tightened. I don't know why Charlie's presence annoyed me. Maybe because he took it for granted I wanted him there, even though I'd clearly told him we'd never be more than friends.

"I like your mother. I admit I don't know her well— yet. But so far, she's been very nice to me." Charlie took one of the chairs and gestured toward the one next to him. "Sit down and talk to me. You look pretty ragged."

"That's just what every woman wants to hear." I sat, but knew I wouldn't be able to stay still long.

Charlie reached for my hand. "Why do you always take what I say the wrong way?"

Because you don't have a clue about how to talk to me? I kept my hands clasped in my lap, not giving him the opportunity to comfort me.

"Where is Cammie?"

"She's in with Mother."

"She sounded pretty distraught when I spoke to her."

"Yes she is." I hoped he wouldn't expect me to carry on a lucid conversation with him. I was much too distracted. I stood up and walked out into the hall. Matt had been gone awhile. Would he be back soon?

Charlie followed. "Is it serious? With your mother, I mean?"

"I'm afraid so."

"You'll probably want to put the sale of your home on hold then."

I whirled around to face him. "Why would you think that?" *Is this why he's here? To see if my mother's condition will have any affect on him?* "Haven't I told you over and over that I'm leaving?"

The shocked look on Charlie's face made me regret my words as much as my tone of voice. "I didn't mean to snap at you."

He immediately composed his features. "Of course you didn't. Come and sit down. Can I get you anything?"

"No, thank you. I'm fine." I wasn't fine, but couldn't begin to describe the turmoil I felt to Charlie. Plus, I didn't know why suddenly he made me so impatient. I returned to my chair and picked up another magazine, hoping to discourage any further conversation.

Charlie took the hint, but managed to irritate me by drumming his fingers on the arm of his chair. Maybe engaging in small talk would stop his fidgeting. "Do you know anything about diabetes?"

"Not a lot. I gather there are two types. One that children get, and the other one comes along later in life. Why? Is that what your mother has?"

94

"Apparently. The doctor thinks Mother's stress contributed to her collapse today. That, and not watching what she ate or taking the proper medicine."

"Knowing you, Sandy, you'll be an expert by the time she's ready to come home."

I shuddered. How could I take on the added responsibility of someone with a life-threatening illness? Who would shuttle her back and forth to the doctor? Monitor her medications? Obviously she hadn't done such a swell job on her own. Yet, if there were nobody else to do it, I knew it would fall to me. I wished I had siblings to help or at least to seek advice from. But my parents never saw fit to have any more children after I was born. Was I an accident in their lives? Or a cranky, difficult child, so awful, they didn't dare try again?

More footsteps. I jerked my head around toward the hall. Matt arrived, holding a bulging paper bag. My spirits lifted when I saw him.

"You're back."

"Sorry I took so long. My phone call took longer than I'd anticipated. Here." He handed the bag to me. "I brought you and Cammie some deli sandwiches. I figured you'd be hungry since we didn't finish our burgers."

"Why, thank you. That was very thoughtful." I peeked into the bag. Then I sensed Charlie's presence moving up close behind me.

"Who are you?" he asked Matt.

"Oh, excuse me. Charlie, this is Matt Boyce. Matt, Charlie Dalan."

Matt stuck out his hand first. "I believe we've spoken on the phone."

"Huh?" *They'd met?*

Matt glanced at me. "He was one of your references. Remember?"

"Of course." My brain cells were definitely slipping away.

Charlie barely returned Matt's handshake. Then he draped an arm over my shoulder. "So you're the one who's been trying to lure our girl to Seattle."

I shrugged off Charlie's arm and moved away. "He is only doing the background stuff. He had nothing to do with my decision to apply for that job."

Matt raised an eyebrow at Charlie. "I'm a little surprised to see you here. I didn't get the impression you and Sandra were all that close."

Charlie glared at Matt, for no reason at all that I could discern. "Is running errands part of your job?" Charlie pointedly looked down at the bag of sandwiches I still held.

What is going on here? These two guys act like enemies. Or would it be rivals? Over me? That's ridiculous.

I pulled a sandwich out, hoping to divert their attention. "Charlie, would you mind taking this in to Cammie? She's right across the hall. And since she is the one who called you, I'm sure she'll be happy to see you."

Charlie took the sandwich like a pouting little child. "Good idea. I'd like to see your mom, too."

I took a deep breath once Charlie left. With luck, Mother's nurses would tell him to go home. Matt had an amused twinkle in his eyes. I could only imagine what he thought about Charlie's rude behavior.

"Let's sit down. You need to eat something." Matt sat in the chair Charlie had vacated.

I had no appetite, but tried to make a show of unwrapping my sandwich and taking a bite. "Ummm. Very good. Thank you." It tasted like sawdust. I chewed and chewed like it was a cheap and gristly piece of beef.

"Somehow I think you're not quite sincere." He grinned, calming me some.

I swallowed, surprised at how difficult that simple action was. "Aren't you having anything?"

"I ate mine while I was on the phone."

"That must have made for interesting conversation."

Matt chuckled. "My boss is used to me by now. Sometimes the only time I have to call him is during my lunch or dinner. I'm pretty good at multi-tasking."

"I'll bet you are." I took another bite.

"I've been called back to Seattle to be briefed on a case the Bureau has assigned me."

Disappointment coursed over me. I'd grown too accustomed to Matt's presence. I'd totally ignored the fact he didn't live or work nearby. "Another background investigation?"

"No. In fact I don't normally do those. It's something else."

"You're not going to tell me, are you?"

"Nope." He smiled, letting me know I shouldn't take his secrecy personally.

"You'll be back?" I needed him to stay. He anchored me.

"Most likely. I can't say when, though. As soon as I can, though. Do you think Charlie would mind driving you and Cammie home?"

"You have to leave so soon?"

Matt's expression softened. "I can stay a few minutes more. In fact, I want to pray with you before I go." He leaned forward, putting his elbows on his knees.

I took another bite. *Pray with me? Oh yeah. He thinks I'm a regular attendee of Cammie's church.* I swallowed and quickly took another bite.

Matt took my sandwich from me, setting it on a napkin on the side table. He waited for me to finish chewing. "Let's bow our heads."

I didn't know what else to do but comply. Nobody had ever personally prayed for me before. Would I be expected to pray aloud, too?

Matt took my hand and started, "Father, we come to You tonight asking for Your comfort and peace. Please make Your presence strongly evident to Sandy and Cammie. Guide the doctors and staff as they take care of Mrs.

Hughes. Give them supernatural knowledge that will speed her healing. I ask that You use this event to bring Sandy closer to You than ever. Fill her heart with love and forgiveness toward her mother, and soften her mother's heart as well. I also pray that Sandy's father would contact her. We ask these things in the name of Your Son, Jesus Christ. Amen."

"Thank you." Matt's short prayer touched me so much I couldn't say anything else.

"I have to go now. Tell Cammie and your mother goodbye. I'll be in touch." He left, but not before he placed a light kiss on my forehead.

I sat there alone, pondering the kiss, and the meaning of Matt's prayer.

The thing he prayed about my mother . . . how would one go about loving the unlovable? Forgive the unforgivable? Surely if I were to forgive her, it would take an act of God to help me. I'd already vowed to be nicer to her. That had lasted all of a few minutes. Until she'd brought out her claws again.

I knew little about how religion worked, but it was plain that my attitude toward Mother was a detriment to my well-being. What kept me from forgiving her? Her attitude toward my pregnancy? Things were different in her generation. When a daughter had a baby out of wedlock, the entire family was shamed.

Mother accepted Cammie now, didn't she? Sure, she picked at *me* at every opportunity, but how would she act if I treated her as if I loved her, the way Cammie loves me? Why was I afraid to try? And why was I afraid to ask God to help me?

I closed my eyes, trying to remember the words in Matt's prayer. Something about me growing close to God. *Was that even possible? Probably it was, for the severely religious. But what about someone like me? Here I am approaching middle age, and I've never so much as given God a thought. I hadn't even said bedtime prayers as a child.*

Cammie spent hours reading her Bible. Perhaps I could find the answers in there. I wouldn't know where to start, though. Maybe if I made an anonymous call to Cammie's pastor, he'd give me some ideas. I discarded the notion of making a personal appointment. After all, if it didn't pan out, I wouldn't want someone hounding me to come to church.

Charlie's return interrupted my thoughts. "The doctor wants to see you in your mother's room. I think you should prepare yourself."

Chapter Eleven

Maude's Journal
July 1990

That boy, Brian, and his family left town after I threatened to go to the police and file rape charges. I can't believe it was so easy to get rid of him. Unfortunately, Sandra dug in her heels and insisted on keeping her baby. I tried everything I could to get her to change her mind. I just know James would spoil Sandra's baby the same way he spoiled her, but he's not going to get the chance. Sandra packed her bags and left. I don't know how I'll explain it to James, but at least there won't be any more tension in this house.

***

When I entered Mother's hospital room, I expected the worst. Instead, she was sitting up in bed, chatting with Cammie and a nurse.

Cammie stood up from the bedside chair. "Why don't you sit here, Mom?"

Charlie moved to the opposite side of Mother's bed and took her hand. Mother gazed up at him as if he were Cary Grant and she was Doris Day. I glared at Charlie. Had he deliberately made me think my mother had taken a bad turn?

As soon as we'd all assembled, the doctor spoke. "Mrs. Hughes is stable." He looked directly at her. "I hope I don't need to emphasize the consequences of further inattention to her condition."

"Could you be more specific?" I asked.

"The diabetes, of course. She'll no longer be able to control it with diet. I'll prescribe insulin for her when she's released. Someone will come around before she leaves the hospital, and show her how to administer it."

Cammie looked up. "Can we take her home now?"

The doctor peered over his glasses at her. "She has to stay overnight so we can monitor her. I've also ordered more tests run to determine her kidney function. I think you should be prepared for her to be on dialysis."

I'd seen some pamphlets in the emergency waiting room. I planned to pick them up on the way out. Since they couldn't very well send her back home with nobody to care for her, Cammie and I needed to educate ourselves.

Trying to juggle taking care of Mother, with selling the house, seemed an insurmountable problem. But we could do it. As a temporary measure.

I concentrated on the rest of what the doctor had to tell us. Then he excused himself and left with the nurse. We were alone with my mother.

Charlie said, "See, I told you everything would work out."

He'd never told me any such thing. He must have been playing the part of comforter for Mother's benefit while I was outside with Matt.

"Charles, you're such a fine young man. I'm looking forward to getting to know you much better." Mother gazed at him with adoration.

Once again, life was out of my control. Would it ever be normal again?

The speaker in the hall blared a warning that visiting hours were over. Cammie kissed her grandmother goodnight.

I hiked my purse strap over my shoulder. "Goodbye, Mother. We'll see you tomorrow."

"Oh don't bother taking time off work. Charles said he'd drive me home."

"Mother, we can't impose on others. Either Cammie or I, or both of us will come."

101

"I thought since Charles is practically a member of the family, it would be alright if he did. Besides, I enjoy his company."

Charlie looked triumphantly at me. I gave up arguing and left the room. Charlie and Cammie met me at the elevator.

"Are you upset about something?" Charlie asked innocently.

How astute. "It's been a long day. I'm anxious to get home."

When we reached the parking lot, I got into the backseat, leaving the front seat next to Charlie for Cammie. His presence and concern smothered me. I needed some distance between us. Some alone time.

He dropped us off at home, obviously disappointed when I didn't ask him in. Dismissing Cammie's offer of help, I spent the next hour cleaning up from our earlier barbeque.

Cammie had already gone to bed when I came back in. The living room seemed unnaturally quiet. I picked up the remote and turned on the TV. The eleven o'clock news had just started. I flipped through the channels till I found what I wanted. A religious station. A repeat telecast from a large church in Portland. Would it have the answers I needed?

The music was upbeat and contemporary, like the music at Cammie's church. But instead of the expected sermon, they showed a series of video clips from the street ministry they ran in downtown Portland. When they mentioned the Union Gospel Mission, I thought it was too bad Cammie had gone to bed. She would have enjoyed seeing the program. I put a blank tape in the VCR to record it for her to see later.

Most of the clips showed teenagers handing out pamphlets and New Testaments. Then they showed others working in a kitchen and serving meals. The long line of people waiting to be fed surprised me. Living in the suburbs insulated me from the hardships of the unemployed and homeless. I wondered if the man who seemed to be leading the volunteer group was the same one who would be coming to Cammie's church. I couldn't see much of his face, so I'd probably never know.

When the program finished, I flipped off the TV. I still wasn't sleepy so I went to the kitchen and fixed myself a cup of herbal tea. Guaranteed to induce slumber, or so it said on the package. I pulled a tablet from its place next to the phone and started a list of things to do the next few days. I'd go ahead with the garage sale, so I needed to place an ad. Pick up garage sale signs. Get small bills for making change. Research Mother's illness, including any possibility it might be genetic.

At last I tore the page out of the tablet, folded it and put it in my purse. One more quick look outside to make sure I'd put everything away, and I went off to bed.

***

I called the hospital the next morning to see if they knew what time they would discharge my mother. After being told it would be late afternoon, Cammie and I both decided we'd go to work. I called again at lunch and didn't get any new information. I thought again of my dad. Had anyone reached him? He'd want to be with us, even if Mother *had* left him. I refused to believe that even someone as bitter as my mother would have harmed him. I had to trust he'd make an appearance any day.

About an hour before quitting time, I got a phone call from the hospital.

"Ms. Hughes? I'm Daisy Brown, your mother's social worker."

My mother has her own social worker?

"What can I do for you?"

"I'd like you to come to the hospital so we can chat about some things. Perhaps you could fill me in where your mother was unable."

She's probably going to tell me about Mother's treatment plan. "I guess so. What time?"

103

"I'll be here until six o'clock. Just ask for me at the desk."

I agreed to come, and hung up to call Cammie to let her know I wouldn't be home to cook dinner till later.

"Do you have to meet this lady tonight?" Cammie sounded a little anxious.

"Yes. Why?"

"Charlie has arranged for us to take a tour of the dialysis center. We really should go together."

Charlie again. I couldn't recall him being so pushy in the past. What had changed to give him the idea he could arrange things on my behalf now? "Charlie shouldn't have done that without checking with me first."

"He's only trying to help, Mom."

I saw no reason to delve into the subject further. As Charlie's summer employee, she shouldn't have to be caught in the middle of any conflict Charlie and I might have.

"Let me speak to him."

"He's not here right now. He went out to buy Gran a welcome home present."

If Charlie were a mosquito, I would have gone for the repellant. But what would repel something way more annoying than a tiny bug? I vowed to find out and use it.

"Then give him the message we won't be going with him."

"Do you mind if I go?"

I weighed the pros and cons. It wouldn't hurt to have as much information as we could get. "Go ahead. But, please don't bring him home with you. I'm too exhausted for company."

"I won't. Thanks. Gotta go, there's another call coming in."

An hour later, a volunteer at the hospital escorted me to Daisy Brown's office. Daisy, as she asked me to call her, was a tall African American woman who looked young

104

enough to be Cammie's schoolmate. She motioned me to sit and opened a folder on her desk.

"I'm glad you could come. I've had a couple of interviews with your mother, and frankly, I'm concerned."

"She can be difficult at times."

Daisy said something under her breath that sounded like "ah." I naturally assumed she'd witnessed one of Mother's tantrums. Probably over something as insignificant as the size of her pillow.

"I get the impression you resent your mother."

Wait a minute. This had taken an ominous direction. "Why is that?"

"I might as well be straight with you. Your mother tells me she's afraid to go home with you. As her social worker, it's my job to ensure she has a safe place to go to when she leaves here."

"Whoa. I have never, nor would I ever, abuse her."

"She was quite distraught when I spoke to her."

I was getting a little agitated myself. If Mother were able to convince people I'd mistreated her, what would that do to my chances of getting the FBI job in Seattle?

"I think you must have misunderstood."

"So you deny you've threatened to put her out on the street?"

My mind raced through the days since Mother had arrived on my doorstep. Sure, we didn't get along, but had she really thought I'd let her be homeless?

"Mother has a perfectly fine home back where she came from. It was her choice to leave it."

Daisy rocked back in her chair, chewing on the stem of her glasses. Why isn't she saying anything? We engaged in a brief stare-down.

At last she spoke. "You know, Sandra—may I call you that? Often when a child grows up in an atmosphere of, let's say violence, the next generation often repeats the dysfunctional behavior."

"What? There wasn't any violence in our home. I don't even know any violent people." The anger welling up in me contradicted my statement. I wanted to take down that fancy, framed diploma of hers and toss it in the garbage can. Then I'd deal with my mother.

"What are you writing?" I gestured toward her file.

"Nothing to concern yourself over."

"Good. Because I don't need any trouble," I said, somewhat under my breath.

Daisy had placed her glasses on again and looked over the top of them. *What twenty-something person wore bifocals, anyway? Was this a weird intimidation tactic?* I shifted in my chair, trying to get a more comfortable position.

"What kind of trouble are you expecting?"

"None. And I don't want any problems based on some imaginary issue my mother has dreamed up."

"So are you saying your mother is welcome in your home?"

"Temporarily, yes. Besides, what other option does she have?"

"None, really. She's certainly not ill enough for a long-term care facility. And it seems you and your daughter are her only family here."

"Well then?" Did this woman drag me down here just to add to my stress?

"I suppose we'll release her to your care. However, be advised I'll be dropping by now and then to see how she's doing." She looked at me meaningfully.

Oh swell. Someone else wants to investigate me. "You understand that both my daughter and I work. She'll be home alone during the day."

"Of course. She doesn't need twenty-four hour supervision. Merely some assistance with her medications and transportation to her medical appointments."

I stood, trying to keep some semblance of dignity. "I think you'll find my mother receiving excellent care." I reached over her desk to shake hands. "It's been nice

106

chatting with you. However, I have a daughter waiting for me at home."

Daisy looked a little shocked at having lost control of our meeting, but covered it well. "I'll see you soon."

I left, before she had a chance to pile any more warnings on me.

***

The doctor decided to keep Mother in the hospital two more days, running every test imaginable on her. Cammie had brought stacks of literature home with her, the night she and Charlie had gone to the dialysis center, so I knew what to expect as far as diagnostic tests and treatment. I hoped she had a good health insurance policy, but didn't know how to broach the subject without setting her off because I was violating her privacy.

Wednesday evening, Teddy came over and took Cammie out for a hamburger and then they were going off to meet friends. I had one more evening with the house to myself. I settled myself in my most comfortable living room chair with Cammie's Bible.

Anytime in the past, when I'd opened that book, I found the Old Testament impossible to understand, so I flipped to the back, and landed in the book of James. Cammie had underlined several passages and I concentrated on those. Then I started in the first chapter and read it all the way through. Twice. *Wow. I've never heard this before. At least not in these words. We should be glad when we're inundated with trials?*

The doorbell interrupted my reading. When I opened the door, Matt stood there, dressed in a suit and tie. The white dress shirt showed off his tan.

"Come on in. It's good to see you."

Matt entered the room, glancing around till his gaze landed on the open Bible. "I see you're studying."

I might have been embarrassed if it had been anyone other than Matt. However, I chose to ignore his comment "Sit down. Can I get you anything?"

107

"No, thanks. I can't stay long." He stayed on his feet.

"Oh. I wondered how it was that you could spend so much time with us. Like a friend would. You're supposed to be impartial in your investigation, right?"

"I'm here for a reason. There's something I have to tell you."

I didn't like the sound of that. That type of statement, almost always preceded bad news. And he looked worried. "Should I be sitting down for this?"

"If you think you'll be more comfortable, that might be a good idea."

This is sounding worse and worse. "I think I'll stand. What is this about?"

"First of all, I want you to know how immensely qualified you are for the job you've applied for in Seattle."

I felt the blood drain from my face. "I hear a 'but' coming."

"Unfortunately, yes."

"Go ahead. There's no use putting it off."

"I can't sign off on your background investigation. I'm sorry."

"But you just said—"

"I said you're qualified. The problem is with the unanswered questions we've uncovered."

"My father."

"Yes. And Cammie's father."

I stood there facing Matt, trying to hold it all together. I wanted to cry with the unfairness of it all.

"Can't you wait a little longer before you make your final decision?"

"If it were up to me, I would. But my boss wants the position filled right away. He's not going to hold it open on the off chance your father and ex-boyfriend show up on your doorstep. Plus, we can't use all our agents to look for people who aren't wanted for a crime."

"So, how long have you known this?"

"That you weren't getting the job?"

There it was. A statement so plain and final, there was no way the door for me could remain open. "Yes."

"I told you from the beginning, we'd have to track Brian down. Your father's absence has merely complicated the issue."

"You said absence, not disappearance. Would you tell me the truth? Do you have any suspicions about his whereabouts?"

Matt shook is head. "I'm not going to speculate with the small amount of information we have. I only know that his car is gone. He hasn't used any credit cards, and there's no sign of foul play in your parents' home. There could be many explanations of why we can't find him."

"But with all the resources the FBI has, can't you issue an all points bulletin, or whatever you call it?"

"If there's no evidence of a crime, the Bureau isn't going to use those resources chasing down someone who could very well have taken a vacation. We have many serious cases clamoring for attention."

I lowered my eyes. "So you're saying you've spent enough time and energy on me already."

"I wouldn't put it quite that bluntly, but yes."

I turned away, not wanting to show him my pain.

Matt placed his hands on my shoulders. "I'm sorry, Sandy."

I stood, facing away from him, stiff as a board. Somewhere, deep within me, anger bubbled to the surface.

"I have to head back to Seattle. I've been given another assignment."

Matt leaving? Was there anything else I'd lose? I'd become accustomed to his presence, and foolishly never gave a thought to the possibility he'd pass right out of my life as quickly as he'd arrived.

I blinked back my tears and turned around. "When are you leaving?" I searched his face for a sign of regret.

"Right away. I've already spent more time here than the job called for."

I couldn't look at him any longer and averted my gaze.

He gently tipped up my chin. "I'd like to see you again. As a friend. Maybe more than a friend."

Chapter Twelve

Today my granddaughter is five years old. I didn't go to her party. I wasn't invited. In fact, I don't even know her address so I couldn't send her a present. James has been grumpy all day. Does he remember what this day is, too? Since he rarely speaks to me anymore, I wouldn't know what he's thinking. The only time I have anyone to talk to is when I visit Mother at the cemetery.

***

I should have been delighted a man as attractive as Matt had expressed interest in me. Instead, my heart lay cold at my feet. While I couldn't dispute the growing attraction between us, I felt as if someone had handed me the booby prize. *Sorry, you're runner up in the Miss America contest, but as a consolation prize, you've won a date with the master of ceremonies. Swell.*

"Matt, I can never thank you enough for the kindness you've shown me and my family. However, I've got too much on my plate now to consider entering into a new relationship."

A brief look of disappointment flitted across Matt's face. "You don't even have room for a friend?"

My feelings for him went beyond simple friendship. I couldn't explain it, even to myself, but Matt was the first man since Brian that had made my heart beat faster. But I didn't trust those feelings. After all, Brian and I had supposedly been in love with each other. Then look at what happened. He moved away without a backward glance.

111

"A casual friendship would be nice," I said in my most non-committal voice. "I imagine we'll be running into each other if you're ever in the area visiting your sister."

Matt took a step back. "I'm sorry. I must have misinterpreted what was happening between us."

So you felt it, too. But how long before he'd find someone else to impress with his dimpled grins? Someone who didn't have a dingbat mother living with her. A missing father and ex-boyfriend? Right then, I couldn't bear the thought of another disappointment in my life.

"Thank you for coming by in person to give me the bad news."

"I wish I didn't have to. But I didn't want you to hear it for the first time in an impersonal letter from the Bureau."

Pain is pain, regardless of how it's communicated. I moved toward my front door. He correctly assumed he needed to leave. "Goodbye, Sandy. I'll see you soon." He let himself out.

As I took in the sight of his broad back and easy stride, the tears I'd been holding back flooded my eyes. I shut the door before he turned to give me the wave I knew was coming.

Inside, I let my emotions go. For a few moments. Then I got out the vacuum, and went over every square inch of the living room. When I finished, I put it back in the hall closet and got out a dust rag. As I walked past the hall mirror, I glanced at my reflection and saw a red, blotchy, swollen-eyed face. If Matt saw me now, he'd rescind his offer to see me again fast enough. Not that I was any beauty, but at least I'd never acted like a blubbering idiot in front of him.

I returned to the living room and swiped at the top of the TV, a few pictures, and an end table. Cammie's Bible still lay open next to the couch. What had I read there? Something about considering it joy when I encountered various trials? Surely that didn't pertain to me. If that were the case, I should have been the giddiest person on earth. People who say religion is a crutch must not have run across that verse.

I sat down and read it again, and then on to the next verses. "*If any of you lacks wisdom, let him ask of God, who gives to all men generously and without reproach, and it will be given to him.*"

Well, God. What do I do now? My own wisdom has been shot full of holes. Do you have any suggestions?

I didn't really expect an answer. As far as I knew, God wasn't in the habit of conversing with ordinary people. Maybe the super spiritual folks occasionally heard from Him. But I wasn't going to hold my breath waiting for a thunder clap and words booming from the sky just for me. I closed the Bible and sat there waiting up for Cammie. I didn't have to look for her for long. I saw headlights flash against the front window, and only a moment later she came through the front door.

"Hi Mom!" She hung her shoulder bag on the hook by the door.

"Sit down, Cammie. I want to talk to you."

Cammie plopped down next to me. "Is Gran OK?"

"This isn't about your grandmother. It's something else. My plans have changed. I'm not getting the job at the FBI."

"So you won't be selling our house?"

"No. At least not at this time." I struggled to hold my emotions in check.

"Then I can stay here, and go to the junior college!" Cammie clapped her hands in joy.

Were all teenagers so self-centered? She hadn't uttered a single word about my job or the disappointment I might have felt. "I didn't say that."

"But I don't want to go to the U. It's too far away. Especially with Gran sick. I could have handled living in a dorm when I knew you would be living nearby. But now you'll be over an hour away."

113

"I can take care of your grandmother. I want you to go to a good school."

"You know I won't get any personal attention from the professors at university. I've heard there are hundreds of students in each class. And what if I can't adapt to college? I've heard it's way different than high school."

"That's the idea. You need to grow. Expand your experiences." I had no desire to go over the same old argument again. It all boiled down to her reluctance to leave Teddy, anyway. "I'm turning in. See you in the morning." I kissed Cammie's cheek and headed off to bed.

***

I got a call at my office from Mort the Realtor, first thing the next morning.

"We've got an offer on your house." His voice boomed over the phone so loudly, I had to hold the receiver away from my ear. "They didn't even flinch at your asking price."

Well why would they? I set the price low enough for a quick sale. After all, I had a wonderful new job waiting for me. I rubbed my jaw, trying to relax the tightness.

"They're coming in this morning with the earnest money."

I'd never sold a house before and tried to remember what I'd signed. Could I get out of this without losing anything? It didn't matter. I knew what I had to do. "Mort, I want to take my house off the market."

"What?" Mort screeched.

I flinched as if he'd taken a swing at me. Not that I could blame him. He'd probably already spent his expected commission on a new car, when for a fraction of the cost, a toupee and a lifetime membership in a fitness gym would have served him much better.

"My circumstances have changed. I won't be moving to Seattle."

114

"B-but you said you wanted to move into a condo. Downsize. I can find something for you right near here," he sputtered.

The thought of selecting another condominium depressed me. I'd never find a new place I'd like as much as the one in Seattle. I might as well stay where I was. At least the house and neighborhood were familiar. I needed that emotional anchor with all the other changes I knew were coming.

"Sorry, but circumstances have changed. I need to stay where I am."

I could feel Mort's anger and frustration coming through the phone line. He spit out a few choice words before he slammed his receiver down. His anger only added to the misery that engulfed me.

I had so looked forward to all Seattle could offer. My co-workers looked at me curiously. I'd soon have to explain everything to them. But not yet. Not when my downfall lived so freshly in my mind. I kept my head down and concentrated on my job. It looked like I'd be there until I could find someplace else to advance. While I liked the accounting firm I worked for, I'd never be promoted again without becoming a CPA. I had neither the time nor the desire for more schooling. At least not now.

I took the afternoon off to bring Mother home and get her settled. If I were expecting an invalid, she proved me wrong. If anything, she had more energy than ever and practically skipped up my front steps.

"I need to get back to work on my book. You should have seen the note I had to sign before they'd release me from that money grabbing hospital. Robbers. All of them!"

I knew nothing about writing and selling books, but I seriously doubted she'd get hers sold in time to pay off her hospital bill. Assuming she ever sold it at all. And that was about as likely as her inviting me to a mother-daughter tea. "You do have health insurance, don't you?"

115

"Of course I do. Your father *did* manage to provide a policy for me. And I have Medicare."

The implication he no longer took care of her didn't escape me. "Don't you think you'll go home again?" I still hoped for reconciliation between my parents.

"Tired of me already? We've barely made it into the house."

A sigh escaped my lips. "That's not what I meant. Let me put it another way. When you first arrived, you said you'd left Daddy. If you mean for your separation to be permanent, are you going to ask him for a settlement? Surely you know you'll have bills to pay. You'll want your own place eventually."

The color drained from her face. "I'm not stupid. Why do you think I'm writing this book? My Social Security check is barely enough to get by on."

"Have you notified the government that you've moved?"

"I don't have to. They put my money in my personal checking account every month. Now I've wasted enough time. I'll be in my room." She walked away.

I went to the kitchen, put a casserole together, and stuck it in the oven. After setting the timer for forty minutes, I headed down the hall. I had just enough time to go through the items Cammie and I had set aside for the garage sale. I'd have to reconsider selling them now. It wouldn't do to have mother stay in Cammie's room any longer. I decided to reassemble the spare bedroom and she could move in there for the duration of her visit.

Is it still a visit? Would Mother ever be able to be on her own? I needed to help her in that direction, but wouldn't that be disloyal to Daddy? Whatever caused her to leave must have been serious. What woman her age suddenly walks out on her husband of more than forty years? Perhaps Daddy wants to reconcile. To be forgiven for whatever imaginary sin he'd committed. Shouldn't Mother give him another chance?

116

I retrieved the bedding I'd set aside for the garage sale and carried it to the bed in the guest room. I had to move the boxes of items I'd marked for the Goodwill store, in order to make up the bed. When I'd finished, and had plumped up the pillow, I carried the boxes out to the garage. I'd never minded doing physical work. It gave me a chance to mull things over.

I didn't relish the new roles I'd been thrust into . . . nurse, caretaker, and marriage counselor. How did these roles fall to me? Who was the mother and who was the daughter? In fact, I couldn't think of how to characterize our relationship. Being friends was out of the question. That would require caring and mutual respect. Yet, we could no longer pretend we didn't have a connection. Fatigue finally sapped my thinking process. I got my headache medicine out of my purse and took it with a glass of water. A commotion at the front door indicated Cammie had come home. The sound of voices told me she'd brought company with her. Cammie burst into the kitchen with Charlie and my neighbor, Mrs. Connely, on her heels. "Charlie brought dinner."

I turned around in time to see Charlie and Cammie set a bucket of fried chicken and all the dinner fixings on the table.

"And I brought you a pie. Made from fruit off the apple tree in my yard." My neighbor set her pie next to the cartons of mashed potatoes and gravy. She pulled a woven cloth off her dish with a flourish.

Had anyone considered asking me first? I glanced toward the oven where my casserole should be bubbling. "You didn't need to do this."

Charlie came around the table, threw his arm around my shoulder, and pulled me close. "We thought you'd like a vacation from cooking tonight. Mrs. Connely must have had the same idea, because we ran into her coming over here at the same time. Where's Ma?"

Ma? Had Charlie suddenly been adopted into the family when I wasn't looking? I pulled away from him. "Who?"

"Ma. Your mother. She said that's what I should call her. Are you upset? You're frowning at me."

Charlie had asked me the same question earlier in the week. It made me wonder if he knew he'd get my goat, but didn't care. Our years of friendship were about to self-destruct. I looked around at the smiling group in my kitchen. The festive atmosphere around the table only made my head pound worse. I pushed my fingers along my temple.

"Mom, why don't you sit down and let us wait on you for a change. Charlie, would you go call Gran?" Cammie pulled out a chair form me and gave me a little nudge toward it. "Mrs. Connely, you'll stay for dinner with us won't you?"

Mrs. Connely pulled up a chair.

Cammie went to the cupboard and pulled out a package of paper plates. "No sense getting a lot of dishes dirty. We can pretend we're having a picnic." She passed out the plates, and then went back for silverware and napkins. "Who wants iced tea?" She put out a six-pack of chilled, bottled drinks.

Mention of a picnic reminded me of the barbeque we'd had in the back yard not so long ago. I could still visualize Matt at the grill. Now *that* was a pleasant thought. Charlie and Mother appeared and took their places around the table. When have we ever had five people sitting around the table at once? I longed for the days when Cammie and I shared our quiet dinners.

Mother reached for a drumstick.

"Wait," Cammie admonished, "we have to ask the blessing."

Three pairs of eyes look at her in surprise. Did they think Cammie only gave thanks when it was merely family

118

around the table? I could see Charlie was annoyed, but Mrs. Connely merely looked curious.

"I don't think it's a good idea to flaunt your religion, dear," my mother whispered.

Cammie ignored her and bowed her head. She thanked God for the food, for her "Gran's" homecoming, and for their other two guests. "Amen."

I had to admire Cammie's convictions. If Matt were there, he would have added his "amen" as well. The only other person in my life who demonstrated a personal faith had been Brian. He'd spoken to me often about the Bible when we were in school together. However, when he moved away without so much as a goodbye, I'd dismissed most, if not all, of what he'd told me. I learned the meaning of hypocrite from Brian. Cammie's faith was genuine.

Changing the subject, I asked, "Mrs. Connely, would you pass me the biscuits, please?"

"Please, call me Hildie. After all these years living next to each other, I don't know why you're so formal."

Mother beamed at our neighbor like a first grader who had discovered a new playmate. "I had no idea we had such a nice woman right next door. We must get together and compare notes about our families." "How many children do you have?"

Mother glanced at me. "Only Sandra, I'm afraid. Of course we wanted a house full of children, but we weren't blessed with any more."

Oh puleeze. You couldn't stand having one.

Mrs. Connely answered, "I know how you feel. My children live clear across the country. I seldom get to see my grandchildren. They've begged me to come live with them, but I want to keep my independence as long as I can."

"You're so lucky your children want you." Mother dabbed her eye with a corner of her napkin.

Charlie reached over and placed his hand over Mother's. "Ma, of course you're more than welcome here.

119

Cammie told me just this morning, how much she's looking forward to getting to know you better."

I looked at Cammie, who avoided meeting my gaze. Was she planning to stay instead of going to the U, knowing how I felt? She certainly had an alliance gathered around the dinner table.

Cammie stuck her nose in the air and sniffed. "Does anyone smell something burning?"

"My casserole!" I jumped up, ran to the oven, and yanked open the door. A cloud of acrid smoke burst forth, nearly obscuring my vision. I grabbed a couple of potholders and pulled the dish out, placing it in the sink. I turned the water on full blast. There was no saving it anyway. Drowning it wouldn't make it any worse. After turning the exhaust fan on, I opened the back door. Everyone at the table sat calmly eating chicken and chatting. They didn't need my casserole. They didn't need me. They had each other. They'd taken over my house and my prerogative to make decisions concerning my life. I looked at each person around the table, then down at the charred mess in my sink. My burnt casserole represented the ashes of my carefully constructed life. I had to rebuild. The problem was, I had no idea where to start.

Chapter Thirteen

Maude's Journal
January 2001

> Today is Camellia's tenth birthday. I wonder if Sandra gave my granddaughter the card I sent. She'd flatly refused to let me speak to her on the phone. I suppose I should be grateful I finally have their address. But never once did anyone acknowledge the birthday and Christmas cards I've sent over the last five years. James is out late again. Ever since he retired, he spends more and more time away from home. I never know if he's going to be home for dinner or not. When he's here, he ignores me. That leaves hardly anyone to talk to except that snoopy neighbor across the street. And of course Mama, when I get the chance to get on a bus and get away from the house. She understands what I'm going through. I wish she could come live with me.

***

The rest of the week passed with no further distractions or emergencies. Mother finally moved her things into the spare room, but still used Cammie's room to write on her book. Several times Cammie hinted she'd like Mother and me to attend church with her again. I didn't object to the church part. I had a few questions I needed answering.

What I really feared was running into Matt. I was in no mood for another reminder of my failure to convince him that Daddy and Brian's whereabouts had nothing to do with my ability to perform the job I'd set my heart on. I suppose I should be comforted with the fact that the FBI is so picky about who they hire. It wouldn't do to have someone like me come along and subvert their organization.

As it turned out, I stayed home with Mother who was complaining about a little nausea and dizziness. None of us were anxious for another trip to the hospital. Mother told me the doctor who treated her at the hospital had referred her to a nephrologist. I had to go for the dictionary to discover that meant kidney specialist. Apparently both Charlie and Hildie, next door, had offered to drive her. I didn't trust either one of them to report back to me on what the doctor said, so arranged for some more time off.

I was glad I'd allowed plenty of sick and vacation time to accumulate. I'd been planning on using my vacation when it came time to move to Seattle. That was off now. As soon as Mother was settled into her new treatment plan, I really wanted to fly back home and find Daddy. Clearly, nobody else cared where he was or if he was OK. The only way I could manage to leave, though, was to give in to Cammie and allow her to stay home and attend junior college her freshman year. *Where is the wisdom I asked for, God?*

Cammie came home from church all enthusiastic about the guest speaker who was recruiting people to go to Portland to minister to the street people. "I stayed after and asked Brian a lot of questions. He gave me some literature for you to look over."

"Brian?" I hadn't heard her mention the man's name before. Why had the mention of the name startled me? Lots of people named their sons "Brian." I shook my head. I'd been carrying that torch long enough. It was time I got over my teenage puppy love and moved on. And I'd finally met a man I might want to move on with, but then I foolishly sent him away.

Cammie heaved a noisy sigh. "Honestly, Mom. Have you been listening to a word I've said? Brian is the man putting the group together from our church. He goes around to all the churches and tells them about his street ministry."

"Sorry. I was thinking of something else. You know I won't be able to go with you. I hope you aren't disappointed."

"Of course I'm sad you won't be able to share that experience with me. But I'm glad you'll be around here to take care of Gran."

I nodded. Although I couldn't quite see myself standing on a corner, handing out tracts, it would have been fun spending the time with Cammie. I waited to see if Cammie would mention seeing Matt at church. Apparently she hadn't, or she would have said something. My mind wandered back to the last time I saw him and the thought warmed me.

Cammie, still excited about the Portland trip, broke into my daydream. She shoved a bunch of papers at me. "Since I'm eighteen now, I won't need a permission slip. But I want you to read this stuff so you won't worry about me."

"Is Teddy going?" *How well will this group be chaperoned?* I remembered the time I'd caught them in a lip lock out in his car.

Cammie's shoulders slumped. "No. He wants to stay behind and work. There are only a few weeks till college starts."

She looked at me with a huge question in her eyes. I knew what the question was without asking. We hadn't really discussed her college plans since Mother's hospitalization.

"I've been thinking."

"Yes?" Cammie's eyes widened with hope. She sensed something big was about to be revealed. Sometimes I was amazed at the way we knew each other. But then, we'd always been very close. Until Mother's visit wedged an uncomfortable space between us.

"I think it would be better if you took your freshman classes at the community college."

123

Cammie jumped up and hugged me. "Oh, Mom. Thank you!"

"Stop strangling me. Just wait a minute. There's a catch."

"Anything. I'll do anything you ask." She rubbed her palms and her smile lit up the room.

"You have to keep your grades up. I don't want anything interfering in your ability to get into the U."

"You know I will." She danced around me. "I can't wait to tell Teddy."

"Not so fast." I waited till she stopped gyrating. "I'm going to need a lot of help transporting your Grandmother to her doctor appointments. And, since you seem to get along so well with her, I need you to encourage her to stick to her diet."

"No problem. Is that all?"

Wasn't that enough? "That's all. Now you can go call Teddy if you like."

I watched her practically skip out of the room. I don't know what I'd done to deserve a daughter like Cammie. And she *did* get along so well with Mother. Unlike Mother and me. Would we ever be able to start over? We'd both need to try. A true reconciliation couldn't be one-sided. I vowed to attend church with Cammie the following week to hear more about that whole forgiveness business.

*****

I worked Monday morning, but took the afternoon off. Over Mother's objections, I, not Charlie, drove her to see the kidney specialist. I hoped she wouldn't be subjected to more tests. Her patience had run out. I was relieved when we were ushered into the doctor's office rather than an examining room.

He didn't waste any time on small talk. "All our tests indicate your mother's kidneys are failing. If we don't get her into dialysis, she won't have long to live. Her blood pressure is dangerously high, too. We'll try to control that with medication. I'm going to refer her to a dialysis center near you. She'll need to go in three times per week.

"How long will each appointment be? Do you think they'll let us arrange them late in the day so I won't have to miss so much work?"

"She'll be there at least four hours each time. You can check and see if they have evening hours available, but they usually reserve those for people who absolutely can't come in the daytime. People who are working to support their families."

Mother didn't say a word during this interchange. I had no idea how the news affected her. Her stoic expression gave no clue. I knew *I'd* be very upset if I were her.

The doctor went on. "I must warn you, many patients find dialysis to be extremely stressful. The only treatment left to consider after that is a kidney transplant. Your mother's heart is strong and she's otherwise in good health, so I wouldn't have any qualms putting her on the waiting list. I would like her to gain some weight, and I'm prescribing something for her nausea."

"I'm not letting you put no dead person's organs in me!" Mother's loud objection startled the doctor and me, since until that moment she hadn't uttered a word.

The doctor faced her. "Cadaver organs are screened just like live donor organs. I assure you, it's very safe."

Mother crossed her arms tightly against her chest. "I'll die first. The very thought makes me want to barf."

The doctor wrote something in his notes. "Of course, we'll respect your wishes. You may want to make sure your husband and daughter are told if you change your mind. If a cadaver organ is the only one available and you need a transplant to save your life . . . well I shouldn't have to tell you the consequences of a refusal. You may not have time to talk it over. We have many other patients waiting for kidneys, too."

"I don't have a husband anymore."

125

"Oh. I'm sorry. I assumed you did." A puzzled look passed briefly over his face.

"She does," I objected. "We're still trying to contact him."

The doctor frowned. "The other option is to find a friend or family member who would be willing to donate one of their kidneys. Have you spoken to a social worker?" He looked meaningfully at me.

The memory of my one and only contact with the hospital social worker still stuck in my craw. "I did, but now that Mother is home, we don't need her." *Would I or could I donate a kidney? I don't know if I could make a decision like that.*

He shuffled through his file and pulled out a page. "It says here you are scheduled for a weekly home visit." He addressed mother directly. "You should consider giving your daughter a durable power of attorney in case you no longer are able to make decisions for yourself."

Mother pushed herself back in her chair, her gaze darting between the door and us. "Nobody is going to have that kind of power over me."

"Mrs. Hughes, you are a very ill woman. Don't be fooled because you feel well right now. Your condition could worsen very quickly. Who better to see you get proper care than your daughter?"

Mother glared at him. *Isn't she listening to what he says?*

"I'm sure the doctor has a lot of experience with people like you," I said.

"What do you mean, *people like me?*"

Groaning inwardly, I sent a weak smile toward the doctor. I understood how shocked Mother must be, but as usual, she was going to try to turn things around and pick a fight with me. I reached out to touch her, but she yanked her hand back like I was a hot stove. *How am I ever going to care for her under these circumstances?*

The doctor stood and came around his desk. He sat on the corner in an exaggerated relaxed position. "Let's take things one at a time," He gently encouraged.

My respect for him grew. He seemed to understand how to reach her much better than I.

Mother perked up a little when she saw his attention rested exclusively on her. "What things do you mean?"

"Let's get you started on the dialysis, and then I'd like to see you again in a week. We'll have a better idea of your tolerance or discomfort, which ever it turns out to be. Once you have settled into a routine, we can discuss the next step in the management of your illness."

Mother nodded her head, but I could see the suspicion on her face. She stood and addresses me. "I'm ready to go home now."

I looked apologetically at the doctor, who nodded his head. He gave me a few final instructions. By the time I gathered up my purse to leave, I could hear Mother's footsteps beating a retreat down the hall. She swept past the receptionist and was standing next to my car by the time I got outside.

"Took you long enough." Her beet red face told me things were back to normal.

I unlocked the car and got in. Mother yanked on her seatbelt several times before she was able to swing it around and lock the clasp. I hoped she'd give me the silent treatment on the way home. Her shrill complaints were bound to affect my driving.

"I suppose you and that doctor have it all figured out."

"Figured what out?"

"All that power of attorney stuff. Next thing I know, you'll force me into one of those homes."

"I'm not planning to do anything of the kind." *Not that the idea of you living somewhere else hadn't crossed my mind.*

"You can always go home to Daddy."

"That's impossible."

Sorry, Mother, but I'm not going to discard that possibility until I speak to Daddy. I glanced at her and saw defiance written all over her face. She looked out her window, but not before

127

glaring at me first. The rest of the ride home, and the rest of the day, was thankfully silent.

***

Cammie came home from work and told me she was able to register at the community college. Since the school year was getting so close, we were afraid she might not be able to get the classes she needed. They must have held some spots open for extremely gifted students, because she got everything she asked for. The best part was that her schedule would allow her to take Mother to dialysis twice a week. I would take her on Saturdays. Hildie next door, promised to check in on Mother during the days Cammie or I weren't around.

I went over to Hildie's to let her know what our schedule would be. She welcomed me into her back yard. There she took me to a shaded area with lounge chairs. When we were seated, I thanked her for all her support and kindness.

"Oh, that's no problem. I'm glad to do it. Your mother seems rather lonesome, so it will be a good chance for us to get acquainted.

"Mother hasn't accumulated any close friends that I know of. I'm sure she'll enjoy your company." I didn't tell her that Mother managed to drive everyone away with her caustic tongue.

"And, I know you'll be glad to hear that my church is praying for your mother's health, too."

"I didn't know you attended church."

"Why of course I do. I can't believe we've lived next door for all this time, and you didn't know that. I must have really slipped up."

"What do you mean?"

"I've been sharing my faith since I was a teenager. Of course I know your Cammie is a Christian, but it never occurred me to have the discussion with you. I guess I just assumed—"

"Of course I'm a Christian. This is America after all."

128

"Lots of Americans aren't Christians, dear. Especially these last few years."

I didn't bother to challenge her beliefs. I knew I was a good person. Someday when I reach those pearly gates, the head angel will look at the column with my faults and see it isn't nearly as long as the list of my good accomplishments.

I looked at Hildie's kind face. Perhaps she'd be willing to answer some questions. "I guess you know a lot about the Bible."

She beamed at me. "I study it all the time. I just can't get enough of God's word."

Is she a fanatic or merely overly enthusiastic? I guess it doesn't matter if she can give me some advice.

I dug my toe into the grass. "I read in James that I should be glad when trials come. Why is it so important to God that we develop endurance? Shouldn't we be learning to know when to cut our losses?"

"Oh my." Hildie's eyes widened. "You didn't pray for patience did you?"

"Did I do something wrong?"

Hildie chuckled. "You can't develop patience without going through some trials. Patience must be tested. Just like our faith must be tested to build perseverance."

"If that's the case, I why do people think religion is a crutch? It seems to me that living a good life is very hard."

"It is. In fact it's impossible."

I didn't want to hear that. Not when I was trying so hard to do the right thing for Mother. "I have to believe it's possible." *If it's not, then I'm working at being a good person for nothing. I need to be able to forgive Mother or I won't be able to tolerate her long enough to care for her. And I must do the right thing.*

"Nope. It says right there in Romans that all our righteousness is nothing better than filthy rags."

Then I can never please God. I got to my feet. "Thank you for this chat, Hildie. I need to get home and start on my chores." I exited her yard without looking back. If I had, she would have seen the tears in my eyes. *What am I going to do now?*

Chapter Fourteen

Maude's Journal
February 2008

I haven't been feeling well lately. I'm petrified I might have cancer like Mama did. I can't talk to James. He's too busy hanging over the fence making goo-goo eyes at the neighbor. Anyway, he quit caring about me a long time ago. My father never took care of Mama. I took care of her right to the end. Who will take care of me? Sandra is barely civil when I call. Not that I could depend on her. She's always favored James, and he doted on her. Besides, she has her own life. If only they lived nearby, I would have had a chance to get to know Camellia. My heart tells me my granddaughter wouldn't let me die alone. I'm scared.

***

I took Mother to her first dialysis treatment. I was afraid at first she'd back out. Especially since she had to go in and have a surgeon prepare her veins the day before. By the time I got her to the center, she was trembling.

"Mother, it's going to be all right," I said as I pulled into a parking space.

"I know. I keep telling myself things could be worse."

"That's right. You have a long life ahead of you."

"I'll bet that's a big disappointment to you."

I wrenched back the emergency brake. *Why does she always have to pick a fight?* "I don't know where you get these ridiculous ideas of yours."

"Humph." She let herself out of the car.

I locked up after checking my purse to make sure I remembered to bring something to read. It was going to be a long four hours.

Mother marched into the building, her back ramrod straight. I had to admire her resolve to be brave. But I had seen her anxiety and knew any show of strength now would be all bluff.

Once we got inside, we were ushered right in to a treatment room. A young man, whose name badge identified him as a technician, weighed Mother, checked her temperature, heart rate and blood pressure. "Have your ankles and feet been swollen lately, Mrs. Hughes?"

"Why? You gonna fit me for a new pair of shoes?" True to form, Mother used sarcasm to cover her stress.

The technician chuckled. "No, Ma'am. Just wondering if you've been retaining fluid."

"The answer is no. Now let's quit all this jabbering and get this over with."

His gaze reflected some concern. "You seem a little tense. That's only normal. Especially the first time. Would you like a sedative?"

"No. Now let's get on with it. I've got better things to do than sit around here and listen to you flap your jaw."

He winked at me and began cleansing the skin on her lower arm. The smell of antiseptic stung my nose.

"Now, Ma'am, you just sit back and relax in this easy chair. Would you like to recline a little?"

"No. I want to see what's going on."

"Hold your arm out, please. I'm going to insert a couple of butterfly needles. This will connect your blood supply to the dialyzer."

"How bad is this going to hurt?"

"It shouldn't hurt at all. If you have any discomfort, let me know and I can give you something for it."

Mother snorted, but I noticed she kept her eyes averted when he inserted the needles and placed tape over them. Then he hooked her up and started the machine. He watched as the process got underway, and then addressed Mother again. "I'll be back to check on you soon."

I took a deep breath. My own tension took me by surprise. In fact, watching the machine exchanging her blood made me a little queasy. Mother kept her eyes directed straight ahead.

The afternoon dragged on. The tech came in several times to check her blood pressure and heart rate. There was a TV in the room, but she refused to watch it. "I need one of those lap computers. Then I could work on my book while I'm lounging around here listening to that thing hum."

"I could let you use mine." *Now why did I say that? I'll probably never get it back from her. Still, it's not doing anybody any good sitting in my closet most of the time.* Guilt spread through me as I realized how selfish my thoughts had been.

"I suppose that would be OK. As long as you don't go snooping around reading my book."

"Cammie can show you how to save your work to a disk. Then there won't be anything for me to see."

"Hand me those papers, will you?" She pointed at her copy of the release she'd signed. When I'd handed them to her, she looked at them as if seeing them for the first time.

Since she had something to occupy her, I pulled my book out and turned to chapter one. I'd only read half a page before she spoke.

"Listen to this. They've given me a list of all the complications I could get from this rotten machine I'm hooked up to."

"Shhh. Keep your voice down. That machine is cleaning all the impurities from your blood. Without it, you could get very sick." Was I going to have to explain everything to her as if she were a child?

"Maybe so, but they don't tell you the bad part till you're already here and distracted by other things. Anemia. Bone diseases. High blood pressure. I've already got that. Maybe it will get higher. Stroke, heart attack, blindness, fluid overload, nerve damage. Good grief. I'll be lucky if I get out of here alive!" She slammed the papers down on her little side table.

"Maybe I should get you a magazine."

"Maybe we should go home."

"They have to tell you about any possible complications. That doesn't mean you'll get them all. Or even get any of them."

"That's easy for you to say. You're sitting there all healthy, reading a murder mystery. Are you hoping you'll get some good ideas about how to bump me off?"

I rolled my eyes. "You're going to bump yourself off with all this worrying you're doing."

"Humph." She brushed some imaginary lint off her dress. I suppose it wouldn't hurt anything if you got me a magazine."

I stood and walked over to a rack on the wall holding several different kinds of magazines. Glancing at the clock on the wall, I saw we still had a couple of hours to go. I felt the familiar tightness in my temples. I needed my migraine medicine. How was Cammie going to stand this twice a week?

I pulled out a half dozen magazines and brought them back to Mother. She looked through them and discarded all but two.

"Maybe you can pick up a copy of Writer's Digest for me before we come here again."

"You're really serious about writing your book, aren't you?"

"Well don't sound so surprised. I told you the day I came here what I was doing."

"I guess I didn't think you'd stick with it. It must be hard."

Mother stuck out her chin. "I'm going to show you and everyone else once it's finished and I'm wealthy."

Wealthy? Mother is living in a fantasy world. "I'll be glad to find your magazine. Maybe I can find some writing books for you too." I didn't have a clue what to look for, but if it

134

would keep Mother occupied, I didn't care if I had to run all over town to find what she needed.

I went back to my reading, and Mother thumbed through her magazines. At last the technician came back and disconnected everything. He put some pressure dressings on her arm and sent us on our way home.

Later that same day, as I loaded our dinner plates and silverware into the dishwasher, Charlie arrived. If I had to describe Charlie in one word, it would be *unremarkable*. That's probably the reason we'd been friends for so many years. He was neither hot nor cold. I don't think we ever had an argument. Nothing ever reached that level of importance.

When I saw him standing in my house, wearing jogging clothes and sporting a new hair style, I suppressed a giggle.

"You look different."

"I've been working out."

"Doesn't golfing provide enough exercise?"

"Not really. I find jogging exhilarating. What they say about endorphins is true. You should join me."

Had Charlie noticed something I hadn't? I'd inherited Mother's genes and had never had an ounce of flab on me anywhere. I felt around my waist. Or was he trying to place doubts about my appearance in my mind so that I'd spend time with him at the gym?

"I won't be having as much free time as I used to."

"Because of your mother?"

"Partially." *And in part because I need to wean you away from smothering me.*

"I told you I'd help you with Ma."

There it was again. *Ma.* Why did he insist on inserting himself in Mother's good graces?

"There's no need. Cammie and I have it covered."

"It grieves me to see you girls stretched so thin."

"Really. We're doing fine."

"Sandy, if you'd only consider marrying me, I could make things so much easier for you. He lowered his voice,

135

probably in an attempt at sounding romantic. Instead it merely sounded creepy.

I slowly exhaled. "We've had this conversation before."

"Maybe you haven't given any thought to what I could do for you. You could move out of this tract house. I can afford a large house with plenty of room for everyone, including a nurse to stay with your mother. You wouldn't even need to work. We'd take vacations, travel anywhere in the world you'd want to go. You wouldn't lack anything you needed."

Except doing anything meaningful with my life. Or being married to someone I truly loved.

"We're friends. We've been good friends. Enjoyed many of the same things. Had fun together. But I've been unfair to you by allowing you to spend so much time with Cammie and I. You could have spent that time finding a woman who could love you the way you deserve."

"Yes, we're friends, and I can't stand by and allow you to go through these troubles alone. You know you're not as strong as you'd like me to believe."

He was right. But he couldn't give me the strength I needed. All he could provide were props.

"You're not saying anything. Does that mean you're finally considering my offer?"

"You've misunderstood my silence. I don't know what else I can say. I want to remain friends, but I can't take this pressure from you to turn it into a romance."

He took a step toward me, entering the close space I reserved for Cammie. "I know you're a reserved person. I don't expect a lot of passion. I merely want to take care of you."

Wouldn't a puppy do just as well?

"Charlie, please! You've got to stop this." I pushed him away.

"It's that FBI guy isn't it? You've fallen for his badge." His mouth clamped into a thin, angry line.

"Matt has nothing to do with it."

"You moron!" Mother suddenly appeared, mad as a crocodile. "You can't be serious. Charles obviously loves you despite all your faults."

Charlie stood there with his jaw hanging. But his astonishment soon changed to pleasure. He smiled like the proverbial Cheshire cat as he strode over to her and enveloped her in a hug. "Ma, don't get yourself upset, now. It's not good for you. Remember what the doctor said."

Mother sniffed and wiped an imaginary tear from her eye. "Sandra can't see what a wonderful loving man you are."

Charlie patted her back. "She'll come around, don't worry. We'll all be a happy family. Don't you worry yourself."

When I'm in the cold, hard ground. Why did I ever think bland Charlie was my friend? And why this sudden change in him? Is he on drugs?

I shot him my meanest glare and jerked my thumb toward the door. At least he wasn't so dense he didn't misinterpret my meaning.

"Ma, I have to get home. You calm down now. Everything will be all right." Charlie favored her with a weak smile.

Mother nodded her head and loudly whispered "thank you."

"Sorry you have to rush off, I said, as I headed for the front door to hasten his exit.

Charlie hesitated before stepping off my front porch. "Please think over what I've said. Consider all the benefits a marriage to me could give you."

"Please give this up. Goodbye, Charlie."

I gently closed the door behind him. *I'm surrounded by lunatics. I need a hot cup of tea to calm my nerves.*

Mother stormed into the kitchen behind me. "What's the matter with you? Don't you know how lucky you are to have someone like Charles love you?"

I whirled around. "I had someone who loved me once. Brian Chapman. Remember? You hated him."

"Because he was not only a religious fanatic, he was a hypocrite to boot."

I heard a gasp. Cammie stepped into the kitchen. "What did you say?"

"Nothing, Cammie. Forget it." I detected her computer-like brain whirring as she digested what she'd heard. The puzzled expression on her face as she stared at me, made me wonder what was going on in her head. Surely she'd heard her grandmother and I argue before.

Mother answered her question in her own warped way. "Charles was just here and proposed marriage to your mother. She not only turned him down, but wasn't very nice about it either. My heart just breaks for that poor man."

I escaped into the back yard before I had to listen to any more. Standing out under a maple tree was about as far away as I could get without getting into my car and leaving. *I've been run out of my own kitchen. Again.*

I looked up through the branches. It wouldn't be long until the leaves turned color and fell. I loved the crisp days fall would bring, but bringing summer to a close also made me sad. This year, it had represented the end of a dream. I took a deep breath of fresh air.

"I've been praying for you."

The words floated over the fence, startling me. I turned and saw Hildie standing in her back yard with an armful of dahlias in her arms. "I thought I was alone out here."

"You're never really alone. Don't you know that yet?"

"It seems so. There's no place I can go for a little peace these days."

"Would you like to come over and talk about it?"

I eyed the flowers in her arms. Gold, red, yellow and orange. They shouted out joy and beauty at a time when I felt the absence of good things in my life. "I'll be fine. I merely needed some fresh air."

"I gather your afternoon at the dialysis center didn't go well?"

"Actually it didn't seem all that bad. Of course Mother may have a different take on things. There was no pain involved, but I imagine the thought of being hooked up to that thing for twelve hours every week, must be depressing."

"I guess so. You're a good daughter to sit with her for the entire time."

I'm not a good daughter at all. "I'm trying, but finding it hard to do the right thing with the right attitude."

"You only have to ask for help, you know."

"Oh, we couldn't impose on your generosity that way."

"I wasn't talking about myself." Hildie pointed a finger skyward. "I was talking about Him."

I shrugged my shoulders. "I'm sure He doesn't have time for my silly problems."

"Your problems aren't silly to him at all. Like any good father, He wants you to come to Him with your troubles."

Hildie certainly had a lot of faith. Was it based on experience, or merely Bible hearsay? "Thank you for sharing that with me. I guess I'd better go in now."

"What are you running away from? Your problems will only follow you into your house."

My problems are in my house. I wanted to experience the things Hildie spoke of, but deep down I knew I'd never measure up. She'd made that clear during our last conversation. So what was I supposed to do?

"Mom, telephone." Cammie stood at the back door, peering out in the twilight.

"I'll be right there." I waved at Hildie, secretly glad I had an excuse to end the conversation. It seemed like every time I saw her, she reminded me how much faith *I* lacked.

I picked up the kitchen phone. "Hello?"

"Hi there, lady."

139

Matt. Hearing his voice made me smile. Probably for the first time that day. What a relief he still cared enough to call after our parting. "Hi, yourself."

"How's your week going?"

"Not so good. Mother started dialysis. It was kind of a long day for her." *And me.*

"How often will she need to go?"

"Three times a week."

"Does that mean you might have a free day now and then?"

"I might. Why do you ask?" Even though I'd brushed Matt off the last time I spoke to him, my heart jumped at the thought of seeing him again.

"Labor Day weekend is coming up in a couple of weeks. I'd like to take you down to Olympia to watch the tugboat races and have dinner out. Would you like to go?"

The thought of getting out of town for a day really appealed to me. Especially with Matt. Even though Olympia was only forty-five minutes away, I'd never taken part in any of their community events.

"Cammie will be in Portland that weekend, but if my neighbor will look in on Mother, I'd love to go." I closed my eyes. An entire day with an attractive man who didn't want anything from me. It sounded like heaven.

"Good. It's a date, then."

"I have to ask Hildie first. And of course if Mother takes a bad spell, I'd have to stay home."

"We'll just have to pray she stays well then."

You'd better do the praying. I'm not sure my prayers are getting much further than the ceiling.

"I'm coming out there to visit my sister this weekend. Will I see you at church?"

I needed to pick his brain and see if he could give me some ideas on locating Daddy. I needed his strength. "Yes, I think so. I'll look for you where they serve coffee, right after the service." We said goodbye and I replaced the receiver. "Finally. I've got something to look forward to again," I said softly.

"I heard you on the phone just now. Who were you talking to?" Mother startled me. I hadn't heard her enter the room.

"It was Matt. He's invited me out."

"When I tell Charles what you're up to, he's not going to like it. When are you going to quit making such foolish decisions?"

Chapter Fifteen

I went to the doctor today. He said I have diabetes. I'm supposed to keep track of my blood sugar and watch what I eat. He sent me to the drug store to get something to poke my finger till it bleeds. A major inconvenience if you ask me. But if it will make me feel better, I guess I could try it. If I don't do what he says, apparently I'll have to have insulin shots. Just another way of them getting my money. But I'll try the diet thing. I've got a book now that tells me what foods are high in sugar. The doctor told me to buy that too. Like I'm so dumb I don't know what has sugar in it. At least I don't have cancer. I decided to tell James what the doctor told me. Maybe he'll pay a little more attention to me when he finds out I'm not well. But, it's eleven o'clock and he's not home yet. I'm going to bed.

***

Mother stood there in my kitchen looking oh, so smug. My conscience wouldn't allow me to throw a sick old woman out on the street. As tempting as it was, I restrained myself. But what would it take to get through to her? "Have you heard a word I said regarding Charlie? We are not a couple. We are friends. That's all. And soon we may not even be that."

Instead of looking chagrinned, as anyone with an ounce of decency would have, she stiffened her back and looked me right in the eyes. "You wouldn't know a good man if the words were written across his forehead. If you had any sense at all, you'd listen to someone much older and wiser than yourself."

"And that would be-?"

"Don't be smart with me! You're never too old to show a little respect for your elders, you know."

"Mother, you're face is getting a little red. Don't you think you should lie down and rest for awhile?"

"You can't get rid of me that easily."

"I'm not trying-oh, what's the use?" I stalked out of the kitchen, down the hall and into my bedroom. Inside with the door closed, I looked forward to five minutes to decompress. A mere few moments. That's all I needed. Then I'd be ready to emerge, ready for the next round.

I flopped on my bed and took several deep, cleansing breaths. I hadn't had to do that since Cammie turned thirteen and came home with pierced ears. But Mother was more exasperating than a houseful of teenagers.

Someone rapped on my bedroom door. I didn't have to guess who.

"Go away!"

"You're wanted on the phone," Mother's shrill voice announced.

I rose and flung open my door. "How interesting. I didn't hear it ring."

Mother jutted out her chin and blessed me with a smirk that raised my blood pressure to a dangerous level. "It didn't. I called him."

"Who?"

"Why Charles of course." She whirled around and went into her own room, shutting the door behind her.

Should I leave him hanging on the phone? It would serve him right. I gave in and picked up the extension in my bedroom.

"What do you want? I thought I'd made it clear earlier that I need some space." I immediately regretted my gruff tone.

"I heard you were making plans to go out of town with someone. Anyone I know?" He jumped right in as if he hadn't heard me.

"Matt is taking me somewhere." *As if it was any of your business.*

"You're wasting your time with that guy."

"That's for me to decide, isn't it?"

"You've had a lot on your mind lately. I'm not sure you're thinking clearly."

"Don't you think that's a little insulting?"

"To you or your friend, Matt?"

"Both."

"Give me a break, Sandy. I've known you a long time. I can tell when your judgment is a little cloudy."

"There's not a thing wrong with my judgment, except that it doesn't agree with your point of view. Isn't that it?"

"You'll see. I'm right about this. That guy is not the kind of man you need in your life. Or Cammie's. Not to mention your mother. She isn't exactly crazy about him. If I see him around here again, I may just tell him that."

"You've discussed Matt with Mother?" *Would it be all right if I kick him in the shin the next time I see him? After all, I hadn't seen that rivalry behavior in a guy since my grade school days on the playground.*

After a period of silence from Charlie, I said, "Aren't you going to say anything?"

I was too furious to continue the conversation another moment.

"Goodnight, Charlie." I replaced the receiver, and then pounded into the other room to replace the one Mother had called Charlie on-assuming she hadn't done so when she was through eavesdropping.

Mother had evidently disappeared into her room again after hanging up, so I grabbed my purse and car keys and walked out the front door. Getting away from her and the phone being paramount at that moment.

I slid into the driver's seat and rested my hands and head on the steering wheel. What is the matter with me? I'm as out of control as Mother. Hot tears flooded my eyes. I

144

couldn't even control my emotions. Anger paralyzed my throat, threatening to cut off my air.

I had tried to set boundaries with Mother, but every attempt failed. Now after all these years, Charlie was pushing me, too. When would I get my life back? I *needed* some harmony. To get through a day without being reminded what a disappointment I was to Mother. Peace with her? I'd tried, but everything I did was wrong. Would always be wrong. She'd never love me. She couldn't even tolerate me. I *knew* it would be like this when I first saw her on my porch. Why didn't I listen to my instincts and send her away?

A sob escaped past the tightness in my throat. The tears were beyond my control and scalded my face as they gushed from my eyes. "I can't do this anymore." I slapped the steering wheel. "I'm empty inside. I've used up all my resources."

Both my hands curled into fists and I buried my face between them. My breath came in huge shudders. "God, if You're really there, please help me. I've come to the end of my rope and don't think I can go on by myself without doing something I'll regret."

I rubbed at my face with the back of my hand. Was God listening? Did He care about a woman who called out for Him from the darkness of her car? Or did I have to meet Him in a church? All I knew for sure was, I couldn't wait around for Sunday to come. I needed some of His wisdom right then.

I lifted my head and gazed into the sky. "Do you hear me, God?" The twinkling lights bore witness to God's existence, but they were so far off. As far off as God. But if He truly was God, He'd hear me no matter how far away He seemed, wouldn't He?

A fresh stream of tears washed down my face. I wiped at them again. I could no longer breathe through my nose and resorted to open mouth breathing.

"Oh how I need strength. Are you listening God? I'm helpless. And here I am slobbering all over my car, hoping to hear from You."

I don't know how long I sat there, but I eventually became aware of someone sitting beside me in the pitch-blackness. *Hildie? Of course not. I'm imagining things. My doors are all locked.* I listened for breathing. A sign of movement. Nothing. Nothing except a sense of peace and well-being.

My fingers remained frozen to the steering wheel, but one by one, they loosened. I leaned my head back on the seat. As my body unwound, the burdens I'd been carrying slipped off my shoulders until with total relaxation, came sleep.

Sometime later, I'm not sure I knew how long, my eyelids fluttered open. It took me a few moments to get my bearings. I quickly sat erect and opened my door, which caused the interior of the car to light up. I jerked my gaze to the passenger seat. No one was there. Had I been dreaming?

I gathered up my purse and keys and after carefully locking my door again, made my way back to the house. Nothing lighted my path. There was no moon, and even the stars I'd looked at earlier had disappeared.

I let myself into the dim living room. A small lamp threw out enough light to keep me from bumping into anything. Peering down the hall, I noticed Mother's door was still closed, and no light spilled into the hall from the small space near the floor. *She must be asleep.*

I took a deep breath, feeling refreshed and relaxed at the same time. My mind flitted back to my dream in the car, instantly recognizing the change in me had a much higher and stronger source. The shift in my emotions hadn't been a dream. God had answered my prayer. He'd been right there with me in my need.

I dropped to my knees next to the couch and bowed my head. "God, I don't know how to go about this, but thank You."

I stayed like that for a long time, basking in a love I'd never before experienced.

***

The next morning I woke, feeling invigorated and energetic. Something wonderful had happened to me. Whatever it was, I wanted more. I looked out my kitchen window while waiting for the coffee to brew. It was as if I'd never seen the beauty in my yard before. The sun shone on a portion of the backyard, creating a lovely mixture of shadows and light. Portions of the lawn and bushes not yet touched by the morning rays were covered with a light sheen of dew. Everything looked new and bright.

Next door, I could see Hildie outside filling her bird feeders. I decided to take my cup of coffee and go over and chat with her about my need to have someone look in on Mother while I was away.

"Good morning, Hildie!" I stepped through the gate separating our two yards.

"You've got a glow about you this morning." Hildie set her bag of millet on the ground.

"You mean you can tell?"

"I'd have to be blind to miss it. Tell me all about it."

"I don't know how to explain it. I had . . . a kind of visitation."

Hildie's eyes widened and her mouth pursed into a perfect O.

"I've shocked you."

"My dear, you haven't been dabbling in the spirit world have you?"

"No. Of course not. It was God. He came here and sat right over there in my car last night." I pointed toward my driveway.

Hildie closed her eyes as if praying.

"What are you doing?"

She opened her eyes and her worried gaze met mine. "I'm testing the spirits. Are you sure it was God?"

"Who else would fill me with love and peace?"

147

"He did that?"

"You, yourself, commented about the glow around me. Why are you so surprised?"

Hildie reached out and tentatively touched my hand. "I've been praying for you. I just didn't expect Him to answer in quite that manner."

I bit my lip. "You don't think I was imagining it do you?"

"Do you?" She tipped her head to the side.

I thought about what had happened. It *had* been a mind-altering experience. Had I dreamed it all up? No, it had been *real*. As real as Hildie standing before me looking all worried and kind of scared.

She paused before speaking. "If you had a God encounter, you'll be changed. Like Paul on the road to Damascus."

"Who? I don't know any Paul."

"He was an apostle. He wrote many of the books in the New Testament."

"Oh. I sure feel changed."

"Do you have a sudden desire to read your Bible? Love your enemies?"

"I don't have a Bible. Not one of my own, anyway. And I don't have any enemies unless you count Mother."

"I think you should seek counsel from a pastor."

"Wait a minute. Just last night you told me He is always with us. Did you mean it or not?"

"Of course I meant it. But He doesn't usually park Himself on someone's front seat."

"But it happened."

"OK, dear. I believe you unless I learn differently. Is this what you came over to tell me this morning?"

I took a deep breath. Talking about it didn't raise any doubts, but only made my experience seem more real. "No. Actually I came over to ask a favor."

"What is it?" Hildie looked a little wary.

148

"I'm wondering if you could look in on Mother next weekend. Cammie is going to Portland with her church group. I've been invited to the tugboat races in Olympia on Saturday and will probably be gone most of the day."

"Why of course. I'd be glad to. I'll even invite her over here for lunch and dinner, if she'd like to come."

"I'll ask her."

"Better yet, let me ask her. Then it won't seem like you're setting her up with a baby sitter."

"Thanks so much." I took a step away. "I have to get back to my place now."

Hildie lifted her hand in an encouraging wave, and I returned to my house and refilled my coffee cup.

Cammie bounced into the kitchen. "Morning, Mom." She kissed my cheek before getting the orange juice out of the fridge.

I smiled at her. I couldn't think of a better way to start the day than getting a smile in return from my daughter. The real test would be when Mother got up. I knew my good intentions in the past had not kept me from anger when dealing with her, but somehow, I felt stronger.

"Is your grandmother up yet?"

"I don't think so. Should I go check on her?"

"No, let her sleep. This will give us a chance to talk."

Cammie's startled expression told me I'd better get right to the subject. "Matt has invited me to go on an outing with him."

"Whew." Cammie smiled in relief. "I was afraid you'd changed your mind about community college."

"Not at all. I'm going to need you close by."

Cammie stuck a couple of slices of wheat bread into the toaster. "Where's Matt taking you?"

"To the tugboat races in Olympia. I know that's your weekend to go to Portland, so I asked Hildie to watch out for Mother." I poured myself a cup of coffee and sat down at the table.

Cammie buttered her toast and joined me.

149

"Is that all you're having for breakfast? I can make pancakes." I realized then, I'd have to start rethinking all our menus in order to accommodate Mother's dietary needs.

"This is fine. I've got to leave soon." Cammie took a sip of her juice. "I've been meaning to ask you a question, too."

"What is it?"

"You didn't tell me my father's name."

I nearly choked on my coffee. I waved my hand back and forth in front of my mouth. "Whew. That was hotter than I expected." I knew my actions wouldn't deter Cammie from following through with her question, but hopefully it would buy me some time to think.

Cammie stared at me, her eyebrows knitted into a frown. "Is it some big secret?"

"No. Of course not. Why do you want to know?"

"Don't you think it's natural I'd *want* to know?"

Of course she'd want to know, but what would her next step be? "I hope you're not thinking of trying to find him."

"I can't very well do that if I don't know his name, can I?"

Knowing Cammie's way of pursuing things once she got something in her mind, I decided to try and discourage her. "The FBI couldn't find him. Besides, he doesn't even know you exist. Think what a shock it would be if you suddenly appeared on his doorstep and announced you are his daughter. Not only to him, but to his family."

"He didn't know you were pregnant? Are you sure?"

"Yes, I'm sure."

Cammie sighed in relief. "Then, it's not like he really abandoned me."

No. He only deserted me. "Of course not. Who would ever think of running off and leaving a sweet, wonderful girl like you behind?"

150

"I'd still like to know his name. I thought I heard you and Gran arguing about him. Were you?"

My heart was torn. What if I gave Cammie his name and she found him, only to be discarded, the way he'd left me? Yet she had a right to know. "We may have. I don't recall. You know how many disagreements we've had lately."

Cammie stood and put her empty glass in the dishwasher. "Never mind. I can see you don't want to tell me." Her voice reeked of disappointment and irritation. "I'll ask Gran."

"Leave your grandmother out of it, please. She never had any use for him."

"Then you were discussing him. His name is Brian Chapman, isn't it?" Cammie placed her fists on her hips.

"Cammie, promise me you won't go looking for him. If anyone should break the news to him that he has a daughter, it should be me."

"Then why haven't you?"

As Cammie stood there staring at me, I couldn't think of any good reason why I hadn't. "Do you really want me to? Is your life so incomplete you want to invite a perfect stranger into it?"

"You just don't understand, do you?" Cammie stormed out of the kitchen and out the front door.

I slumped over my coffee cup. *Boy I handled that well, didn't I, God? I didn't know my first test would come so soon.*

Chapter Sixteen

Maude's Journal
July 2008

> James came home late every night this week. I decided to confront him and lay down the law. That was a big mistake. Come to find out, he'd been snooping through my journals and found out I'd chased Brian Chapman and his family out of town. James was furious at what I'd done. Said Brian should have had a chance to make things right. His face got all red and he shook his finger right in my face! I told him he should have been thanking me for keeping Sandra from making another huge mistake. No way is any daughter of mine going to marry some religious hypocrite. James just kept on yelling at me. Accusing me of chasing Sandra away and depriving him of knowing his grandchild. I was afraid he'd have a heart attack. Instead, he lost his mind and told me to pack my bags and get out of his house. What am I supposed to do? He knows I have no place to go.

***

I'd hoped, when I broke down and asked God for help, that things would get a little easier. At the very least, I expected my close relationship with Cammie would continue. I certainly never expected her to rush off in a huff. I should have known my past mistakes would come home to roost someday.

I heard Mother come shuffling down the hall. Glancing at my watch, I saw it was nearly nine o'clock. "You must have slept in. Did you sleep well?" I was determined to start my day off with her in a positive manner.

Mother headed for the cupboard and pulled out a box of cold bran cereal. "Considering how you upset me last night, I suppose so." She slammed the box onto the table.

"Here, let me help you." I got out a bowl, spoon and the two-percent milk and set it at her place.

She looked at me rather suspiciously and poured some cereal into her bowl.

I forced a smile. "I thought perhaps you and I could go shopping today. I'm sure we can find some delicious things at the grocery, which will be fine for you to eat on your new diet."

She poured some milk over her cereal. "I'm working on my book this morning. I'm just getting to the good part and can't stop."

"Well, perhaps this afternoon after your dialysis?"

"Charles is taking me for a ride later."

God, my patience is being tested here. Are you still around? "Where are you going?"

"He's looking at houses for sale and thought I'd like to come along."

"Are you thinking of buying a house?" *Would that even be possible? She evidently can't even afford her own apartment.*

"Of course not. It's for Charles. And the rest of us if you ever come to your senses."

That's about as likely as me being asked to be a Miss America body double. I knew the Bible said to honor our parents. I hoped that command wouldn't extend to honoring my Mother's warped desire to pick a husband for me. "Are you sure you feel well enough to go tramping through a bunch of houses? There will probably be stairs."

"Charles will take good care of me."

If Mother wanted to go traipsing around with Charlie, there wasn't a thing I could do about it. She was an adult after all, even though she didn't always act like one. "I hope you have a nice time. Would you like to leave me a list of things for me to pick up at the store?"

"If I have time. Right now, I'd like to finish my breakfast and get back to my book." She took another bite and refused to meet my gaze.

I've been dismissed. That's OK. There are worse things. We haven't had a fight yet today. Besides, a free afternoon is something I haven't had in awhile. I should use the time to go shop for my own Bible and to figure out how to smooth things over with Cammie.

I left Mother eating her breakfast and ran the vacuum in the living room. Once done, it didn't take long to dust and fluff up the throw pillows. I glanced around the room. Summer was nearly over and soon it would be time to wash all the windows, inside and out. It had to be done before the rains began. I couldn't help recalling that I'd planned on being out of my house and living in Seattle soon. How different my life would have been if Mother hadn't come to visit.

I put the vacuum back in the closet and went down the hall to clean the bathrooms. My Saturday morning routine hadn't varied much in the last few years. It was different when I spent Saturday's running Cammie around to soccer practice or swimming lessons. Where had the time gone? Cammie was practically an adult. Soon she'd be gone. Would she ever come back and visit? Or had I upset her so much she'd spend the next few years avoiding me. Just as I had stayed clear from Mother.

One thing I knew for certain, I had to find Brian before Cammie did. Not that she had the resources the FBI did. Still, the Internet had dozens of places where people could look for their biological parents or children. Open adoption hadn't been widely accepted until recently. Fortunately Brian wouldn't be looking for her, but what if Cammie sent out a plea for anyone knowing someone named Brian Chapman who was in his late thirties? Or worse yet, what if she got a lead and left college to pursue it?

I got out the old toothbrush I used to scrub the grout around the bathtub. Within an hour, the master bath

154

sparkled. I had just picked up my rubber gloves and bucket of cleaning supplies, when the phone rang.

"Hi Sandy." Matt's voice soothed my anxiety like hot tea and honey.

"Hi yourself." I set my supplies next to my feet and sat on the edge of my bed.

"I'm calling to see if your neighbor agreed to stay with your mother so you can come to Olympia with me."

"Yes, she did." The fact that Matt seemed to look forward to their day together as much as I did, warmed me all over.

"Good. I've made tentative dinner reservations at a very special place, and need to call back and confirm."

"I was planning on dressing casual for the races. Do I need to bring a change of clothes?"

"Not at all. Casual is fine."

"Matt?"

"Yes."

"I was wondering-I mean I have this friend who is kind of searching for spiritual meaning in her life. Do you know of any good books I could recommend to her?"

"The Bible, of course. If your friend isn't familiar with the Bible, I suggest the NIV It's easy to read and some come with great study guides."

There's more than one version? I grabbed a pen and notepad off my nightstand and wrote down what Matt said. "Is there a particular part of the Bible you'd recommend?"

"You say your friend is searching? Meaning she's not a believer yet?"

"Uh, I'd say so. She's a real beginner."

"Then I'd recommend the Gospel of John. Don't you agree?"

I wrote "Gospel of John" on my notepad. "That sounds good to me."

"Let me know how it turns out. It's such a thrill to lead someone to the saving knowledge of Christ."

155

Another term I'm unfamiliar with. If I'm going to hang around church people, I'd better learn the language or they'll realize I'm a fraud. Not really an imposter; merely uniformed.

"Thanks for your input. I know she'll appreciate it."

"You wouldn't be speaking of your mother, would you?"

I was glad I didn't have anything in my mouth at the time, or I would have spewed it all over the phone. "Not a chance."

"I'm sorry to hear that. Well, whoever it is, she is lucky to have a friend like you."

I'd better change the subject before he figures out the friend is me. "I'm glad you called. I'm really looking forward to our outing."

"Me too. I've got another call coming in. See you next weekend."

I sat on the bed for a few moments after we said our "goodbyes." I tried to picture Matt's face. His dark eyes and hair. The deep dimples. With my eyes closed, I could imagine the broad shoulders. Wide enough to protect me from any storm.

What am I thinking? It's only a casual date. Was it a date? What else could it be called? I lurched to my feet, and bent to grab my cleaning supplies. Daydreaming like a teenager wasn't getting my chores done.

Cammie came in a little while later. I was on my knees, wiping the lower shelf of the refrigerator. I looked up, fully expecting her to want to continue our conversation. Instead she ignored me. Didn't even say hello. I couldn't let that pass. "Are you sure you want to take your grandmother for her dialysis today? I can do it if you're busy."

"No, thank you. I want to take her. It's important for her to have someone with her she's close to,"

Touché. A stab of pain seared my heart. Cammie had never said anything so cruel to me or anyone else before. I'd drastically underestimated the impact that keeping secrets from her would have.

"Cammie, I'm so sorry I hurt you."

"Then why did you?" She reached over me and got a soda out of the refrigerator."

"If you'll sit down and talk to me, I'll try to explain."

"Not now, Mom. I'm very busy this morning."

Too busy to talk? A niggling of annoyance rose up in me. When had I ever been to busy for her? So I'm not a perfect mom. Nobody had tried harder than I had. Didn't any of that matter? One mistake and suddenly I'm out in the cold. The outsider in my own home. *God, I sure hope there's some answers in that book of yours.*

I returned to my cleaning. When I finished, and as I peeled off my latex gloves, I heard the front door close. Then the sound of two car doors closing reached me through an open window. Neither Cammie nor Mother had come in to tell me goodbye.

The silence of my empty house swirled around me like a cold wind. I looked around at my perfectly clean kitchen. The satisfaction it usually brought sat in my stomach like a rock.

***

Later that day, I walked into the Christian bookstore. It took me all of three minutes for confusion to set in. Rows upon rows of books, greeting cards, T-shirts, and various gifts stretched out before me like a potpourri of foreign languages. I walked up and down the rows, attempting to look as if I shopped there every day. The music coming from some unseen speakers gave credence to the kind of store I had come to, but I still wasn't altogether sure I really belonged.

I strolled through the store nonchalantly, stopping to pick up a book here and there, and reading the back covers for clues to their relevance to my life. The book shelves marked *family living* and *women's issues* caught my interest. I ran my forefinger across the titles. So much to choose from. How was I supposed to know which books pertained to someone like me?

157

I decided to pass those sections up and went in search for the Bibles. Again, my mind spun with the vast array or choices. If Matt hadn't given me his recommendation, I never would have figured out which one to buy.

"May I help you find something?"

At last. Help. "I guess I should have read 'Bible Buying for Dummies' before coming here."

My weak attempt at humor brought a frown to the clerk's face.

"What I meant was, I want to buy a New International Version of the Bible, but there seems to be so many to choose from."

"Is this for yourself, or a gift?"

"It's a gift. For myself."

The clerk pulled a Bible from the shelf. "This one has study helps just for women."

"I'll take it." I took the bible from her hand.

"Will there be anything else? Concordance? Commentary? Dictionary? We have several nice ones to choose from."

Dictionary? They published religious dictionaries? "Yes. I'd like a dictionary of all the terms that church goers use."

This request brought another frown to her face. "I'm not sure what you mean. Could you give me an example?"

"Church-speak. The layman's guide to the insider's language."

"Perhaps you should browse through that section over there to see if it has what you're looking for." Her tone suggested I wouldn't find it, but she felt compelled to direct me somewhere.

Another thought occurred to me. "Maybe you could tell me what your most popular books are."

Relief filled the clerk's eyes. "That's easy. We have a rack of all our best sellers right up front."

"Oh, good. I don't suppose you have anything pertaining to dealing with difficult family members?"

She squinted at me. Apparently she'd never met anyone in the store who had relationship problems.

"Never mind. I'll just browse around some more."

I finally walked out of the store with my brand new Bible, which I declined having my name written on it in gold. Also, several books, including a best selling fiction novel, and a double CD of praise and worship songs. I stopped myself from buying a framed print of a restful scene that the clerk said was all the rage. As lovely as it was, I couldn't quite envision a lighthouse fitting in with my decor. It would have been perfect, though, in a Seattle condo overlooking Elliot Bay.

I'd cringed a little at the total cost of my purchases, but justified the expenditure by telling myself I needed something to read during Mother's dialysis treatments. Besides, a Bible was a lifetime item. And I'd read enough of Cammie's to know I wouldn't be able to read it once and have a total understanding of the contents.

My next stop was a large chain bookstore near the mall. As promised, I picked up several books for Mother. A thesaurus and several how-to books on writing. Again, I had to get help from a sales clerk. She wasn't any more knowledgeable than me, but fortunately all the books I needed were grouped in one alcove of the store.

The grocery store was next. I glanced at my watch. I still had a couple of hours to shop, get home, and put my purchases away. The shopping part challenged my habits of many years. I wasn't used to reading the labels so closely. Yikes. Do they put sugar in everything, even spaghetti sauce? No wonder Mother had such a difficult time controlling her glucose levels. I finally finished, drove home, and put all the food in its proper place. I separated the sugar-free items from what I already had.

I then went down the hall and stacked Mother's books on her dresser. I took my books into my room. Taking my new Bible from its box, I put it in the drawer of my bedside table. I wasn't ready to share my newfound interest with

Cammie yet. And especially not with Mother. The books on prayer and forgiveness went in the drawer too. I set the novel on my bed, and picked up the last book. The back cover touted it as the perfect answer for the new believer. Would I find the answers to some of my questions inside? If I was going to go down the path of religion, I wanted to do it right.

The slam of the front door startled me. It was too early for Cammie and Mother. I jumped up and went out in the hall.

"Mom!" It was Cammie.

My heart fluttered. Something was wrong. I met her in the hall. "What is it? Why are you back so soon?"

"It's Gran." Cammie's face was blotchy as if she'd been crying. "She was fine for the first two hours, and then she started pitching a fit. They tried to talk to her and I tried to calm her down. They finally had someone come in and unhook her from the machine."

Just then, Mother came in the house. "I suppose that daughter of yours is in here tattling on me."

"Cammie is worried about you. Would you mind telling me what happened?"

"Nothing happened. Except that I exercised my right to get up and leave."

"You shouldn't have done that. Didn't you hear what your doctor told us? Without dialysis, you'll go into total kidney failure and die."

"Well then I die. I'm not going to spend the rest of my life hooked up to that machine." She went to the phone and dialed.

Cammie looked at me and shrugged.

"Hi, it's me." Whoever Mother had called must have been very familiar to her. She had memorized their phone number, and expected them to know her voice.

Cammie went to her room, but I stayed within earshot of Mother. I didn't like eavesdropping, but her behavior was seriously detrimental to her health.

160

"I got done early. Just thought I'd let you know I'm ready to go anytime. OK." She hung up.

"Who was that?"

"Charles. I told you he was taking me out this afternoon." She went into her room and shut the door, leaving me to fume by myself.

I took a deep breath. Cammie hadn't been able to persuade Mother to stay for her treatment. I probably wouldn't have had any better success. Would she listen to Charlie? She seemed to think he was the next best thing to the proverbial action hero.

I stepped outside and sat on my front porch. I had to speak to Charlie alone. Would he help me deal with Mother? And would he expect something in return for granting me a favor? My hands trembled as I waited for the sight of his car coming up the street.

Chapter Seventeen

Maude's Journal
August 10, 2008

> *I thought things would blow over between James and me. Not so. He told me to get out weeks ago, and he's still angry. When he bothers to look my way, he only glares. I can plainly see the hatred in his eyes. Clearly he wants to hit me. I never would have thought we would end up like this. Like my parents' marriage. All I've ever wanted is the perfect union. Only I'm not about to stick around to see if James beats me up. To think he once loved me. I'm sure I didn't imagine it. Can't he see I merely wanted to protect Sandra? We no longer want the same things. I'm too old to be homeless. I MUST come up with a plan.*

***

I could see Charlie's car turning into the cul-de-sac. *God, are you there? Could You please give me the right words to say to him? I don't want to encourage him to pursue a relationship with me, but I need his help with Mother.*

The closer his car came, the more my hands trembled. I stood. I hadn't heard any word from God, but what was I expecting? An audible voice blaring from the clouds? Maybe I hadn't given myself enough credit. I'd handled difficulties by myself for more than eighteen years. Why complicate this problem by dragging Charlie into it, when he obviously represented an additional source of trouble for me? I shoved my hands in my pockets to still their shaking.

Charlie's brand new luxury sedan came to a stop in my driveway. I backed up till my shoulders brushed my front door. Too late to make an escape. He'd seen me.

"Hi, beautiful!" His voice, once a source of friendly comfort, grated on my nerves.

"Hello, Charlie." I watched him amble toward the porch. "I gather you're taking Mother somewhere."

"I'm hoping you'll come along too."

Is he serious? "I have other plans." Pain stabbed through my stomach. I rubbed the spot where it hurt. Was I getting an ulcer?

Charlie reached around me and opened my front door. "Anything I should worry about?"

I stepped aside to let him in the house. He brushed past me. "It's a personal matter, and you needn't waste any concern." My head began to pound and little black specs crossed my vision. *Oh, great! A migraine and an ulcer.* "Besides, why would you worry about anything I do?"

"Have you forgotten how many years we've been friends?"

"No. But you have to admit, that lately things between us have been strained."

"They don't have to be. If you'd relax and let me take care of you . . ." He reached toward me.

"I'm used to taking care of myself." I snapped my mouth shut before my temper got the best of me.

"I know. But at what cost?"

"What are you implying?"

"Merely that a woman like you shouldn't be saddled with so much responsibility."

I stiffened my spine. *A woman like me? I'm not even sure what that means any more.* "I've handled it well, haven't I? Cammie is growing up into a beautiful and competent young woman."

"I couldn't agree with you more. But once she's gone, how will you cope with your loneliness? Who will you shower all that love and concern on?" He took a step closer to me.

Well, there's still Mother. "We've been over this ground before. I don't understand you anymore. Why the sudden interest in having a romantic relationship? You've always seemed content with the way things were."

"To tell you the truth, I didn't realize how much you meant to me till I realized you were serious about leaving. Now that you're not moving to Seattle, we can resume our time together. And more."

It's the "and more" that's bothering me. My stomach screamed for an antacid.

"Are you sure you don't want to go with us today?"

"I'm sure."

"I'm glad we had this little talk. Do you see how pleasant things can be between us when you're not fighting me?" Charlie stepped into my home.

I followed him into my living room. "I don't *want* to fight with you." *But you leave me no choice.* "Why don't you have a seat? I'll go get Mother." I escaped down the hall, not realizing until I got to her door, that I'd been gritting my teeth.

Mother opened her door. She'd changed her clothes after coming home and was wearing a dress I hadn't seen before. She entered the hallway and headed toward the living room, without acknowledging me.

"You look very pretty, Mother."

She kept walking as if she hadn't heard me. I couldn't help staring at the way her shoulder blades protruded from the back of her dress. The skirt was an A-line which exposed the fact she'd lost weight in the short time she'd stayed with us. Guilt overcame me when I realized I had overlooked her physical condition far too long.

Charlie stood as we entered the room. I grimaced when Mother lifted her cheek for his kiss.

"Mother, have you eaten anything since this morning?"

"I'm not hungry after the way they tortured me today at that clinic."

"But you have to eat. How else will you keep your glucose levels where they're supposed to be?"

164

"I'll take her out for dinner after we have our outing," Charlie chimed in.

I glared at him. Maybe it wasn't safe to let her go with him after all. "At least drink a glass of fruit juice before you go."

"All right, if it will shut you up." She sat on the couch, clearly expecting me to go get her drink.

I left and returned right away with a full glass of orange juice. Charlie had moved to the couch and his arm rested along the back, as if to protect Mother from harm.

"Mom, could you come here for a minute?" Cammie's voice drifted down the hallway.

"Excuse me." I left Mother and Charlie chatting together in the living room.

"What is it?" I entered Cammie's room where she had some papers spread across her bed.

"Can we talk about Gran?"

"Of course. I'm sorry your day with her turned out to be so stressful."

"I thought I'd be able to talk her into staying there. I feel so bad." Her face showed evidence of recent crying.

"It's not your fault. She's not an easy woman to get along with."

"I'm beginning to see that now." She handed me some papers. "I picked up some literature. Did you know there's an option for home dialysis? Then she wouldn't have to go to the center three times a week."

I took the pamphlets she offered me and began reading. After I'd finished the first one, I said, "I'm not sure this would be a good idea. It looks like it would require some monitoring none of us are equipped for right now."

Cammie began to cry. "I don't want her to die."

"I don't either, Sweetie. We'll figure something out."

"Promise?" Cammie swiped at her damp face with the back of her sleeve. That action reminded me of when she was a little girl. But these were grownup tears.

"I promise. Right now, I need to go tell Charlie to watch what she orders when they go out to eat."

I left Cammie's room, taking a pamphlet with me. When I reached the living room, I found it empty, except for Mother's half finished juice. A glance out the window revealed a vacant driveway where Charlie's car had parked.

I picked up the glass and took it to the kitchen. While I rinsed it out and placed it in the dishwasher, I debated the wisdom of leaving Mother at home the following weekend. Would she run all over Hildie? Asking Charlie for help would be a last resort. Perhaps I should stay home. I decided to wait a couple of days before breaking my date with Matt. Perhaps I could turn things around.

***

Cammie left a few hours later to have dinner with Teddy and his parents. I spent a few moments fluffing the pillows on the living room couch, and then headed out to the kitchen to fix myself a salad. I took my dish, a bottle of juice, and my notepad and pen out to the patio. Raising a daughter on my own had taught me to multi-task, and it had become second nature. I alternated between bites of my meal, and making a list of things to accomplish before the holiday weekend. I looked forward to three days off. Especially seeing Matt again. I hoped I wouldn't have to cancel our date.

The highest priority on my list was getting Mother back into dialysis. Unless that issue was resolved, there was no point in getting a new outfit to impress Matt. I took a sip of my juice. Helping Cammie get ready for her weekend in Portland was a given. I always had time for my daughter. Going to church the next day was a priority. I vowed to let nothing interfere this time. Maybe I'd even ask for an appointment with the pastor.

I'd already retired for the night when I heard Mother let herself in the front door. I turned over, burying my face in the pillow. I didn't see any point getting up to hear about her evening. She'd tell me anything she wanted me to know

166

the next day. And probably a lot more I didn't want to know.

***

Sunday morning, Cammie, Mother, and I were loading into my car when Hildie's voice drifted across the yard between our houses.

"Good morning, ladies."

We turned to see her, dressed for church, and waving her Bible in the air. Instead of getting into her own car, she came across the grass toward us.

I waved at her. "Mornin' Hildie. You've usually left by now."

"I was hoping you'd let me come along with you this morning."

I frowned at this unexpected announcement. "Of course. But won't you be missed at your own church?"

"I made arrangements for someone else to teach my Sunday school class. Besides, the Good Lord doesn't care which building we worship in, as long as it's Him we're focused on. Maude, I'll sit in the back seat with you."

Cammie went around the car and got in the front passenger seat.

I opened the driver's door, slid in, and fastened my seat belt. Since we were running a little late, I saw no reason to question Hildie further. However, her request to accompany us seemed not only unusual, but had been totally unexpected.

"Maude, I imagine you're thrilled to share these Sunday mornings at church with your family." Hildie's voice held all the enthusiasm of a junior high girl on the way to her first pep rally.

"I'm only along because if I stayed home, Sandra would stay with me and nag me to death."

"Oh, I'm sure that's not true. Your daughter is a loving and kind person. And now that she's found Jesus, all your lives will do nothing but improve."

167

Mother slipped into a coughing fit. If I weren't such a cautious driver, I would have run up onto the curb. I wasn't ready to announce my newfound faith to the world yet. And especially not to Mother. What if I had imagined the entire episode? Why did Hildie have to go and say what she did?

I glanced in the rear view mirror. Mother's glaring eyes took up the entire image. Hildie's announcement had been equivalent to my cutting Mother's heart out. I knew it and Mother knew I knew it. I opened my mouth to try and soften Hildie's statement.

Cammie spoke up. "What? Mom, you never said a word to me about finding Jesus."

My hands gripped the steering wheel as I concentrated on staying on the road. I had planned on broaching the subject of my conversion with Cammie *after* I'd had a chance to speak with the pastor of her church. Mother and Hildie's presence had not been part of my strategy.

By the time we arrived at the church and pulled into the parking lot, I figured the back of my head had been bloodied by the imaginary poison arrows Mother shot at me. Cammie ran around to my side of the car and gave me a hug. I didn't have to ask why.

"Are we going in or not? If not, let's blow this pop stand and go to the mall." Mother hadn't missed the hug, and true to form, tried to divert the attention back to her.

As we headed across the parking lot, my heart skipped a little beat when I caught a glimpse of Matt entering the church with his sister. When he told me he'd see me the following weekend, I assumed he wouldn't be in church this Sunday. Even from a distance his stride spoke volumes about his self-confidence, with none of the arrogance one would expect from a federal agent.

I stumbled over the curb, teetering a little as I tried to catch my balance.

"Quit yer gawking before you break your neck."

Didn't anything escape Mother's beady eyes?

168

Hildie put an arm around her and led her off to the side. "Are you feeling well this morning, dear? You seem a little stressed."

Mother shook off Hildie's arm and marched ahead as if she were looking forward to the church service. Fat chance.

Once inside I scanned the crowd for another glimpse of Matt, but he was nowhere in sight. When I felt a strong masculine arm around my shoulder, I whirled around with a huge smile. A smile that dimmed when I saw it was Charlie.

"What are you doing here?" *In church?*

"Your mother invited me."

Oh swell. I turned and sure enough, Mother stood a little way off, beaming as if she'd won the lottery. I gritted my teeth. If she invited him, she could sit with him.

"I need to stop in the restroom. Why don't you folks go on ahead and get seats?"

I stalked off without waiting for an answer. I glanced over my shoulder to make sure nobody followed. It would be just like Charlie come along and to stand outside the door and wait for me.

I went inside and examined my makeup in the mirror. Were those frown lines? They must have appeared overnight. I tried to smooth them with my fingertips but they remained etched in. Permanent-like. How long before I looked like an old dried up prune? Would any man care about me then? Perhaps if I pointed out my flaws to Charlie, he'd go away.

I used a dollop of hand cream, rubbing it slowly onto each hand, covering each finger several times.

I knew I'd stalled long enough and finally picked up my purse and left the restroom. I could hear the beat of the music coming from the sanctuary, and the last few stragglers were rushing inside. I slipped through the double doors and stood in the rear. The people were on their feet, clapping to the upbeat melody. How was I supposed to find anyone in a crowd of that size? Especially when I couldn't

169

see over their heads. I decided to wait till everyone was seated. With luck, I'd spot Matt. I needed the anchor of his presence after all the craziness of the morning.

But it wasn't to be. Charlie loomed into view, approaching me before I had a chance to escape him once again.

"What took you so long? You had us worried. Come on. We've saved you a seat."

If I could have figured out a way to decline without causing a scene, I would have found my own seat. Next to Matt.

The pew Charlie led me to, was only five rows back from the stage. There was no way I would be able to look around the auditorium and find Matt from that location. Even Mother wouldn't have wanted to sit so close to the front. Yet there she was, motioning me to the empty space next to her.

This was church. A place to begin exercising Godly values. I didn't know how I could entertain Christian thoughts sitting between her and Charlie.

The music soon took my mind off my surroundings. They sang praise to Jesus, the One whom I'd put my trust in. Could I trust Him to show me how to keep from slapping Charlie, who had inched over till I could feel his arm touching mine? I clapped along with the others, aware of Charlie and Mother who, although standing, both kept their arms stiffly to their sides. I clapped harder, purposefully swinging my elbows outward to keep Charlie at a distance.

Lord, I know it would be wrong to wish someone wouldn't come to church, so could You please direct Charlie to a church on the other side of town next time?

The music stopped and a hush came over the crowd as the pastor approached the podium. He motioned for everyone to be seated and launched into his message.

I don't know how he knew what I needed, but I soon forgot everything and everyone around me as I got caught up in the message. At the end, he invited anyone who needed prayer or who wanted to make a commitment to the Lord, to come forward. I reached for my purse. It was now or never. As I readied myself to stand, Mother clutched my wrist, digging her fingernails into the skin.

"Don't you dare!" she hissed.

Chapter Eighteen

Maude's Journal
August, 17, 2008

> *I've finally arrived in Washington. I don't think Sandra recognized me at first. When she did, her cool reception was no big surprise. She always favored her father over me. Somebody had to be the disciplinarian. James sure wasn't cut out for it. I'm sure James and Sandra would have been perfectly content if I had disappeared from the face of the earth long ago.*
>
> *Even so, I have to find a way to make a home here with Sandra and Camelia. I have nowhere else to go. I admit I was surprised that Sandra named her daughter after my mother since I had rarely spoken of her. Camelia seems to like me. She may be able to persuade Sandra to let me stay on till I get my book written, and the big checks start rolling in. I am so tired. I felt ill on most of the train ride. I'll be fit as a fiddle as soon as I have a good night's sleep.*

***

Shouldering my way though the crowd, I sensed Charlie a few steps behind me. Would I have to seek refuge in the rest room again? Bringing Mother to church once more had been a mistake. What was the point? She would never change her mind about religion. I rubbed my wrist, still feeling the sting of her nails. Glancing down at the redness, I expected to see drops of blood, but mercifully, she hadn't broken the skin. What was wrong with her anyway? I'm a grown woman. What I do is none of her business. Yet she persists in trying to control my every action, even though she can't even properly run her own life.

172

Evidently today wasn't the day. I found myself moving along with everyone else to the back. The crowd in front of me slowed to a standstill as they filed past the pastor, shaking hands and exchanging greetings. Only three people remained ahead of me. I would ask for an appointment when I reached him.

The couple directly in front of me moved away from the pastor. Just as I stepped forward, an arm reached around me.

"Pastor." Charlie shook the pastor's hand before I had a chance to speak. "Fine sermon this morning."

"Thank you. And you are . . .?"

"Charlie Dalan. You know Cammie of course. I'm a close friend of the family." Charlie draped his arm over my shoulder in the proprietary way men use to broadcast their brand on a woman. I attempted to squirm away, but his hold was firm.

"Well, it was nice meeting you." Charlie slipped his hand across my back and grasped my elbow, leading me away before I could open my mouth.

Angry with both Charlie for his nervy performance, and myself for letting him get away with it, I wrenched my arm away. Attending church this morning had not only failed to make me a better person, it had renewed my resolve to remove Charlie completely from my life. Why had I ever thought I could manage his presence in exchange for his help with Mother?

I stormed out the door toward the parking lot and my car. This time I hoped I *wouldn't* see Matt. My anger would only disappoint him. Where had this temper come from? I'd never come so close to losing it before. Even Mother had never made me so furious. My anger with her had always been tinged with my hurt feelings. My feelings for Charlie had never been strong enough for him to wound me.

I slid into the driver's seat and started the engine, fighting the temptation to drive off and let Mother go home

173

with Charlie. However, that would only give him another excuse to come to my house.

I felt a migraine coming on and rifled through my purse looking for my pills. I usually had a bottle of water in my car, but I'd failed to replace the last one I'd drank. I tossed the pill toward the back of my tongue, gagging as I tried to swallow it dry.

After what seemed like at least a half hour, I heard Cammie and Hildie chatting as they approached the car. Where was Mother? I swung my head around. I spotted her walking along behind them. Charlie was nowhere in sight. Had God heard my prayer or would this be merely a momentary reprieve?

The front car door opened. "Mom, why did you run off? I wanted to introduce you some more of my friends?"

"I'm sorry, Cammie. I have a headache and need to go home."

"Oh dear, I hoped we could all go out for Sunday brunch," Hildie offered from the backseat.

I raised my gaze to my rearview mirror. Mother had again positioned herself so I had a clear view of her angry face. I reached up and flipped the mirror to the left. *Now at least I won't have to view her disapproval of me all the way home.*

"I've got it," Hildie said. "I'll fix something for all of us at my place. I've never had you over for a meal and I'd say it's about time."

"I have to work on my book," Mother claimed.

"Mother, I think you should go. Cammie too. I'll lie down for a nap while the house is quiet."

"Mom's headache will be gone after she's slept an hour or so. Hildie, Gran and I would love to come over," Cammie said.

"It's settled then."

"But my book. I'm just hitting my stride."

"Sunday is the day of rest, Gran." You'll have plenty of time to work on your book tomorrow. By the way, Mom, is Charlie coming over later?"

174

"No." I cringed. "Why do you ask?"

"He told Gran and me that he had a wonderful surprise for you."

I didn't think I could stand any more surprises from Charlie, unless he planned on announcing his move to some remote village in Tibet. "Did he give any indication of what it might be?"

"Only that it would motivate you to stay in this area."

Oh groan. What had he dreamed up this time? Or rather what had he and Mother cooked up? It was getting harder to stay ahead of those two. "Hildie, I think I'd like to come over for brunch after all." The more information I could drag out of Mother, the better prepared I'd be to defend my position as the boss of my own life.

"Is your headache going away, dear?"

"I took a pain pill a little while ago, and I think it's beginning to work now. I'm looking forward to coming to your house."

Later at Hildie's we had a lovely brunch on her patio. I tried to pry more information out of Mother about Charlie's latest scheme, but she only smirked and changed the subject.

After we finished, Mother and Cammie left for home and I stayed behind to help Hildie clean up. I had been pleased that Hildie had chosen to serve us fruit rather than the frosting covered cinnamon buns I'd spotted on her kitchen counter. When I thanked her and commented on it, she patted my hand.

"My late husband, rest his soul, was a diabetic. I learned to select foods that wouldn't throw his insulin level off.

"Did he have to have dialysis?"

"No. He was able to control it through diet at first, and then learned to give himself insulin shots. "He died of a heart attack."

"I'm so sorry."

"He was a believer and is with the Lord now."

"How long has he been gone?"

"Going on three years now. I still miss him. We had no children of our own. But I still have our church family."

I suddenly felt ashamed. Hildie's husband had died right next-door and I hadn't even noticed. I hadn't been there for my neighbor at all. Yet she treated me like we'd been the closest of friends. Who else besides Cammie would have offered to help me with Mother? Except Charlie, whose help was definitely suspect. I vowed to do better in the future and treat Hildie with the same kindness she'd shown me.

I hugged Hildie before I left for home. Being so wrapped up in my own life, I'd missed out on the blessing of getting to know her. My loss.

When I arrived home, I sought Mother out. "You seemed to enjoy our visit to Hildie's today."

"She's OK, I guess."

"Her late husband was diabetic. Did you know that?"

"Is that what he died of?" I noticed a slight tremor in Mother's voice.

"No. It was his heart. Are you aware of all the complications of your disease and the importance of taking care of yourself?"

"What do you care, anyway?"

I reached for Mother's hand but she slipped it from my grasp. "I do care. But why do you make it so hard?"

Mother stared hard at me, the way a stray dog would look at a stranger as if it were waiting to be kicked.

I took a deep breath. "I'd like you to consider returning to the dialysis center tomorrow. I'll go with you this time."

"No." Her lips pressed together in a thin hard line.

"Can you at least tell me why?"

"I could die there, you know. I overheard some people talking. Someone died right there while they were hooked up to the machine."

I gasped. So that was it. Evidently Cammie had missed that exchange or hadn't considered it important enough to Mother to put two and two together.

"I admit I'm not familiar with all the risks involved. But I know this-you will die for sure if you don't have your treatment." I waited for Mother to respond, but she turned away, looking out the window.

"Mother, I won't let you stay here and commit suicide in front of Cammie. If you're not going to take care of yourself, you'll have to go. Maybe we can find you one of those assisted living apartments."

Mother whirled around. "If it means so much to you, I'll try it one more time. But I'm warning you, if one more person croaks in there, I will quit for good."

I sighed with relief.

***

On Monday, I took Mother to dialysis and sat with her till her session was over.

Tuesday morning, my boss, and owner of the business, called us all into the conference room. All twenty-five employees entered the room, single file. There weren't enough seats around the walnut table for everyone, so most of us stood against the wall.

The last time we'd been called together like this, he'd announced there had been a slump in business. Three people had been let go. Today, the tension spread through us all, especially those recently hired. As the sole bread winner in my family, my anxiety level rose a little, but business had been very good for the past year. I couldn't imagine why there'd be any more layoffs.

"Good morning, everyone." My boss took the seat at the head of the table. "Before I begin, I'd like to say I've enjoyed working with each one of you. You've done well. In fact our earnings this year so far are up twelve percent over last year."

Several people let out sighs of relief. It couldn't be bad news then.

177

He continued, "After many discussions with my wife, we've decided this is the perfect time to retire and do some traveling. I've received a very generous offer from a buyer looking to expand his business holdings."

"Oh, no." We all looked at each other in shock. Most of us had worked for this same company for years. The only reason I'd even considered leaving was because the opportunity in Seattle had been too good to pass up. While I enjoyed my current job, the promotional opportunities in a small company just weren't there.

"The new owner doesn't expect to handle the day-to-day supervision here. And, the good news is, he's promised to keep everyone on, as long as his or her work shows merit. I don't think any of you have anything to worry about there."

I glanced at Jane, my boss's personal secretary. She must have known about this ahead of time. Still, her eyes shone with unshed tears.

Stan, my immediate supervisor, raised his hand.

"Do you have a question, Stan?"

"Yes. Who will be managing the daily operations then?"

"I've urged the new owner to select someone from the group in this room. There are several good candidates to choose from. However, he may very well bring in someone from the outside."

I heard a few nervous murmurs from around the room. No one welcomed the change that new management was bound to bring in. Things had been running smoothly. However, the current owner was correct. This was a good time to sell.

"Who is the new owner?" someone asked.

"He prefers to remain anonymous for the time being. At least until all the paperwork is completed and filed." He looked around the room. "Any more questions?"

I think most of us were too stunned to think clearly. Nobody responded.

While, I knew out boss had done the best he could to keep our jobs safe, there was no guarantee the new owner would keep my fellow workers and me. What if my job wasn't secure? Should I start putting out my resume just in case? Having to worry about employment right now, when I had the added responsibility of Mother, made my loss of the Seattle job all that more upsetting.

Later at home, I pulled the newspaper out of the recycling container and flipped through till I found the classifieds. Skimming through the ads, I grimaced when I noted most of the jobs I qualified for, otherwise required college degrees. While I had taken many night school classes, there hadn't been the time or money to get a degree with a child to support. I tossed the paper back. Didn't experience count for anything?

The sound of the front door slamming captured my attention. Mother had already gone to her room to write, so it had to be Cammie. I followed her as she stomped down the hall to her room.

"Since when do we slam doors around here?"

Cammie stormed into her room and threw herself face down on the bed.

"I'm waiting for your explanation."

Cammie sobbed into her pillow. My heart softened, and I sat on the bed next to her.

"What's got you so upset, Sweetie?"

Her muffled words and shaking shoulders told me I wouldn't get an answer right away. Should I wait, or give her some time to herself? I gave her a tentative pat on the back. "I'll be in the kitchen if you need me."

I closed Cammie's door behind me when I left. What could have brought on such a burst of emotion from my easygoing daughter? And why wouldn't she confide in me? We had always been so close and she had shared secrets with me that girls usually confided in their friends.

I often wished I'd had someone to share confidences with. Mother certainly never filled that role. Daddy had, up

179

to a point. That is, if I was ever able to have some alone time with him.

I picked up my neatly folded dishrag from that morning, and ran it under the faucet. I'd noticed a smudge on the refrigerator door that hadn't been there yesterday. Scrubbing the door till it sparkled again gave me a little comfort, but didn't take my mind off Cammie.

What had the pastor said Sunday morning? Something about the Lord being a Father to the orphans and a husband to the widows? I wasn't a widow, and Cammie was only half an orphan. Still, would He be at least willing to listen to my problems?

I rinsed out the rag, wrung it out and folded it into thirds to hang over the faucet to dry. Nothing smelled worse than a damp, dirty dishrag.

"I broke up with Teddy."

I hadn't heard Cammie enter the kitchen and whirled around at the sound of her voice.

"I thought you were getting along well."

"We were . . . except he's been putting a lot of pressure on me to go all the way."

I stiffened my spine. How dare he try to take advantage of my daughter!

"You did the right thing then."

"I kept thinking about growing up without a father. I wouldn't want that to happen to a child of mine."

Heat rose in my face. Cammie hadn't deliberately set out to hurt me, but her words stung. My recklessness as a teenager had impacted her, and I'd never even considered the consequences at the time.

"I'm so sorry."

"You did the best you could."

"I tried. And to see what a fine young woman you've grown into at least proves I did something right."

"I want to find my father. I want to see him and talk to him. Face to face."

Why had I never prepared myself for this need in her? I had let my fear of further rejection from Brian influence me. I should have expected that Cammie would one day insist on finding her father. I knew she wouldn't be put off.

I brushed Cammie's hair back from her face. "OK. We'll talk about this when you get back from Portland. But let's keep this between you and me. Your grandmother hated him and I don't want to give her anything else to get upset about."

"I hope you mean it, Mom. I really want to find him. If you won't help me, I'll find someone who will."

Seeing the determination in Cammie's eyes made me realize my need for wise counsel. First thing in the morning, I would call the church and make that appointment to talk to the pastor.

Chapter Nineteen

Maude's Journal
August 20, 2008

>*I'm finally settling into Sandra's home. I have a room to myself, where I can go through my journals and have some privacy. I'm mostly comfortable. I'll say one thing for Sandra, she keeps a clean house. If only she'd listened to everything else I tried to teach her. This church stuff is a lot of rot. It's a plot designed for men to keep their women under their thumbs. I figured this out when I was only a child. I tried to teach Sandra the facts, but she deliberately chose to ignore me. Camelia is so steeped in the church's propaganda I doubt if she'll ever see the truth. It's downright criminal. My granddaughter seems like such a nice girl. But it's all that sweetness which will ruin her in the end.*

>*I'm going to turn out the light and go to bed now. I'm having difficulty sleeping. I still don't feel well. Lying in bed and staring into the darkness only makes me miss James. I wonder if he misses me.*

***

Cammie stood at our front door, surrounded by enough luggage to last at least three weeks instead of three days.

"Have you got your cell phone?" I pulled my phone from my purse. "Here, program my new cell number into it. Drop me a text message when you arrive. I'll keep it on while you're in Portland."

A twinge of sadness pierced my heart. This would be the first time so many miles had separated us.

"Don't worry about me, Mom. We'll always be with a group."

I reached for her and hugged her tightly. She stood as tall as me. I forced back a choke. It wouldn't be long till she'd be off on her own. Raising a great kid like her was every parent's dream. And I had no husband to share it with. I thought back to Cammie's high school graduation just months before. Cammie must have looked out into the audience seeing all the fathers and grandparents there. I had been the only one there for her.

"I'll always be there for you," I whispered.

"What?" Cammie stepped out of our embrace first.

"Nothing. Just thinking out loud." I helped her outside with her bags and watched until the church van carrying her and her friends from church drove off out of sight.

My daughter's departure wrenched my heart as I reentered my living room. The silence in the house was nearly more than I felt I could bear. How would I ever cope with the loneliness that stretched ahead of me for years down the road when her absence was permanent?

***

Mother's treatments went well during the week. Charlie stayed away from church on Sunday morning. I dared hope his *big surprise* involved his retreat from our lives. Despite Cammie's absence, I was starting to feel pretty cheerful and saw no reason to cancel my weekend plans.

Matt picked me up early Saturday morning. He looked wonderful in his casual slacks and shirt. As we walked to his car, I caught a whiff of soap and spicy aftershave. I breathed in the scent, pleased he'd gone to the trouble for me. Minutes later we merged onto Highway 512, headed for I-5.

As we neared Olympia, I noticed a few of the maples along the freeway were beginning to display their fall colors. I hated to see summer end but loved the change in seasons. Each one brought a promise of new things to come. Like my friendship with Matt maybe turning into something more.

183

We made small talk for the duration of the ride. It felt good to get away, relax, and enjoy his company. Matt turned off at the State Capital exit. We passed several government buildings then turned down the hill toward the waterfront. This was my third visit to the capital city. The other two times, no handsome man walked by my side. Only Cammie and her classmates.

"I wanted to get here early enough to find a good parking place midway between Farmer's Market and the Harbor Days craft booths." Matt helped me from the car, locking it afterward.

We strolled down the boardwalk. My nose tickled as I breathed in the tangy salt air of Puget Sound, mingled with the diesel fumes of some of the boats.

"What would you like to do first? Visit the booths? Get something to eat? Or take a tour on of the tugboats?" Matt spoke with the enthusiasm of a child facing a day at a carnival.

"I had breakfast already. Let's just wander around looking at things. Unless, of course, you're hungry."

"Nope. I already ate too." Matt reached for my hand. "Let's go."

Over half of the vendors were selling items with boat or marine themes. Calendars with photos of tugboats, T-shirts with lighthouses, Orcas, or sailboats stamped on them. Smiling people in flag-covered tents sold everything from windsocks to paintings.

"See anything you'd like?" Matt nodded his head toward a booth full of original paintings. The artist sat in their midst, his brush touching a canvas with light strokes.

I would have loved to bring home a souvenir of my date with Matt, hopefully the first of many outings. However, the painting titled "Orcas Playing" that I fell in love with was beyond my means.

"I think I'd like to look around a bit more before deciding if I want to buy anything."

184

The crowd increased and we had to weave our way around mothers pushing baby strollers, a group of teens, one of which carried a blaring boom box, and small groups of people who had stopped to chat with one another.

"This is a popular festival." Matt pulled me close as we navigated through the crowd, keeping me protected from being trampled.

I welcomed Matt's guidance. "Since Labor Day signals the beginning of the rainy season around here, I imagine everyone wants to get out and enjoy all this sunshine."

Would you like me to take your jacket back to my car?"

I noted the brisk breeze coming off the water. "No, I think I'll keep it on for awhile."

"Let's walk down to the market, then."

The market was four or five blocks from where we'd started, only in the opposite direction. Going the other way, even off the boardwalk and away from all the booths, the walk was just as crowded with people. We finally entered the market where everyone moved along slowly, practically bumping shoulders.

Tons of autumn produce, from pumpkins and peppers, to apples and pears, overflowed the tables on each side of the walkway. Buckets of Dahlias in reds, oranges, and yellow called to anyone who wanted to take home their blaze of color before the gray days of winter set in. Matt still held my hand, as if he were afraid I'd wander off and get lost. I loved that feeling of connectedness with him.

Just outside the covered area, we stopped to listen to some musicians who sang along with their fiddles and banjos. Matt left me for a moment and returned with a bag of sticky, nut-covered cinnamon rolls. "Let's get away from this crowd."

Matt guided me down toward the bay, right next to a large waterfront restaurant, and we sat on a bench nearly surrounded by foliage. The music in the distance could still be heard. We ate the gooey pastries, stopping to lick our

185

fingers in between bites. Matt's gaze met mine, his eye's twinkling. I guess four napkins weren't enough."

I laughed, but felt self-conscious as he watched me try to finish my treat with some degree of dignity. "I would have been a lot less messy eating it with a fork." I dropped a piece on the ground and seagull flew down, landing merely a couple of feet away. Its obsidian eyes focused on the fallen crumbs, and I could tell by the speed of its arrival that he was used to people's leftovers.

Matt grinned, showing a dimple I hadn't noticed before. "I have something special planned for an early dinner. I promise there will be silverware involved."

"That's quite alright. I have just the thing we need in my purse." I pulled a couple of foil-wrapped moist hand-wipes out of the side pocket, and handed one to Matt. The gull finally rushed in and grabbed the morsel he wanted, taking flight as soon as he had it safely in his beak. I barely took note of it, though. Matt had my full attention.

After we finished wiping the goo off our fingers, Matt took my hand again. He brought it to his lips, brushing my palm with a gentle kiss. My heart hadn't beat like that since I'd been a teenager. My arm tingled all the way up to my shoulder. The emotions it conjured up scared me and thrilled me at the same time. I had thought all those old feelings had died long ago.

Still holding my hand, he pulled me in close, tipping his head till our lips nearly met.

My cell phone vibrated then rang. *What rotten timing.* I reluctantly moved away from Matt and reached inside my purse. I fumbled around before I was able to pull it out from under my wallet. Was something wrong with Mother? I glanced at the screen. It was Cammie calling.

"Hello? Cammie? Is everything all right?"

"Hi Mom. Yes, it's more than all right. I've found him."

"Found who?"

"My dad. He's here with our ministry group."

186

I glanced at Matt, his face reflecting curiosity, and I stood and turned my back.

"How do you know it's him? Did you ask him?" I lowered my voice to a near whisper and walked away a few steps.

"I just know. His name is Brain Chapman. That *is* my father's name, isn't it?"

I felt the blood rush from my face. This was the Brian who headed up their group? It may not even be the same person. After all, the name wasn't all that unusual.

"Have you told him who you are?"

"No. I'm scared. Could you come down here? So we can tell him together?"

Of course she was scared. Of rejection. I knew the feeling well.

"I don't think that would be a good idea, Cammie."

"Mom! This is important." I pulled my phone away from my ear to avoid a pierced eardrum. I glanced over my shoulder. Matt looked as if he was fascinated with watching the seagull that had returned. I knew he was only trying to be polite.

"I know how important this is to you. But you're over a hundred miles away from here. It's bad enough I left your grandmother for a couple of hours. Let's talk about this before we rush into anything."

"I don't want to talk about it. I've waited long enough." Her voice took on a petulant tone. "If you can't come here, I have no choice but to tell him myself. Maybe I can get him to come home with me after this weekend is over."

I could only imagine what kind of reunion that would be. Me, standing there with a red face, and Mother screaming in the background. Still, I'd rather be in my own living room than in a strange city on Brian's turf.

I made one more desperate effort to put off the inevitable. "Think of how this will affect him. He probably has a wife and family."

"He isn't wearing a wedding ring. Besides, wouldn't his wife be with him if he were married? You can't talk me out of this. I've made up my mind."

I heard a click, which signaled Cammie had broken the connection. I turned back to Matt, trying to keep my expression neutral.

"Is something wrong?" Genuine concern filled his voice.

I shoved the phone back into my purse. "Cammie may have found her father." My voice came out flat.

"How can she be sure? The Bureau didn't have any luck locating him."

"I've been wondering about that. I mean, how hard did you look for him? Apparently he lives in the next state. For all I know, the FBI never tried to find my father either." I tried unsuccessfully to avoid sounding resentful.

"There are hundreds of Brian Chapman's. None of them we found were the right age." Matt paused, and then asked, "Do you still have feelings for this man?"

"Yes. No. Oh, I don't know. That isn't the issue."

Matt's dark eyes met my gaze. "It's an issue with me. Surely you know I've developed feelings for you. I thought we had something special."

"Don't you see? I have to get this thing with Cammie's father straightened out before I can even consider moving on with anyone else." Maybe I *was* still carrying a torch for my high-school boyfriend. Didn't I owe it to myself and Matt to find out?

"And I'm merely anyone." Matt didn't couch the phrase as a question. His expression went blank.

"You are much more than that. You're the first man I've even come close to caring about since Brian left." I pleaded for his understanding with my eyes.

Matt nodded his head without conviction that he believed me. "I'm glad to hear you say that." But then he smiled and reached for me.

188

I let Matt draw me into an embrace. Where could anyone find a more patient and understanding man? His arms protected me as I nestled my head against his shoulder. My heart soared when he placed a kiss on my head. How could I compare this man with the boy Brian had been when I knew him?

I gave Matt a squeeze and stepped from his arms. When I looked into his face I saw someone I could count on. Had Brian grown into a man like this? Did I owe Brian anything because we'd had a child together?

"I can see you have a lot to think about. What is your next step?"

I loved it that Matt had enough respect for me that he didn't try to tell me what to do. Yet, I knew that all I had to do was ask, and he'd give me his opinion. "It depends on Cammie. She wants me to come to Portland. When I told her I couldn't, she said she would bring Brian to our house. I'm assuming she means Monday evening, after their street ministry has concluded."

"That gives you tomorrow and all day Monday to think about how you want to proceed, then."

I knew Matt said that partly to remind me that he and I were supposed to be on a date. I had enjoyed myself so far. Until Cammie's phone call. I vowed to myself that I wouldn't let her discovery ruin the rest of the day. I smiled up at Matt. "Let's go have some more fun."

We tossed our napkins and the empty pastry bag into a nearby receptacle and headed back toward the Harbor Days festival. There must have been a couple of dozen tugboats, all different sizes, tied up to the docks just below the boardwalk. Most had tires hanging along their sides, which I guessed was to keep them or the dock from damage when they bumped.

Matt took my arm as we descended one of the ramps leading down to the water. According to the signs, many of the larger tugboats had invited the public on board for a tour. "Shall we?" When I smiled in agreement, Matt motioned me toward the nearest boat and helped me up the steps to the deck. "Have you ever been on one of these?"

"Nope," I said as I picked my way over a few ropes strewn around on the floor. The tug we were on let out a shrill whistle. I gasped and jumped. "

"Don't be startled. The captain is probably letting one of the youngsters toot the horn."

"Sounds more like a blast than a toot."

A young man, just a little older than Cammie approached us and introduced himself as a member of the crew. "If you'll follow me, I'll show you the galley."

The tug's small interior surprised me, but it was well equipped with stove, sink, cupboards, refrigerator, and even a TV. There were even sleeping quarters.

"All the appliances are tied down in case we enter rough waters." We followed him to the engine room, back to the deck and then up to the captain's pilothouse, which was surrounded on every side by windows.

I got lost in all the talk about horsepower, radar monitors, tachometers, and GPS systems, but Matt didn't have any problem following the conversation with the captain.

"I confess that all I know about tugs is they pull the big boats into the harbors."

"Ships. They're called ships." The deckhand corrected me.

Matt threw his arm around my shoulders, giving me a squeeze. "That's the whole idea of your open house; I mean boat, isn't it? So the public can learn?" His warm laughter rumbled in my ear.

The boy's face reddened and he half-heartedly gave me a smile. "Guess so."

I thrust out my hand to shake his. "Thanks so much for the tour. I really enjoyed it."

Relief washed over the young deckhand's expression as he took my hand.

As Matt and I left the tug, I said, "Wasn't he the cutest thing? He didn't look old enough to have a job on a tugboat. I'll bet the work is dangerous too."

Matt chuckled. "I hope he didn't hear you. It might have further eroded his pride." He stopped and looked around. "We still have a couple of hours before our early dinner. What would you like to do?"

As I tried to decide, Matt reached for his belt. "Excuse me, it's my pager." He grasped it in such a way as to read the digital message. "Wait right here. I have to make a call."

I watched him walk away, admiring the confidant way he carried himself. Even in a large crowd, he stood out as someone special. I didn't have to wait long. He returned within minutes.

"I'm so sorry, Sandy. I have to get back right away. They're sending me to Quantico to fill in for one of the instructors at the academy."

"Oh, no. That's clear on the other side of the country. Will you be gone long?"

"It could be for several weeks. Ever since 9/11, we've been spread out pretty thin. I knew leaving was a possibility, but didn't think it would be this soon."

My former happiness being with Matt faded. With all the turmoil in my life, I'd been subconsciously counting on him to be around. "I don't know how I'll deal with Mother and Cammie, and now Brian, without you to turn to."

Matt grasped both my shoulders, and looked me full in the face. "I'll call you often. And remember, you have the Lord with you at all times and He wants you to turn to him for help."

I want a flesh and blood man standing next to me. Is that so wrong? "I'll try to remember."

"Good. And I wish we didn't have to leave here right away. I booked us on a dinner cruise."

Matt's disappointed countenance matched how I felt. Could anything else happen to ruin our day together?

191

We walked back to the parking lot while I thought of all that lay ahead at home. In the beginning, when Cammie was still a toddler, I used to dream about Brian coming back into my life. As the years passed, I realized the futility of such a notion. Brian could have easily found me if he'd really wanted to.

"Are you going to give me the silent treatment all the way home?" Matt's voice, kinder than I deserved, broke into my thoughts.

I shook my head and returned to reality. I didn't even remember getting on the freeway, but here we were already passing Fort Lewis.

"I'm sorry. None of this is your fault, so I have no right to be rude." I touched his arm, not satisfied with merely sitting next to him.

"I understand, you know. And I've been praying for you since we left Olympia."

I melted, but Matt's words served as another reminder that while he relied on God, I was used to relying on myself. In another twenty minutes, Matt dropped me off at my house. He was in a hurry. There was no goodbye kiss.

Chapter Twenty

Maude's Journal
August 30, 2008

> *Sandra insists on spending time with that FBI guy. I told her about that TV program that showed cops are more likely to abuse their wives than men in other professions. But did she listen to me? No! She took off with him for the day and left me with the next-door neighbor watching me like a hawk, like I need a babysitter or something. Sandra wouldn't even sit down and watch the program with me. She rarely watches television. How, then, is she supposed to hear about all the dangers out there? She should be teaching my granddaughter these things. She's lucky to have me to look out for her.*

***

"Mother, I have something to tell you." I found her in the kitchen after Matt dropped me off.

The suspicion in her eyes reminded me of the feral cats that occasionally wandered into our yard to sit under the bird feeder. One false move from me, and their retreat became a blur.

"Sit down."

Mother didn't move from her spot in the kitchen doorway.

"It's nothing bad, I promise."

What was she afraid of now? I hadn't asked her about Daddy in ages. I knew that would be a waste of time. So what had she to worry about?

"I don't know what your promises are worth." She sidled up to the table, keeping one eye out for some imaginary threat.

As soon as she sat down, I poured her a cup of her favorite tea.

"Don't try to butter me up first. You've got something on your mind. Out with it." She reached for the sugar substitute and dumped some in her cup.

A heavy sigh escaped my lips before I could call it back. I didn't know where to start.

"I'm waiting. Or don't you think I have better things to do with my time?" She tasted her tea with her sugar spoon, and made distasteful face.

"Cammie has been wondering—asking about her father."

Mother slammed the spoon to the table. "She don't have to know anything about him. Leave the past where it belongs."

"But she *does* need to know. Besides, it's too late to stop it now."

Mother sat up straight like her back had been cranked up a flagpole. "What are you talking about?"

"She called me from Portland. She says she's found him and wants to bring him here."

"Absolutely not!" Mother's face hinted at an imminent purple rage.

"I'm sorry, Mother, but you have no say in the matter. I'm only forewarning you so you don't go into shock when he arrives. Or worse yet, cause a scene."

Mother stood so fast the kitchen chair clattered to the floor. "I'm a sick old woman. Doesn't anyone care?" She clutched the area over her heart with her right hand.

"Of course we care. And what are you doing? Feigning a heart attack?"

"Didn't you say your neighbor's husband died of a heart attack? Is that what you want me to do?"

"Nobody wants you to die. Yes, you are not well, but you can't hold us hostage with your diabetes. Especially since you won't even take care of yourself. You've always managed to get your own way, but you need to learn that

194

nobody gets what they want all the time." My breath came in short spurts. However, my frustration hadn't yet risen to the level of anger. Maybe I was learning something after all. I watched her march out of the room, knowing if I called her back, nothing would change.

As soon as Mother was out of earshot, I tried calling Daddy again. My heart cried out for some loving words. *Oh please answer this time.* The phone rang three times and I heard the pickup. My heart jumped. Finally, I'd hear my father's voice. He could tell me what to do.

However, the person that answered my call was a stranger— a recording. "The number you have called has been disconnected. If you feel you have reached this message in error, please hang up and dial again."

Could I have misdialed? I called once more. The same impersonal voice greeted me. I clenched my fist in frustration. If only I could fly back there and find out for myself what was going on. Did Daddy forget to pay the phone bill? I couldn't make sense out of his absence. How many weeks have I been trying to reach him?

I smashed my lips together in anger. Why couldn't the FBI at least look into his disappearance? What would it take to get them involved? But then they hadn't even found Brian and he apparently lived in the next state.

I called information to get the number for the police in my hometown, Detroit.

"Good morning? How may I direct your call?"

Well at least I'd connected with a real person. "I need someone to investigate the disappearance of my father."

"How long has he been gone?"

"I'm not sure. At least three weeks. Maybe longer."

"Could you give me a description of him? Where was he last seen? What was he wearing?" The woman on the other end of the line shot questions at me as fast as I could answer them. Not that I could answer very many.

"I'm sorry I can't be more specific. My home is miles away from there. I haven't seen my father for years."

I heard an exasperated sigh from the other end of the line. "You'll have to give us more information-"

"Can't you just send someone to his house? His phone has been disconnected. I don't know any of his neighbors. You are my last hope."

"Do you think he might have met up with foul play?"

My mind raced back to my suspicions about Mother. She always referred to Daddy in the past tense. *And* she had an unreasonable temper. Yet I couldn't force myself to believe she'd actually harm him.

"All I know for sure is I can't reach him."

"OK. We'll send a car around to check out his house. There's not much else we can do without more information."

"How long will that take. Could you call me right back?"

"I can't promise anything. There may not be anyone available right now."

"Anything you could do, I'd be so grateful." I answered a few more questions then replaced the receiver. I'd barely been able to choke back tears during the call, but it had to be done. "Lord I'm getting real scared. Please let everything be all right." I waited all evening for a callback but it never came.

The next day arrived too quickly. Since it was Labor Day weekend, Cammie wasn't due home until Monday evening. Would she call me again and let me know if she were bringing a visitor home? What in the world would I say to him-after all this time? Would he be happy about Cammie? Angry with me? Only my Heavenly Father knew what had gone on in my heart all these years. First, grief and total devastation at being deserted. Anger came along later. After I'd been forced to leave my parents' home.

Finally I had accepted Brian's lack of involvement in our lives. What else was there to do? Hire a detective? All my resources had gone for Cammie. Food and shelter first, and then all those other things every little girl should have.

My arms folded tightly across my chest, I paced the living room floor. He'd have no right to be angry. After all, Brian was the guilty deserter.

I'd been too distracted to go to church that morning, which I'm sure made Mother happy. How I wished I had told the pastor about Brian. Maybe he could have counseled me on what to do. Or maybe he would have been so shocked that he wouldn't want me in his church. Instead, we'd spent an hour outlining the steps for me to take as a new Christian. I'd come home with a study book he'd given me, and a promise that I'd be contacted by one of the women so I'd have a prayer and accountability partner.

Nothing was said about my past sin rearing its proverbial ugly head.

So far, no one from the church had contacted me. The knowledge that Matt was praying for me comforted me somewhat, but shouldn't I be praying too? Prayer seemed to come so easy for others. Why was it so hard for me? I knew that the traditional "Now I lay me down to sleep" was not what God expected of me. But what did He want?

I plopped down on the couch and pulled my new Bible off the end table and onto my lap. Where do I start? Matt's words came back to me. God wanted to help me. I flipped through the pages looking for anything that would catch my eye. I refused to resort to the eeny meenie minie mo method, but didn't know what else to do.

I settled on the Gospel of John and began reading where I'd left off the week before.

***

Monday morning, I found Hildie working in her garden.

"Hildie, I'm wondering if you could do me a favor."

"Of course, what is it?

"Cammie is bringing someone home who is special to her. For reasons I can't go into right now, it would be better if Mother weren't here. Do you suppose you could take her to dinner and a movie? My treat of course."

"I guess I can." Hildie glanced toward my house. "Have you tried to resolve whatever issues there are between you and Maude?"

"Issues?" I asked innocently.

"I don't like to butt in, but it's obvious there's a lot of tension between you two."

I debated how much to share with Hildie. Certainly not enough to poison Hildie's mind against Mother. I couldn't be that mean. Still, right now I needed a friend. "Mother and I have never been what you'd call *close*. Now that I've become a Christian, I'm afraid the gap between us will only widen."

"Have you prayed about it?"

I didn't need Hildie to remind me of my weak prayer life. "A few times, but I'd welcome your prayers. I'm sure He's more used to hearing from you."

"Sandy! God knows your voice intimately. He doesn't play favorites. He loves you as much as He loves anybody."

I gazed past Hildie, not seeing anything, but inwardly recounting my inadequacies as a Christian. "I'm sure you're right, but I don't know the correct words. Somehow I had expected them to come out naturally, but they don't."

"He knows your heart, child. That's all that counts."

I took a deep breath and looked her full in the face. "So you'll take Mother for the evening?"

Hildie looked slightly disappointed when I changed the subject, but smiled and nodded her head.

After making a few comments about the beauty of her garden, I escaped back to my place. I wanted to check my answering machine for any messages from the Detroit police. Instead, I found Mother hanging up the phone.

"Was there a call for me?"

"It depends."

"Come on, Mother. Who was that just now on the phone?"

"Well, it seems you called the police about your father. Did you think I'd bashed his head in and thrown him in the river?"

No way was I going to admit the thought had crossed my mind. "Aren't you the least bit worried about him? It's like he's dropped off the face of the earth." I willed myself not to cry in front of her.

"Perhaps he ran off with the floozy across the street."

"That's ridiculous. But it would serve you right. After all you ran out on him."

Mother glared at me. "It figures you'd take his side. Again."

"There's no point discussing this any further. Did the caller leave a name and number for me?" I glanced at the pad I kept near the phone.

"I guess I forgot to write it down."

"Will they be calling me back?" It wouldn't do me any good to call back. The office would be closed on a Sunday and this certainly wasn't an emergency.

"Do I look like a clairvoyant to you?"

I felt the blood rushing to my face. "No. You look like someone with something to hide." I left her standing there, hoping something I'd said had made an impression, but knowing she'd never offer an ounce of help finding Daddy.

***

I busied myself the rest of the day cleaning house and trying to decide what to wear for Brian's arrival. After I'd examined my entire wardrobe at least three times without making a selection, I flopped on my bed in aggravation. Who was I trying to impress? I hadn't gone to this much trouble getting ready for my date with Matt who had turned my insides to Jell-o only a couple of days ago.

I rolled over onto my back and stared at the ceiling. Brian probably couldn't care less whether I dressed like a frump or a fashion queen. The foremost thing on his mind would be his daughter, and the fact she'd grown up without him. I needed to spend my energy planning damage control.

My desire to impress would have to take a backseat to protecting Cammie from possible abandonment by her father for the second time in her young life.

If Brian was involved in the street ministry in Portland, it was logical to assume his Christianity would guide his actions. I could only hope that included forgiveness. After all, I was willing to put aside my anger at him for leaving me. *Oh, Cammie, I pray you don't get hurt.*

I rose from the bed and went to the mirror. Brian used to tell me how pretty I looked. I ran my fingers through my hair. He'd have to look closely to see the few gray strands I'd given up on pulling out. Still, my hair didn't have the bounce and sheen it had when I was a teenager. Were those crows' feet around my eyes?

How had the years treated Brian? Had he gone bald? Put on weight? Did he still have that twinkle in his eyes when he teased? So many men lost their sense of humor and enthusiasm as they aged.

A soft knock on my front door interrupted my daydreaming. Hildie came in after I opened the door. "You're early!"

"I thought I'd take Maude to one of those waterfront restaurants in Tacoma, and it's a fair drive."

"She'll love that. I haven't had a chance to take her around sightseeing." I pulled a couple of twenty's out of my purse and thrust them at Hildie.

She waved them off. "I don't need that."

"But when I asked you, I said it would be my treat. Please take the money." I shoved the bills at her and she stuffed them in her coat pocket.

I heard Mother shuffling down the hall. "So my babysitter is here, is she?"

Hildie looked a little taken back, but said, "Why don't you think of it as two grand dams out for a night on the town."

"As long as you put it that way, I can't refuse. It'll do me good to get away and do something fun for a change.

Everybody else gets to." Mother glared at me before getting her coat and scarf out of the hall closet.

"Well, let's be on our way, then." Hildie turned and let herself out the front door.

I watched Mother button her coat. "I hope you have a wonderful time."

"Don't think I don't know what you're up to," she hissed. "And I'm warning you right now, you're not getting away with it. I've seen to it." Mother strode out the door, slamming it behind her.

"Oh, Mother. What have you done now?" A feeling of dread surrounded me like a cloud of cheap perfume.

I looked at my watch. Cammie should be arriving home within the next two hours. Then I glanced at the phone. I hadn't heard from Matt since he brought me home Saturday afternoon. The Detroit police hadn't called me back . . . maybe that was good news. I wish Mother had taken a message. If I called back now, I'd get the dispatcher again and I didn't even know whom the case had been assigned to or who to ask for. And of course, Daddy hadn't seen fit to call me. I could only hope it was because he was embarrassed that Mother had left him and he didn't want to deal with any questions.

I walked through the house, looking for something to fill a couple of hours. There were only so many times I could mop the kitchen floor before I wore the design off the tiles. *Perhaps I should re-arrange the pantry.*

By the time I'd alphabetically sorted the soup cans, my stomach was rumbling. Had I eaten lunch? It was already suppertime. I prepared myself a chicken sandwich and leaned against the kitchen counter while I ate. However, filling my stomach didn't do much to stop the butterflies that flitted around in there.

A car stopped outside. *They're here!* I tossed my napkin under the sink and headed for the living room. I forced myself away from the front window, not wanting to appear over-anxious.

201

The mirror hanging next to the front door gave me one last chance to check my appearance. My hands shook as I smoothed my hair. A car door slammed outside.

Would they ring the doorbell to warn me, or would Cammie bring him right in? I heard footsteps approaching the front door. *Lord, are you still with me? I need You here to give me strength.*

The doorbell rang and I flung open the door.

"It's you."

Chapter Twenty-One

Maude's Journal
August 31, 2008

> *The most awful thing has happened. Cammie has found her father. Now they'll find out that I caused his parents to move away with my threats. No amount of explaining that I had a valid reason will help me out of this mess. My days here at Sandra's are numbered. Cammie will hate me, and I'll be out on the street. Where will I go? Charlie won't take me in unless Sandra is part of the deal. I have hardly any money. My only possible source of extra income is from the novel I'm writing. Sandra bought me a book that lists all the publishers. I'd better send them the chapter I wrote and hope they'll send me a huge advance.*

***

"Who were you expecting? Charlie's tone of voice told me he knew very well whom I expected and I knew who told him.

"Cammie is due home any moment, and she's bringing company." I stood square in my doorway, not inviting Charlie in. So much for exercising the gift of hospitality.

"I know. Your mother called me. She said you could use some moral support." He smiled, clearly oblivious to the fact that it was Mother, not me, who had invited him over.

My mind snapped back to Mother's warning just before she left with Hildie. What was it about Charlie that garnered her approval when Matt, my obvious choice, was so worthy of her disdain? Was it Charlie's money? Or merely that he catered to her because he wanted an ally?

"This isn't a good time for you to visit, Charlie."

"Oh, contraire. I think you could use someone here who's on your side. By the way, you look exceptionally pretty this evening."

He winked! I gripped the door handle, fighting the temptation to close it, leaving him standing on the porch. How could such a successful executive and owner of his own company be so lacking in understanding of the English language?

"I don't know what Mother told you, but this is a private matter concerning Cammie and me."

"And her mysterious guest." Charlie shifted his weight, showing his fist sign of impatience since his arrival. "When will you learn that I only have your best interests at heart? There's so much I could do for you, if you'd only let me."

"I can't think of a thing I need, so why would I want you to do anything for me?" It seemed like we'd had this conversation before. Many times.

Charlie lifted an eyebrow. "Have you forgotten I gave Cammie a job this summer?"

"You said yourself; Cammie was one of the best people you've ever had at your front desk." I resented him bringing up how he'd helped us out when Cammie hadn't been able to find a good paying job. "You should have told me at the time there were strings attached."

Charlie took a step closer. "Of course I meant no such thing. I merely pointed that out as an example of how I love doing nice things for you. *And* Cammie." His voice lowered, taking on an intimate quality.

I glanced over Charlie's shoulder. Was that a strange car coming down the street? My heart thudded.

"You seem nervous." He turned to see what I was looking at. "Oh. Do you suppose that's Cammie?"

All doubt was erased when the car pulled in behind Charlie's. There would be no getting rid of him now. I stepped aside. "Why don't you go in and help yourself to a cup of coffee?"

He smirked, and in three strides, he was inside my house, where he'd wanted to be all along.

I stepped out to the porch, pulling the door closed behind me. The man got out of the car first, but went back to the trunk so I couldn't get a good look at him. Then Cammie got out. She waved and then turned and lifted one of her suitcases out of the back seat.

My knees threatened to give out. I had imagined this moment many times. But I had never expected I'd have an audience. As much as I loved my daughter, I wanted some private time with Brian. Not much chance of that with Cammie right there and Charlie lurking behind my front door. I tried to compose something witty to say. Or welcoming. My mind went blank.

"Mom. I'm glad you're home." Cammie ran the last few feet to where I waited, dropped her suitcase, and threw her arms around me.

I hugged her back, but had gotten a brief look at her face. "You've been crying." I wanted to wring Brian's neck. Had he hurt her? "Please tell me those were tears of joy."

Cammie sobbed. I could feel her wet tears on my neck. "Oh, Mom. He says it's not true. He denies even knowing you."

I've been afraid of this. I moved back a little and brushed the hair off her forehead. "I'm sure his reaction was one of shock. Remember, I warned you about this."

The man in question came up the sidewalk, carrying Cammie's other two suitcases. I turned on him. "If you want to argue with someone, here I am, but don't take out your disbelief on our daughter."

The door opened behind me. "Coffee anyone?" Charlie came out carrying my coffee carafe and mugs on a tray.

I waved him away. "Please take that stuff back inside. We'll be there in a moment." By playing host, Charlie sent a strong message regarding his alleged place in our family.

205

"I'll just put everything on the coffee table. I'm sure everyone is ready for some refreshment after the long drive." Charlie moved back inside, but left the front door wide open.

Cammie pulled on my arm. "Mom, tell him that it's true." She nodded toward Brian who had set both suitcases on the sidewalk at the bottom of the steps.

I took a hard look at him, searching for anything of the young man I'd gone through high school with.

"Mrs. Hughes, I ordinarily wouldn't have given any credence to such a ridiculous claim, but your daughter was so upset, I felt it best to bring her home and clear this up right away. Besides, one of the other kids needed a ride to his house just five miles south of here. May I come in and we'll straighten this out?" He glanced at a nearby yard. One of my neighbors held a hose, watering his rose bushes, but his full attention was on us.

I squinted at Brian, still not seeing in the man, the boy I'd loved as a teenager. And why would he call me Mrs. Hughes? He knew Hughes was my maiden name. I darted a glance at the neighbor who had moved closer to the property line. "Yes, let's go in the house." I led the way.

Brian and Cammie picked up her suitcases and carried them inside, setting them on the floor next to the hall closet. Charlie, still acting the host, immediately introduced himself and invited Brian to sit down.

I couldn't take my attention away from Brian. On the other hand, he never once looked in my direction. What was he feeling? Trapped? Would he persist in his denial?

I took in his appearance. His thinning hair didn't compare with the thick wavy brown style I remembered. His face was much fuller. His waist was certainly thicker. I wanted him to look at me. I wanted to see that spark of recognition that he knew we'd once pledged to love each other forever.

He turned and said something to Cammie and I looked hard at the side view of his face. His nose and chin! Even age, maturity, and weight gain wouldn't have changed his profile from Roman to a Bob Hope look-alike. "You're not him."

"Mom. What are you saying? Of course it's him." The plea in Cammie's eyes nearly broke my heart.

"I tell you, he's not your father." I didn't know whether to cry for Cammie, or laugh in relief.

"That's what I've been telling you all along," Brian said to my daughter. "Not that I wouldn't be proud to have a daughter like you." He looked at her kindly, not unlike teacher trying to praise a child's first effort at finger painting.

Cammie's face reddened in anger. "You're lying. Both of you." She pointed an accusing finger at me. "You never wanted me to find my father."

Charlie strode to Cammie's side and patted her back. "There, there, now. You don't need a complete stranger in your life. And that's what he is, an outsider, your father or not."

I fought the urge to smack Charlie. "This man is not Cammie's father. Maybe he has the same name, but that's all."

"My daughter is right." We all whirled around toward the new voice coming from the open front door.

"Daddy!" I ran to my dad, nearly knocking him down. Weeks of futile calls, no help from the FBI or police, and certainly no help from Mother, and here he stood. I couldn't decide whether to keep hugging him, or to keep looking into his kindly face. If I were Cammie's age, I would have jumped up and down.

Cammie shoved her way in, not wanting to be left out of a family hug. "Grandpa! You're an answer to my prayers. The only thing missing now is for my Dad to admit he knows my mom." She glanced over her shoulder at the man who'd driven her home from Portland. "If you're telling the truth, I guess you won't mind taking a DNA test."

"Cammie!" I sent an apologetic look to Brian, the wrong one, Chapman.

"That's quite all right, Ma'am. If it will put your daughter's mind at ease, I'll be glad to."

Daddy pulled away from our entwined arms. "That won't be necessary." He took a long look at me, sympathy in his eyes. "Sandy, dear. I hate to bring you bad news. I was hoping for a different outcome. I'm afraid your Brian passed away many years ago."

Shock ripped through me, dampening the thrill of the reunion with my dad. "Why? And how is it you know?"

Daddy looked around my living room, taking in Charlie, who looked relieved, and the other Brian, who decided that now would be a good time to pour himself a cup of coffee. "I expected your mother to be here."

"She *is* staying here, but she's out with a friend, our neighbor woman, this evening." Of course. Daddy had come all this way to see Mother. He missed her. Even despite her running out on him. He must have been out of his mind with worry.

Brian raised the coffee carafe toward us. "Anyone else?"

"Good idea," my dad said. "Why don't we all sit down?"

We all took our places on the couch and chairs, me, sitting as close as possible to Daddy. Of course Charlie didn't miss the opportunity to introduce himself. "It's a pleasure to meet you sir," he said, shaking Daddy's hand before sitting down.

Brian, now that the pressure of instant fatherhood was no longer an issue, did the same. "I'd like to add that your granddaughter, Cammie is a fine young woman. I've had the delight of getting to know her this weekend." He turned to face me. "Getting to know you better would be a pleasure, also."

"There's no need for that." Charlie, true to form, tried to establish his place in our lives.

208

I ignored Charlie, hoping the others would too. "Bringing Cammie all this way home was very nice of you."

"As I said before, I couldn't very well deny her the opportunity for us to meet." He smiled broadly, his good nature covering his entire face. "However, I don't want to intrude on this reunion with your father. As soon as I finish my coffee, I must get back on the road and return to Portland." He looked meaningfully at Charlie.

I fought a smile. It hadn't taken this virtual stranger long to figure out Charlie's agenda. "I can't send you off without even a bite to eat. It's the least I could do after the patience you've shown Cammie." I stood, planning to go to the kitchen. "Daddy, you must be hungry after your trip, too."

"I ate on the plane. I'm content with sitting here feasting my eyes on you and my granddaughter." Daddy's words didn't come close to the warm feeling I had merely knowing he was safe with us at last.

Cammie dropped down on the couch next to Daddy. "You're going to stay, aren't you? You and Gran can have Mom's room since she has a double bed."

Daddy glanced at me, at Charlie and Brian, and then back at Cammie. "I don't want to put anyone out."

I didn't think this public forum was the place to discuss my parents' recent separation. "We'll settle this later." I touched my father's arm. "You said Brian had passed away. Could you fill me in with the details?"

"After the Chapman's left Detroit, they settled in New York. Brian went to school there for a few years, and then joined an overseas mission organization. They appointed him to a post somewhere in the Middle East. The area had a bad reputation for capturing and imprisoning Christians. Brian didn't care. He wanted to take the Gospel to the people he said needed it most. People who wouldn't hear it unless someone from the outside brought the message in."

"Why did his parents allow him to go to such a dangerous place?" Cammie expressed shock.

Daddy patted her hand. "They didn't have a choice. Brian was of age." He looked directly at me. "I can imagine the fear and loss they felt when their son left. It must have been every parent's nightmare."

I felt heat rising in my face. Was that how Daddy felt when I left home?

"Did he die overseas then?" Cammie's voice caught, ready to break into a sob over the father she'd never met.

"When I finally found his parents they told me Brian had disappeared after he'd been there only six months. They traveled to the last place he'd been seen and spent weeks trying to locate anyone who knew of their son's whereabouts. They came up with nothing. After years went by, and even the private investigators the Chapman's hired couldn't help, the State Department listed him as *presumed dead*."

Cammie perked up. "Then he could be alive somewhere. They didn't find a body."

"It's been what? At least twelve or thirteen years since anyone's seen him? Realistically—"

"Charlie! Show a little sensitivity." I darted imaginary arrows at him with my eyes.

Cammie slumped back into the cushions of the couch. I wanted to take her in my arms and comfort her, but the truth was, I also needed comforting myself. *What a waste of his life.* Even now that I'd become a Christian, I couldn't understand how God would allow such a thing to happen.

Brian emptied his coffee cup and set it down. "This is a family moment. I really need to be going." He stood. "It's been a pleasure meeting you all. Charlie? Why don't you walk me out and direct me back to the freeway?"

To say I was grateful to Brian was an understatement. Charlie's indecision grated on my nerves. I stood, and when Daddy did the same, Charlie must have realized protesting would be futile. He shook hands with my father. "Hope to see you again soon." He followed Brian outside.

After I heard both cars pull away, I turned and gave Daddy another hug. "You can't know how happy I am to see you. I have so many questions. And I need your help."

He took my hand and led me back to the couch, sitting down between Cammie and me. "What kind of help do you need?"

"Could you answer a couple of questions first?"

"Shoot."

"How long have you known about Brian? That he's gone, I mean."

Daddy still had my hand in his and gave it a squeeze. "I learned it a few days ago. I've been looking for his parents for the last couple of weeks."

Disbelief surged through me. "But why would you be looking for them? Why now?"

"Because of something I learned recently. Something you best ask your ma about."

"Does it have anything to do with the reason she ran out on you?"

"I'm not going to say anything more about it. At least until your ma gets here."

Cammie sat quietly during this exchange. I had a feeling she hadn't given the circumstances surrounding my leaving Detroit much thought. I'd never seen a need to tell her that Mother had tried to drag me to an abortionist. I certainly didn't plan to tell her now. Especially since she'd formed such an attachment to her grandmother during the last few weeks.

"I will tell you something." Daddy's words interrupted my thoughts. "The Chapman's are very decent people. When I told them they have a granddaughter, they were overjoyed. They want to meet you, Cammie."

Cammie's eyes widened. "You mean they didn't know about me?"

The sternness on my father's face startled me. "No. And your father didn't know about you either. That wasn't right. And that's why I went looking for them."

211

The news stunned me. I thought Brian must have suspected we'd conceived a baby. And then Mother told me he knew, and that's why their family left Detroit . . . or sneaked out of town as she so eloquently put it.

Daddy reached across me and picked up my Bible from the end table. "I see somebody here has learned something about faith in God." He stroked the leather cover with his wrinkled hands. "Brian's folks shared their beliefs with me. Beliefs their son, and your father, Cammie, died for. I'd like to learn more about this God."

My eyes burned from the salty tears welling in them. *Thank You, Lord, for bringing my dad to us. And to You."*

The front door swung open and Mother came in. "Whose car is that out front?" Then she spotted Daddy. "Well. Lookie what the cat drug in.

Chapter Twenty-Two

Maude's Journal
September 1, 2008

> *I should be further along with my book. I've managed to skim through most of my journals. I'd hoped to find a clear answer about why my marriage failed. This was what my novel is about. People want answers. My readers will be looking to me for solutions to their own problems, even in a fictitious story. These how-to books Sandra gave me are worthless. I don't have time to read them, and need to get this story finished so I can send it in. Then I can start thinking about who should play me in the movie.*
>
> *I'm making a list of warning signs to look for in a potential husband so I can insert them along the way, like clues in a mystery novel. But every time I get on a roll, some dumb little thing in those journals distracts me. Like the time James surprised me on our fifth wedding anniversary with a trip to Atlantic City. We called it our second honeymoon. I must have spent an entire evening, going over all the things we did together on that trip. There were certainly no warning signs there.*

***

"Mother, that was really mean." Couldn't she have at least said hello before she tried to pick a fight?

"Gran? Aren't you excited to see Grandpa?" Cammie looked very unhappy to hear her newest family member getting picked on, especially by none other than her *sweet Gran.*

Daddy stayed put and didn't say a word. Of course he was used to her verbal stabs.

"What do you think?" Mother swiped at a tear, but I saw it before she hid it. "Did you think I moved all the way out here because I wanted him around?" Another tear rolled down her face before she could react.

How would I smooth things over if Mother couldn't soften up? "Weren't you and Hildie going to the movies?" Maybe if I could draw her attention away from her bitterness, we could have a little peace.

"She wanted to see some stupid fairy tale about some bratty kids who think there's a magic world in the back of a closet."

"Do you mean the *Chronicles of Narnia* movie? I saw it and really liked it. You would too," Cammie spoke up.

"I hope you didn't insult Hildie. It's too bad you couldn't have reached a compromise." Was that the real reason she came home early? Or had she intended on interfering with Brian's visit? "An evening out would have been good for you."

Mother answered my unspoken question. "Good for you, you mean."

"Daddy, did you know Mother has been very ill?" I asked, hoping to deflect another argument.

Finally giving some sign other than the stoic expression he'd displayed since her arrival, his head jerked up.

Mother sashayed across the room. "That certainly woke you up from the dead. I guess you still have a life insurance policy on me."

I moved into position in front of her. *Who knows what she'll do next?*

"Sit down, Sandy. I've been taking care of myself for most of my life." Daddy's sharp command made me wonder if he welcomed Mother's barbs. "What's wrong with you, Maude?" he asked softly.

Mother didn't deserve the concern I heard in Daddy's voice. She had attacked him the moment she came in the door, just like she had always done while I was growing up.

214

Mother took one of the vacant chairs. "Nothing much. Some people make a big deal over nothing."

Daddy sent a puzzled look in my direction, but I figured Mother needed to 'fess up and tell him herself. Besides, he'd just reminded me not to get between them during one of their "discussions." She did look pale and thin. Daddy had to notice that. We waited for her to answer.

Daddy sighed. "Well then, if you don't want to talk about your health, perhaps we should talk about Brian." He pinned her with a stare like I'd never seen from him.

Mother paled even more. *What is going on here? She actually looks afraid.* She glowered and gestured around the room. "Not much to talk about. I understand he was supposed to be here tonight, but evidently he's chosen not to come. Just proves what I've said about him all along."

Cammie burst into tears, rose from the couch, and ran from the room.

"Now you've done it, Mother. Could you be any less sensitive?"

"I have no idea what you're talking about. Camelia is nearly an adult. She has a right to know what a shirker he is."

"That's enough, Maude." Daddy's voice was soft, but carried some hidden meaning I couldn't understand. He clenched his jaw and glared.

"I suppose you've come here to make trouble for me." Mother's voice held a tremor not there before. Underneath her bravado, I sensed strong emotion.

I began gathering the coffee cups from our earlier guests. "I'm going to load these in the dishwasher and give you two some time to catch up."

"Sandy, the dishes can wait. There's something that needs to get out in the open." Daddy spoke in a firm voice. "Maude, I'm giving you a chance to tell her yourself."

"I don't know what you're talking about," Mother huffed.

215

I stood. "Really. I need to clear this stuff away." The tension between my parents brought back too many unpleasant memories. Only I never recalled Daddy having the upper hand. He usually dealt with conflict by withdrawing behind his newspaper, or puttering outside in the garage.

I started toward the kitchen.

"Sit down, Sandy."

My hands shook, causing the coffee mugs to rattle together. "Daddy, during the last eighteen years I've done my best to provide Cammie with a peaceful environment. Since Mother has arrived, harmony in this house has become a thing of the past. Now you're here, and your presence is adding to the tension. As much as I love you, I can't stand by and watch, while everything I've striven for is destroyed. I wish you'd take Mother home."

I felt my heart pounding, not believing what I'd just said. Daddy stood and took the tray from my hands, making me feel as if I were six years old again.

He carried it into the kitchen, but came right back. "I blame myself for the turmoil in our home. I took the easy way out and let your ma run things. I told myself you'd be better off if she and I never argued."

"It wasn't all—"

"Don't interrupt." He glanced at Mother who had slumped into the chair cushions. "Now your mother may have been sincere in her desire to protect you, but her actions were sorely misguided."

"I did the best I could!" Mother piped up.

"I'm sure you did, Maude. Just as I think your upbringing had something to do with some of your notions about child rearing. But my stars, woman, why do you think the Good Lord planned for children to have two parents?"

"Oh no. Don't try to shore up your arguments with religion." Mother slammed her purse down on the floor. "You've never set foot in a church your whole life. Besides, Sandra had two parents."

216

Daddy's face turned red. "I'm talking about Cammie, too. She needed a father. And Sandy needed a husband to help her all these years."

"Well she didn't have one."

"And whose fault was that?" He strode across the room, sticking his finger at her. "Tell her."

All the blood drained from Mother's face.

"Daddy, Mother isn't well. I don't think—"

"Tell her, Maude, or I will."

"Daddy, please."

"Just listen, Sandy. I promise I'll leave as soon as your ma comes clean about what she did."

The color started to return to Mother's face, but she still looked shaky.

"What I did? I saved our daughter from a life of heartbreak, that's what. That boy would have ruined her life. He came from one of those religious fanatical families who treat their women like slaves. Is that what you wanted for her?"

What is she talking about? How did she save me from anything? My father stood poised over Mother like a lion tamer. I expected her to snarl at him at any moment.

"Go ahead, Maude. Tell Sandy why the Chapman's left Detroit."

I still wanted to escape their confrontation, but my fascination with the shift of power from Mother to Daddy kept me rooted to the floor. Besides, was Daddy saying Mother had some knowledge about why Brian and his parents had left?

Mother crossed her arms over her chest. Her face twisted into a grimace of both anger and fear. "Tell her yourself, you self-righteous old coot. Stand there and gloat while I lose my last chance for a roof over my head."

"I think our daughter should hear it from you. Or if you're too cowardly, perhaps you'd like to give her your journals so she can read it for herself like I did. I know you brought them with you."

217

Mother gasped and sputtered, "If you weren't such an old snoop, this whole subject would never have come up. Do what you like. I'm going to bed." Mother rose and exited down the hall faster than I'd seen her move since she'd arrived.

Daddy looked at me, sadness in his eyes. "I gave her every chance to explain herself."

My gut whirled, threatening to lose its contents. I dreaded what I knew Daddy was about to tell me. I always thought I'd escaped from Mother's influence over my life, but now I knew she'd done something to make me lose Brian for good.

Daddy came and enveloped me in those big comforting arms of his. "I'm so sorry. If I'd known, I would have stopped her."

"Tell me everything."

"It's not too complicated. When she found out you were carrying Cammie, she went to the Chapman's and threatened to have Brian jailed for rape. According to what they told me, and what I read in the journals, she never told them about the baby. They spoke to their son, and were convinced he hadn't forced you, but they moved away, rather than put you kids through the public agony of a trial."

Rage coursed through every vein in my body. "But why didn't Brian try to get in touch with me?"

"Your ma convinced them that you had made the accusation."

"Is that why Mother left you? You argued over me?"

"I asked her to leave when I found out what she'd done. I shouldn't have been so harsh. I was as angry with myself as I was with her. As soon as she was gone, I went looking for Brian to try and set things right."

I suddenly felt very tired. I looked at my watch. It had been a long emotionally exhausting day. I needed to pray. My anger toward Mother exceeded what I could handle on my own.

218

"Thank you for trying, Daddy. I need to go check on Cammie. Why don't you go get settled in my room? It's the last door on the left. I'll bunk out here on the couch. It's really very comfortable."

"Are you sure you're all right?"

"Of course. I merely have a lot of information to sort through, that's all." Plus I had to figure out some way to explain to Cammie the real reason she grew up without a father.

Dad enveloped me in a hug. "I'll stay on the couch, so I can be here when your mother comes back.

I was glad Mother had gone to her room. I couldn't have stood to see her face. I'd already extended her more hospitality than she deserved. She might think she could justify her actions to herself, but she'd never convince me to forgive her.

I stepped into Cammie's room. Her light was off, but the outside streetlamp shone through the window. She was asleep, her hair fanned out on her pillow. I tiptoed to her side and kissed her forehead.

When I walked across the hall to my own room, I could see down the hall to the living room. Daddy sat next to the end table lamp, thumbing through my Bible. *Lord, let my dad find the strength he needs to help us all through this.*

I hoped the soft click of my bedroom door didn't disturb him. I got in my shower, turning the water as hot as I could stand it. I could finally cry where no one could hear me. For Cammie. For me. For Daddy, who had sacrificed so much over the years to keep the peace, and for Brian. Brian, who would be alive and part of our family, instead of dead someplace on the other side of the world. All because of my mother.

***

The next morning, I crept down the hall to the kitchen, hoping I wouldn't wake Cammie or Mother. Cammie didn't have to be at school till Wednesday, and the less I saw of my mother, the better.

219

Daddy, holding a hot cup of coffee, greeted me in the kitchen. "Good morning, Honey." He handed me my coffee and gave me a peck on the cheek. "Did you sleep well?"

I took a sip of the steaming coffee before answering. "I slept very little." I grabbed a banana off the counter and sat down. "I'm glad you're up. I have to leave for work soon, but need to talk to you alone first."

"You never were afraid of getting to the point, even as a little girl." He pulled up a chair opposite me where his own mug sat half-finished.

"Thanks. I appreciate your willingness to listen." I took a deep breath, knowing what I had to say might not set well with him. "I have a fulltime job. It pays for this house plus some of Cammie's tuition. I've been missing work lately because I've been taking Mother to dialysis." I saw the shock in Daddy's eyes, but continued on before he could ask any questions.

"She has to go three times a week. Each time she's there about four hours. After what we learned last night, I'm not willing to ask Cammie to take her. I also hesitate to call on Hildie, our neighbor, unless it's an emergency."

Daddy was no dummy. He knew what was coming next. "You want me to take her." He rubbed his head. "I had no idea she was so ill."

"That would be a big help. I know you two are separated now. But what I don't know is if there's any chance you'll reconcile. If you get divorced, I'm going to take steps to put her in an adult care facility. I can't have her here any longer." I waited to hear his response.

He pushed his mug away. "I asked your mother to leave, you know. I was furious with her and hoped it would force some sense into her. To tell you the truth, I don't know if we'll get back together or not. It depends on her. But I'm unwilling to go on as we were before."

"I hope you'll make a decision soon. I honestly don't know how much longer I can stand to have her in this

220

house. My stomach has been tied up in knots every day since her arrival."

Daddy reached across the table, covering my hand with his. "I'm not going to abandon her, or you either. I'll take her to her treatments. If she'll let me."

After seeing the way he'd handled her the night before, I had no doubts about his ability to wrestle her into the car and into the dialysis center. His willingness was the only thing in question.

"I married her for better or worse. I'm not going to abandon her when she's ill." Tears pooled in his eyes. "It sounds serious."

"It is. Her kidneys are failing."

"You go on to work. I'll take care of everything here."

I gave my father all the information on Mother and the directions to the clinic, then went in and dressed for work.

***

I got to work fifteen minutes early and headed straight for my office. Libby, one of the section managers stood at my desk, piling my personal things into a cardboard box. My heart stopped. *Lord, I can't take any more! I thought you promised to take care of me.*

"What is going on in here?" As if I couldn't see with my own eyes. The new owner had begun restructuring already. *So much for his promises to keep everyone on.*

Libby didn't meet my eyes, but continued pulling things out of my desk drawer in quick, angry movements.

I strode to my desk and pulled the box away from her. "The least they could do is allow me to do this myself."

Her dark eyes met mine. "I was instructed to pack everything up."

"By who?" Was the new owner on the premises? I clenched my fists, preparing myself to storm into whatever office he'd commandeered.

"You don't have to play dumb." Libby's pupils contracted to tiny points. "It will be all over the office by the time everyone arrives." She dumped my stash of teabags, a tube of hand cream, and other personal items of mine into another box and walked out of my office with them.

"Where are you going with my things? And why are you angry with me? We've always had a great working relationship. Or at least I thought we had," I mumbled as I followed her down the hall.

I fully expected her to cart my belongings to the dumpster outside. Instead, she made a beeline down the hall to our boss's office. I had to break into a trot to keep up with her. I followed her inside. I'd never before entered his office without knocking first.

My boss stood at the large bank of windows, looking out toward the employee parking lot. Libby dropped the box on the floor next to his handcrafted walnut desk and left. Now that I was there, I didn't know what to say. The only thing I could think of was, "You said all our jobs would be safe. I'm fired. Right?"

He turned, and removed his glasses, brushing the lenses across his shirtsleeve. "I didn't tell you the entire story."

My shoulders drooped. I'd trusted him. Mother's fear of being out on the street suddenly took on new meaning for me.

"My health isn't all that good. My wife and I want to spend time together while we still can. As the sale of my business progressed, it became clear that, shall we say, certain terms must be met."

I stared at him in unbelief. "And somehow this affects me? What are the terms? Tell me, please." I waited for his answer. The sooner he said it out loud, the sooner I could head for the unemployment office.

"The sale was dependent upon you becoming the CEO of this company."

222

Chapter Twenty-Three

Maude's Journal
September 2, 2008

> *James is here. At first I thought he'd had a change of heart and had come for me. I smarted off to him, hoping he'd get the idea I wasn't going to make it too easy for him. I would have given in. Eventually. After letting him grovel a bit. I've got too much pride to let him know I miss knowing that he's sleeping right next to me at night.*
>
> *But I should have known. He didn't come here on my account. He came to see Sandra. It was always about Sandra. Made me look like a fool in front of my daughter and granddaughter. As if he could make anything worse than it is already. I'm afraid Camelia has turned against me too. My only hope now is Charles. If he doesn't come through, I'll end up walking around with all my stuff in a shopping cart.*

***

My jaw must have dropped to my knees. "There must be some mistake."

"There's no more need for you to keep it a secret. The papers are all signed. Payroll will make the appropriate adjustments to your salary effective today." Our boss glowered at me.

No hearty congratulations, only thinly disguised resentment. I couldn't blame him. Everyone figured his former second in command, and Libby's immediate supervisor, would take over the reigns of the company. He deserved it and would have had everyone's support.

"Wait. This is the first I've heard of any of this. I'm telling you, some monster error has been made. You and I both know how ridiculous this is."

223

"I wish what you say is true. For your sake, as well as my company's."

The import of his words weren't lost on me. Nobody would accept my appointment to such a position of authority. What did I know about running a business?

Libby returned with another box of my things. "A catalog arrived from an office furniture and supply firm, with instructions for you to return it with your preferences to refurbish this office. A decorator will be here right after lunch."

"Libby, take all this back to my office. Someone is playing a huge prank. And even if any truth existed in what you both are telling me, I wouldn't accept."

"Wait." Our boss raised his hand like some traffic cop, hoping to prevent a major collision. "It's gone too far, and I no longer have any say. The agreement I thought I had with the buyer was never put in writing. He's threatened to lay everyone off if you don't step up and lead this company."

I couldn't come up with one coherent explanation for such a preposterous event.

"Who *is* this lying, blackmailing, trickster? I want to speak to him." The thought of my friends and coworkers losing their jobs on account of me made me feel sick.

"Nobody, including me, will ever believe you and this so-called anonymous buyer haven't been cooking this up for months." Libby's mouth crunched into an angry grimace as she stood twisting the office supply catalog.

Suddenly the entire ludicrous situation overcame me. "So does this mean you won't be applying for the position as my administrative assistant?"

Libby spun around and ran out the door, but not before I saw her tears.

"Libby, Wait! I didn't mean to be flippant." Only the sound or her footsteps retreating down the hall answered me.

I slumped into one of the guest chairs next to my boss's desk. Life was so much simpler when my only enemy was Mother. Now it appeared I'd garnered an entire office full of adversaries. *Lord what have I done to deserve this? What am I doing wrong? Tell me. Please?*

"I would have thought you'd be *thanking* God instead of complaining."

I lifted my head to see my boss hadn't left on Libby's heels. "I didn't realize I was speaking out loud." I'd always liked and admired the man in front of me. I thought I'd earned his respect over the years. It hurt to think I'd lost that through no design of my own.

"You know I haven't planned any of this. I was surprised as everyone else when you announced you were selling. Besides, I told you I had applied for that job in Seattle. Would I have done that if I planned to take over your company and run it into the ground?"

The muscles in his face relaxed a little. "I'll admit, I was shocked when he named you as my successor. You'd never given any indication your ambitions pointed in that direction."

"He? You keep referring to the buyer as *he*. Not *they*. Not *she*. Won't you tell me who he is? How does he know me? Was I selected at random? My name picked out of a hat?"

My boss picked up his briefcase. "I'm sure you'll be filled in soon. After all, it's in his best interest to protect his investment by keeping his new CEO happy." He walked around his desk stopping to place his hand on my shoulder. "Good luck. I've got a feeling you'll need it."

He walked out leaving me stunned and alone.

What does one do at a time like this? Phone everyone you know and share the great news? Call a staff meeting? Sit in here by myself and wait for further instructions? I covered my face with my hands. Splaying my fingers, I peeked through and looked at the phone. A friendly voice would transport me back to my real life. Whatever *that* was. My other life hadn't been too stellar lately. Still, there had been a few bright spots illuminating the dark periods.

Of course Cammie topped the list of people who brought me joy. However, she had enough to contend with without me adding another burden. Daddy. He'd been my rock while I was growing up. Granted we hadn't communicated much at all during the second half of my life. Anyway, he'd be on his way to the clinic with Mother by now.

Then there was Matt. I closed my eyes, willing the image of his handsome face to materialize into a flesh and blood man. I perked up. Matt would at least give me some ideas about how to identify this phantom new owner who had turned my life upside down. Why had fate arranged for him to be on the other side of the continent when I needed him here? I don't suppose the FBI would take kindly to me calling and interrupting his class merely to tell him I'd been promoted. I'd probably be compromising national security or something.

The phone sat on the desk, inviting me to call someone. Anyone. Using my boss's phone for a personal call seemed a little presumptuous, but since he'd indicated he wasn't coming back, he probably wouldn't care who used it. Nevertheless, I reached into my purse and pulled out my cell-phone. I scrolled through my contact list till I found Hildie's name and number. I'd ask her to pray for me.

I rose to shut the office door. Privacy for this conversation seemed to be the wise choice.

"Oh excuse me, Ms. Hughes." My boss's secretary nearly collided with me as we reached the doorway at the same time.

"For crying out loud, Jane, you've been calling me Sandy for the last five years. Don't start treating me like a stranger."

"I'm sorry. I was trying to show respect." Jane wrung her hands and looked at her feet.

"We've always treated each other with respect. I know we haven't been close friends. I haven't had time to

226

socialize—raising my daughter alone like I have, but I intend to change that."

"I didn't know you had a daughter." Jane's gaze met mine, but slid away again.

"Look. I need to pick your brain. Why don't we get a cup of coffee?"

"I'll get it for you. How do you take it?"

"Why don't we walk down to the lunchroom?" No way was I going to let her wait on me.

"That might not be a good idea."

"Why not?"

"Some of the others are having a meeting there."

It didn't take a genius to figure out what the meeting was about. Since I hadn't been invited, my presence would only put a damper on their agenda.

Jane fidgeted, apparently waiting for my instructions.

"Why aren't you at the meeting?" Perhaps she'd been selected to keep me busy.

"To tell you the truth, I need this job. I understand if you want to pick out your own private secretary, but I'd like it if you'd consider me."

"I'm flattered. I gather I'm not the most popular person around here right now."

Jane's face flushed. "It's just, ahem, just that my kids are in private school. I wouldn't be able to afford the tuition if it weren't for this job. I'll be right back."

I waited in my old office for Jane to bring the coffee. My photos were gone from my desk, presumably packed away in a cardboard box. As my gaze traveled around the small area that had been my workplace for several years, I saw that no one would find a single clue as to who the last occupant had been. Instead, it looked like someone had hastily left, leaving behind only scraps of paper and an old company policy manual, which I'd been instrumental in updating. It contained nothing that pertained to this situation.

After what seemed like enough time for someone to go to Starbucks and back with a dozen lattes, Jane returned with two paper cups. One taste convinced me I didn't need any coffee after all.

"Sorry. The pots were all empty. Everybody must have filled up before their meeting. All I could find was instant." Her eager-to-please expression kept me from making an unkind comment.

"Let me get right to the point. I'm completely taken by surprise that number one, we've lost our leader," I paused for effect," and two, that the new owner, whoever he is has somehow confused me with someone else in this company."

Jane's eyes widened. "Oh, Ms. Hughes, I'm sure you'll do a wonderful job. And if there's anything you need, you just let me know."

I wondered if there was anything in Jane's cup besides coffee. Granted, she probably thought my reaction was unusual. Anyone else would be celebrating and counting their blessings. *Lord, this is a blessing I didn't need. Could you take it away and think of something else?*

"Jane, you were the executive secretary for a long time. I'm sure you were privy to information not available to the rest of us. Who is the new owner?"

"Honest, I don't know."

"Think. Have you seen anyone new around here lately meeting with your boss? Secret meetings? Someone who looked like they had a lot of money?" I couldn't imagine what the price tag of the building and business had amounted to. Easily more than a million. Probably more. The building alone was worth at least that.

"No. I don't remember anybody like that."

"How about in his files? Any chance the information would be there?"

"He took all his personal files with him."

"Do you keep an appointment calendar for him?"

"Of course. That's one of my duties. I'll do that for you, too." Again, the hopeful look returned to her eyes.

"Why don't you go get it for me? In the meantime, I think I'll drop by the lunchroom and attend a meeting.

***

Over twenty pair of guilty looking eyes turned toward me as I barged in on the impromptu employee's meeting. It seemed as if everyone was there, from the managers, down to the mailroom clerk. Seeing the women there, who I supervised in the general accounting pool, disturbed me enough that I fumbled for words.

"I gather you've all heard the news. I want all of you to go back to your desks. Work on what you'd normally do, until I get this figured out. In case you're wondering, I did not ask for this position. But until the right person is appointed, I'm apparently stuck with it. Rest assured, I am not planning on making any personnel changes." I hoped my little speech would calm everybody's fears.

The only sound came from the bubbling coffee pot at the far end of the room.

I looked around, seeking some support. "Are there any questions?"

A hand raised in the back of the room. "Yeah. Who did you sleep with to get that cushy job?"

A migraine had waited in slumber all morning for an occasion like this. *Isn't this swell? I'm trying to make the best of a bad situation and what happens? Certainly not a thank you from anyone.*

I tried to make myself a little taller. "I'm going to forget you said that since you're new here and obviously don't know me very well. However, even though I said I won't make any changes," I looked directly at the only one who had the nerve to ask out loud what many must have been thinking, "anyone who feels they can't cut it during the transition is welcome to take this afternoon off to look for employment elsewhere."

I could have lived without all the mumbling as they filed out of the lunchroom, but at least no one openly threatened an insurrection.

I spent the better part of the morning placing everything back where it belonged in my old office.

Jane watched me anxiously. "Don't you think you'll command more respect if you take the CEO's office?"

"The trappings of a position I'm not qualified for won't make anybody accept me any faster. The best thing I can do is correct the problem before the company loses face with its clients." I held out my hand for the calendar Jane had brought me from her office. "Why don't you go to lunch with some of your friends and see if you can sooth their concerns.

After Jane left, I went over every entry in the appointment book over the past six months, looking for any clues about the identity of the new owner. The only name I didn't recognize came up dozens of times. Each time the appointment was for lunch, never for a meeting at the office. The name was C.A.D. Inc. *Hmm. Cad. How appropriate. This has to be it.* I tugged the phone book out of my desk drawer and thumbed through it, looking for a listing.

"Rats!" I plopped the directory back in the desk drawer. Who was behind this phantom corporation? Maybe the owner was from Seattle or Tacoma. Made sense. Someone who bought up other businesses would probably be based in a big city.

Before I had a chance for further investigation, Jane popped her head back in my office. "We've got some potential clients coming in who would like to talk to someone in charge."

"Don't the managers usually handle that?"

"They're all busy, except the new guy who went home sick."

I pressed the heel of my hand to my forehead. We couldn't very well turn away business. Every account meant job security for everyone who worked here. "Are any of the conference rooms available?"

"They're all being used. I checked." Jane fidgeted, just like a kid does when they're expecting to be punished.

"Obviously my office isn't large enough. I guess there's no choice but to use the office our boss vacated."

"I'll show them in." Jane scurried out, leaving me wondering if I could adequately represent our firm. *Oh well, it'll be good practice for when I interview for my next job.*

***

Between trying to do my old job, and attempting to make sense of the new responsibilities, which had been thrust on me, I couldn't carve out a scrap of time to do any more investigation into the C.A.D. Corporation. By the time five o'clock rolled around, I was exhausted, both mentally and emotionally. I escaped out the back door to my car headed back to my family.

Daddy met me at the door. For the first time in days, I'd been eager to get home and though seeing his face reminded me of all the issues waiting for me, I smiled and gave him a hug.

"How did it go with Mother today?"

"Not too bad. I got a chance to speak to her nephrologist. You were right. Her situation is worsening. However, he held out hope for a kidney transplant."

"Mother will never agree to that. We've already discussed it."

"Leave your mother to me. I'm used to her tactics."

Relief surged through me filling me with the first burst of confidence I'd experienced all day. This was exactly what I'd hoped for if Daddy were found.

"I've started dinner."

My heart overflowed with love for my father. It had been a long time since I'd been the recipient of such kindness. "Is Cammie home?"

"She said she was meeting with some kids from her church for some kind of debriefing. Your mother is lying down in her room."

"Good. I'm looking forward to some alone time with you. We've got a lot to catch up on. I'll go change my clothes and meet you in the kitchen." I decided not to share my day at work with him. With any luck, I'd have the problem solved within a day or two.

Back in the kitchen, wearing jeans, a T-shirt and in my bare feet, I gratefully accepted the cup of coffee Daddy handed me. "What's that cooking on the stove?"

"Not much. I put together a pot of stew." Daddy's eyes twinkled as if he knew how the meal surprised me.

"I'm sure it'll be good. I missed lunch today and am famished."

Daddy seated himself across the table from me. "You know, I've been thinking a lot today. I'd like to sell our house and move out here to be closer to you and Cammie."

"But, Daddy, Detroit is your home. All your friends are back there."

He chuckled. "Does that mean you don't want your old dad around?"

"Not at all. I'd love it."

"That's what I wanted to hear. I'll start putting things in motion tomorrow. Of course I need to discuss it with your mother first."

We sat together, drinking our coffee and chatting. Daddy shared things about home, and I told him about Cammie as she grew up. Our time together filled me with happiness. Having him around all the time was a dream come true. The only problem was that now, he wouldn't be taking Mother back to Detroit.

Chapter Twenty-Four

Maude's Journal
September 2, 2008

> *Sandra got her new job today. Now that finances are looking up for her, and she has all those big responsibilities, she'll be too busy to make my life difficult. I've written another five hundred words in my novel. Charles says he knows the publisher of a small press who might be willing to give my book a look when it's finished. James has taken over driving me to the clinic. At first I didn't want him butting in, but then changed my mind when I saw how he made the staff treat me good. Maybe he's forgiven me.*
>
> *I'm exhausted this evening. James is in Sandra's kitchen cooking something, but all I want to do is lie down and sleep.*

***

Daddy tiptoed down the hall and back to check on Mother. "She's still resting."

"The dialysis seems to wear her out." I took my coffee mug to the sink. "I'd love to have a bowl of that beef stew now, if it's ready."

He lifted the cover off the pot and stuck in a fork. "The potatoes and carrots are done, so go ahead and dig in. Sorry I don't know how to make biscuits like your Ma, but we can have bread instead."

I ladled the yummy smelling dinner into a bowl and set it on the table. When I grabbed the butter and jam out of the refrigerator, I notice a cream pie on the bottom shelf. I waited for Daddy to get his food and sit down with me. Getting off on the wrong foot with someone who had never been anything but nice to me wouldn't fly. "I've been

233

pretty careful to keep sweets out of the house lately. It's too much of a temptation for Mother."

"You'll be glad to know that beautiful concoction is sugar free. While I waited for your Ma this morning, I had time to read through some of the clinic's literature." Daddy's eyes twinkled, recognizing my surprise at this accomplishment.

I picked up my spoon, ready to dip into my stew.

"Do you say grace before meals? If so, go ahead. I'd like that."

My spoon clattered to the table. It was one thing to pray in the privacy of my shower. It was something else to pray out loud, especially in front of my dad. *If I could only remember the words Cammie uses.* Somehow, I managed to bumble through a short prayer, nearly forgetting to ask God to bless the food.

Raising my eyes, I noted the big grin on Daddy's face. I'd forgotten how much his approval meant to me. I certainly didn't expect any from my pitiful little attempt at saying grace. "We never asked the blessing when I lived at home with you and Mother."

"Never to late to start." He winked and took a mouthful of his stew.

How long had Daddy felt like this? Did he secretly disagree with Mother's stance on religion all these years and only kept quiet to keep the peace? Or was this something new?"

"I understand you and Cammie go to church. You've even managed to get your mother to go." Daddy sure seemed interested in staying on the subject.

"I don't imagine Mother had anything nice to say about that."

"True. But why don't you tell me about it?"

When I asked Jesus into my life, I never thought I'd be sharing something so personal and precious with my dad. I never thought we'd be sitting across the table from each other discussing the experience I had with God in the car

234

that night, either. I never thought he'd understand. But he listened, nodding his head as I described my confusion and inadequacy as a new Christian.

Daddy silently chewed his food, gazing out the window. I took the opportunity to really study him. The last eighteen years had changed him from a strong looking man, middle-aged, and still working for a living, to someone with thinning wisps of white hair, and prominent blue veins under the transparent skin on his hands. My realization of his age shook me. I had been the one that chose to leave home resulting in lost years with my dad.

"I'm sorry, Daddy, that I ran so far away. I should have come home." My guilt for abandoning him filled me with tearful remorse. The thought of my only daughter leaving me someday, and traveling to a far-off place terrified me. Who would watch out for her? Was that how Daddy felt when I left?

"I didn't know you were pregnant till after you left. I wish you would have come to me." He continued staring outside, as if he couldn't look at me.

"I couldn't bear to face you, and see the disappointment in your eyes. And I couldn't stay and keep Cammie, too." I silently prayed for Daddy's understanding and forgiveness.

He turned his gaze back to me. "Don't you know I'd do anything for you?" The hoarseness in Daddy's voice gave away his deep feelings.

"But, Mother—"

"I know. I love your ma, but at times she's been a hard woman to live with."

"Why does she act like that? She behaves as if she hates me, yet she seems determined to stay here in my house." I kept my voice low, in case Mother could overhear.

"She doesn't hate you. I can't say I understand the workings of her mind. I believe though, that down deep, she's a caring person who wanted the best for you." Daddy smiled kindly at me.

235

Down deep was an understatement. If Mother harbored any affection for me at all, it was buried so deep it would never see the light of day. As a teenager, I assumed I wasn't lovable enough. Not good enough to win her approval. My best efforts always resulted in a less than adequate response. I knew Daddy loved me, but I don't remember him ever saying the words. Brian was the first one who ever said he loved me.

"It's OK, Daddy. I've accepted things will never be different between us. I dealt with it a lot better when we were two thousand miles apart, though. I didn't have to be reminded of her disdain on a daily basis."

"I'll start looking for another place tomorrow. Don't worry about a thing." He patted my hand. "Say! Your Ma says you have a special man in your life. Tell me about him. I'm assuming he was the one I met here last night?" He took a piece of bread from the loaf and tore it into pieces, dropping it into his stew.

I laughed. "It's been a while since I've seen anyone do that."

"You're changing the subject, young lady." He stirred the bread around till every piece soaked up the broth from the stew.

"There's not much to tell. We're only beginning to get acquainted. In fact, we've only had one date so far and it was cut short. He was called back to Virginia to teach some classes at the FBI academy there." The reminder of Matt sent waves of warmth through me. I could hardly wait till I told him all about the latest developments in my life.

Daddy raised an eyebrow. "That doesn't sound like the man your ma described. She said you'd been seeing a successful man who owns his own construction business, and had been seeing each other for several years."

"I'm afraid that's wishful thinking on Mother's part. She likes Charlie because he caters to her and he has money for a fancy car and house. But he's nothing more than a friend, although lately he's been pressuring me to escalate

236

our friendship into a romance." I felt the muscles in my face stiffen as I spoke of Charlie.

"Many a good marriage began with a solid friendship. And there's nothing wrong with financial stability." Daddy lifted his head and gazed around my kitchen. "Not that you've done too bad for yourself. This is very nice. I'm proud of you."

I could feel my face beam at his compliment. Still . . . "I may be new at being a Christian, but somehow I think that if I'm going to let a man into my life, we should share the same beliefs. Matt does."

"Your ma said Charlie had gone to church with you because he knew it would please you."

I frowned. "That's the only reason he went. To make an impression. Matt goes to please God and himself."

Daddy nodded. "I see the difference."

"Besides," I said, letting my resentment of Charlie's recent behaviors drive my words, "Charlie has been doing some underhanded things lately. For example, he's trying to use Mother to manipulate me into making decisions I don't want. I never realized how controlling he was till recently." The reminder renewed my pledge to avoid Charlie from then on, which would be easier with Mother moving out. Everything would be more comfortable then.

"It sounds as if your feet are solidly on the ground." Daddy stood and took his dishes to the sink. "I'm going to check on your Ma again. Then I'd like to check the paper for your local real estate prices. I don't suppose you know a good agent, do you?"

I chuckled to myself. I knew one I wouldn't recommend. On the other hand, maybe I owed it to Mort, after backing out of listing my house, to send some business his way. "I'll try to think of someone, Daddy." As I watched him head toward Mother's room, I couldn't help but think how homey his presence made my house seem. Not like the war zone it had been lately.

***

237

Once I'd finished eating and loading the dishwasher, I went looking for my Bible. I searched everywhere and looked in my room, the last place I remember having it, at least three times. I finally found it tucked between the arm and cushion of one of the living room's easy chairs. *I hardly ever sit here. Daddy? Has he been reading my Bible?*

I curled up on the end of the couch and opened it to where I'd left off in the Gospel of John. I read through most of a chapter before I had to stop to answer the phone.

As soon as I heard Matt's voice, my heart did that pitter-pat thing. "It's so good to hear your voice. But it must be late back there."

"There's only a three hour time difference. I'm done for the day and back in my room getting ready for tomorrow's lessons. Thought I'd call and see how you're doing before I head to bed." His deep voice rumbled through the phone line.

I closed my eyes, picturing the way Matt's face looked as we walked the boardwalk at the Harbor Days Festival. "A lot has happened. The best thing is that Daddy is here!"

"That's certainly good news. I assume he had an explanation for why nobody could find him." Matt paused, as if searching for words. "And how did your meeting with Cammie's father go?"

"As it turns out, the man wasn't her father at all."

I heard Matt exhale, then, "I'm sure she's disappointed."

"More than that." I gulped before going on. "Brian is supposedly dead. Someplace in the Middle East." It still hadn't sunk in, and wrenched my heart to say the words out loud. "You know, I understand why Daddy couldn't be found since he was traveling, but I would have thought the FBI would have found a record of Brian's death."

"I'll look into it when I come back. I'm so sorry, especially for Cammie's sake that things turned out this way. How's she taking it?" I could hear the concern in Matt's voice.

"It was a huge disappointment, but having her grandpa here has mitigated the loss."

"Sounds like you have a lot going on there. Do you miss me?"

Matt's sudden change of subject made me chuckle. "Yes. I do. Very much." I took a deep breath." I wish you were here. I could use your advice."

"What's going on?"

"It's my job. I can't remember if I told you, but the owner of the firm I work for has sold the business. The entire transaction has been shrouded in secrecy and the new owner still hasn't been revealed. I'm afraid things are going to get very upsetting. I wish I could have gone to work for the FBI. Is there any chance now that Daddy is here?"

"I'm sorry, Sandy. The position you applied for has been filled. Perhaps in the future."

"Oh," I said, feeling letdown. "I'd been holding out hope there'd be a place for me there." Seeing Matt more often would have provided an additional benefit in addition to escaping the situation at work.

"You said you needed some advice."

"Like I said, nobody seems to know who this new owner is. However, before the old owner left, he told me that part of the bargain had been my appointment as the new CEO. There has to be a humungous mistake, but I have no way of correcting it without talking to this phantom owner."

"So what's the bad news?"

"That's not funny, Matt." Didn't he see the problem? "I'm not qualified for that job and everybody, meaning every employee of the firm, knows it."

"My advice would be to wait and let him, or her, contact you."

"But I don't know when that would be. I have enough problems right now with Mother living here. I've enlisted the executive secretary's help, but so far, all we've come up

239

with as a possible clue, is a corporation which isn't listed in the phone book."

"If it's a corporation, it will be registered with the Secretary of State's office. Go on-line and look it up. They have to list the owner, or at least their registered agent."

"What's that?"

"Most states require that a corporation have a Registered Agent who maintains an office within the state of incorporation. The main purpose is to provide potential claimants against the corporation with a person, whose whereabouts are available in public records, and who may accept service of process on behalf of the corporation."

"That's great information. I knew you'd know the answer. Thanks. I'll look it up when I get off the phone." I heaved a sigh of relief. By tomorrow, the problem at work would be cleared up.

"Yeah, I need to hang up here and get ready for tomorrow." His voice lowered. "I want to see you again when I get home."

"I'd like that too. Thanks for calling me. That means a lot."

After we ended the call, I leaned back and remembered the way Matt had protectively guided me through the crowds last weekend. No one had ever made me feel so special. I never would have expected that kind of treatment from someone like him. *I can't wait to see him again.*

"Sandy! Come in here!" Daddy's voice thundered down the hall. He sounded frantic.

I didn't lose any time rushing down the hall. Mother's door stood open and Daddy bent over the bed holding her by the shoulders and shaking her.

"What's wrong?"

"I can't wake her up. Maude! Can you hear me?"

"Is-is she breathing?"

"Yes. I checked that first thing, but something is very wrong."

"When did she eat last?"

240

"I don't know. You'd better call the medics."

I hurried to the phone and called 911. The ambulance arrived quickly and two young men in blue uniforms came in with their EMT trauma bags. It hadn't been that long since they'd been to my home before, so I was prepared for their routine and questions.

They donned their gloves. "Sir, could you step away and let us check her?"

Daddy lowered her from being cradled in his arms, back to the bed. "She's diabetic. And her kidneys are failing. Please help her." He reluctantly stepped back to allow the medics to do their work.

Two more medics came in, and one took Mother's history and list of medications from me. I knew the information could be important, but wondered if they also did that to keep family members out of the way while they worked on the patient. All the while, I kept an eye on my parents, neither one looking very healthy. Daddy staggered back and plopped on the chair Mother used when using the computer.

The medic who had been talking to me saw and said, "Are you OK, Sir? Do you need medical attention too?"

Daddy waved. "I'm fine. Just take care of her." He motioned toward Mother.

They continued to work on Mother while Daddy and I hovered in the background. Finally one turned to address us. "We've given her some glucose, and she's coming around, but not as quickly as we'd like. We think it's a good idea to take her to the emergency room."

"Is she going to be OK?" Daddy stood and tried to peer over a medic's shoulder to see Mother.

"It's best that she be seen by a specialist. She's stabilized now, but that's all we're able to do at this point."

"By all means, take her. Should I bring her insulin along?"

"They'll have everything she needs at the hospital."

241

Two of the men left and came back with a gurney. After they got Mother settled and strapped on, they turned to Daddy, "We'll meet you at the hospital."

Daddy only briefly glanced at me before saying yes. He followed them outside and watched while they loaded her in the ambulance, and hooked her up to an IV.

"I'll lock up the house and then we'll go."

Daddy nodded, but his attention was on Mother.

Once again, I found myself traveling to the emergency room, wondering if Mother could survive another crisis.

Chapter Twenty-Five

I left a note for Cammie on her door. I had decided not to call her until we knew more about Mother's condition. My daughter had been through enough turmoil lately, without spending hours at the hospital with us. I had a sinking feeling that this time, the situation was more serious. To my shame, I didn't think Mother deserved Cammie's concern after what she'd done before Cammie's birth. But I suspected Cammie's threshold for forgiveness was different from mine.

I found Daddy in the waiting room, sitting in a chair with his head in his hands. Putting my arms around him, I realized he'd probably never been faced with potentially losing his wife. As far as I knew, other than the last few weeks, they'd never been apart. I shook my head. How could he love such a demanding, critical, woman?

"They kicked me out of there. They said I'd only be in the way." Daddy's voice cracked.

"That's normal. I'm sure they'll come out and get you when it's OK for you to go in. Did Mother seem any better the last time you saw her?"

"She was awake, but not talking." They did tell me it looked as if she had been in a diabetic comma." Daddy ran his fingers through his thinning hair.

"Can I get you anything? A cup of coffee? Magazine?" I knew we'd probably spend most of the evening there.

"I couldn't concentrate on anything right now. How did she get into such bad shape? She was always after me to take care of myself. Why didn't she take her own advice?"

Was it a rhetorical question? "I don't know the reason for anything she does. Sometimes it seems as if she doesn't even care about herself or anyone else for that matter. The only one I've ever seen her show any caring toward is

Cammie, even though she called Cammie a religious fanatic."

Daddy looked me square in the eye. "Your ma loves Cammie. I can tell."

"I'm glad. I don't want Cammie to have to deal with the same constant put-downs that I have."

"You need to cut your ma a little slack."

"How can you say that? Especially after what came out when you arrived and forced the issue." My insides did a slow burn, threatening to expel the beef stew I'd eaten earlier.

Daddy pursed his lips. I could see he'd heard enough from me. "I think I'll have that coffee now."

So I'd been dismissed? I guess I couldn't blame him. Who needs two women who can't stop haranguing on each other? "I'll be right back." I headed out of the waiting area and down the hall to the cafeteria. The espresso bar had closed for the evening, so I had to settle for vending machine coffee. I juggled two paper cups of hot coffee and my purse as I returned to the waiting room.

Daddy sat where I'd left him. Poor guy. He'd come for a visit and hadn't even been here two full days when this happened. I promised myself I'd stop criticizing Mother and be more of a support to him. Besides, I'm sure he knew her flaws better than I anyway. He's merely learned how to cope better than I had.

"Here's your coffee, Daddy."

"Thanks," he said, with little enthusiasm.

I sat next to him. "This hospital has an excellent reputation. Try not to worry."

He didn't look reassured. By then he'd probably realized I wasn't exactly a vast storehouse of medical knowledge.

I took a sip of my coffee, grimaced at the bitterness, and looked around the room. Unlike weekends, Tuesday evening must be slow. The waiting room wasn't even half-full. The upside being, we probably wouldn't have to wait long.

The double doors to the examining rooms opened, and a woman wearing green scrubs approached. "Hughes family?"

Daddy and I stood in unison.

She strode over to us, her face displaying frown lines. She addressed Daddy. "I'm Dr. Graham. Are you the husband?"

"Yes. Can I see my wife now?"

"In a bit." She nodded at me." I'm afraid she can have only one visitor at a time." I need to talk to you first." She spoke to Daddy, and then glanced around the room at the other people. "Could you follow me back to the conference room?"

Daddy stumbled backward. "It's bad, isn't it?" he gasped.

She took his arm and began leading him away.

"Do you want me to go with you, Daddy?"

"No. I'll be OK. I'd like you to wait here for me, though."

"I will." I continued standing until they walked out of sight.

Slumping back into a chair, I felt strangely useless and unwanted. In the short time Mother had been in my home, I'd taken on the responsibility for her health. Now Daddy has taken over. I felt relief, but at the same time, was dying to know what the Doctor had to tell my father. But even though he is trying to be strong and to take charge, Daddy won't be able to care for her alone.

Lord, forgive me for my thoughts. I confess being just as concerned with how this will affect me, as how my Mother is doing. What is wrong with me that I can't put her welfare above my own?

I felt a hand on my shoulder.

"Sandy, dear. I saw the ambulance leave and thought I'd come right down here to see if I could help. It's your mother, right?" Hildie's voice soothed my troubled soul.

How like God to send someone at the right moment. Just like the stories I'd read in the Bible.

I accepted Hildie's hug. "Mother went into some kind of coma and Daddy couldn't rouse her."

"Daddy? Your father is here?"

"Yes. I'm so happy to see him. He arrived last night."

"I wondered whose car was sitting in your driveway." Hildie plopped down in a chair. I noticed she'd brought a tote with her with an unfinished knitting project.

"It's a rental. He flew out here. He's taken over getting Mother to the clinic. The best part is, he's talking about moving out here." I watched Hildie pull out her needles and a ball of yarn.

"I wish I had something to do like that to distract me."

"It relaxes me. Also I need to get this layette done for our missionary circle. We keep a cupboard at church for visiting missionaries to raid whenever they're home on furlough." She began clacking her knitting needles together.

Daddy returned and I introduced him to our neighbor.

"Nice to meet you." He abruptly turned to me. "I'm afraid it's not good news."

Hildie's head bobbed up and I put my hand to my throat.

"Your ma is heading into renal failure. If she doesn't get a transplant soon, we're going to lose her." He reached a hand toward me. "I'm sorry to have to tell you this. It doesn't look good right now. She could only have a matter of weeks left. A woman her age probably won't go to the top of the transplant list, no matter how ill she is." His voice broke.

"Let's pray." Hildie jumped up and took Daddy's hand.

"Uh—" Daddy jerked away from her.

"It's OK, Daddy. I think we should all hold hands while we pray," I said, standing and intertwined my fingers with theirs.

246

Hildie prayed for Mother, the doctors, Daddy, Cammie, and the donor the Lord would send. She asked for peace, wisdom, and strength. I'd never heard such a fervent prayer. *Lord, please, everything that Hildie just said.*

"Amen."

"Amen."

"Thank you."

Daddy wiped his eyes. "I need to get back. They said I could sit with her while they get a room upstairs ready. It looks as if she'll be here for a while." He hugged me again. "I think it might be a good idea if you called Cammie." He nodded at Hildie and walked away toward the emergency area.

"You look pale." Hildie's eyes filled with compassion. "Would you like me to call Cammie?"

"No, I'll do it." I headed outside for some fresh air and privacy while I called my daughter.

Cammie answered her cell phone immediately. "Where are you? I've been home for over an hour."

"We're at the hospital. It's your grandmother again. Grandpa wants you to come."

"I'll be right there."

A million jumbled thoughts raced through my mind as I walked back toward the waiting room. Mother had already said she didn't want a transplant. But would she change her mind if it meant she'd die without it? And then there was the issue of a donor. Did the hospital keep some kind of list?

"Did you reach her?" Hildie looked up from her knitting.

"Yes. She'll be here soon."

Hildie and I sat in silence for a while. Someone had turned on the TV to the news, and a toddler ran up and down the room between the chairs, escaping his mother with a baby in her arms.

"I'd like to talk to you about something before Cammie gets here."

"Nothing like that tone of voice to make a person wary."

"I don't mean to butt in. However, there's something you need to think about. If you don't at least consider it, weighing all the pros and cons, mind you, I'm afraid you'll regret it later.

I could almost hear the warning bells going off in my head, but asked anyway. "What is it?"

"Has it occurred to you that you may be eligible to be the kidney donor?"

I gulped. The thought had pushed its way to the forefront several times, but I'd knocked it back with so much force, I'd nearly passed out from the effort.

"I've never had any surgery. The thought of it scares me."

"If it were Cammie instead of your mother who needed a kidney, what would your answer be?"

"I'd give Cammie anything. Any mother would sacrifice anything for her child." *Except my mother.*

"Like Jesus sacrificed everything for you." Kindness covered Hildie's face. But was she judging me? And what she said about Jesus—how could I complain about not having a mother's love when I had Him now?

"But Jesus gave everything up for the whole world, not merely one child."

"That's right, dear. And that includes your Mother, too."

"I'm afraid Mother will never be counted among His children."

"You never know. But she might not have the chance to get to know Him if she dies."

It is a guilt trip! What If I died? Who would watch out for Cammie?

I would. Just as I've always watched over you.

OK, God. But what about my job? I can't afford to take much time off right now.

What's more important? Following me, or your job?

248

"Sandy? You seem a million miles away." Hildie's voice brought me back to earth.

"Sorry. I zoned out for a minute."

"What do you think about what I said?"

"I'll talk to Daddy about it. The last I knew, Mother didn't want a transplant."

"Don't wait too long to decide. Would you like me to pray with you about it?"

I already knew what the answer would be.

Hildie reached over and patted my hand. "I know you'll do the right thing."

Hildie, I'm afraid you don't know me at all.

Cammie burst through the doors of the waiting room, bringing with her the first sign of crisp fall air.

I met her halfway across the room and she nearly knocked me off my feet with her hug. Would she still want to hug me if she knew what I'd been thinking?

"I think your Grandpa would want to know you're here. Why don't you go tell the nurse at the desk?"

Cammie rushed off, not even noticing Hildie.

"She didn't even see you sitting there."

"Of course not. She has her mind on one thing. Her grandmother."

I flipped through a magazine. Hospitals and doctors' offices must have a lot of readers for patients. Magazines and occasional newspaper covered the surface of every table in the waiting room. Not finding anything to interest me in the periodical I held, set it aside and amused myself by doing a little people watching. Anything to escape thinking about Hildie's advice.

I glanced at her from the corner of my eye. What if she brought it up again? I wasn't prepared to have that discussion. I looked at my watch. "Hildie, it's getting late. Why don't you go on home?"

"Oh, my. I wouldn't dream of leaving you here alone."

"Grandpa says we should all go home." Cammie appeared, startling me. "Hi Hildie. I'm glad you were here to sit with Mom."

"You weren't in there very long."

"They only want one person with her. Grandpa insists on staying. They're getting ready to take her to a room and he's going to sit with her till she falls asleep. The hospital has guest rooms down the hall from the critical care unit and he's going to stay there for the night. He said he'd call if we need to come back."

I felt guilty leaving Daddy alone there, but I knew I could be back in less than fifteen minutes if need be. Hildie gathered up her purse and knitting and we all walked out to the parking lot together.

That night I slept fitfully.

After kissing Cammie goodbye the next morning, I left for the office a half hour early. I'd already heard from Daddy and learned Mother had a restful night. I couldn't say the same for him. His usual cheerful voice didn't sound at all as if he'd slept.

"You go ahead and go to work. She's stable and they're keeping a watchful eye on her."

"How do I reach you today?" I asked knowing he didn't have a cell phone.

"Call the switchboard and ask for her room number. That's where I'll be."

"I hope you take time out to eat something."

"There's a vending machine right down the hall."

"You forget I've been there before. Those machines are full of bitter coffee and junk food. Go to the cafeteria and get a real meal. The nurses will page you if they need you."

Daddy signed off without promising me anything.

When I pulled into the parking lot at work, I noticed everyone else seemed to be there ahead of me. Another employee meeting?

My old office looked the same as I'd left it. My new secretary had commandeered the desk nearest my door and sat at her chair, flipping through some phone messages. She looked up as I approached. "Can I get you a cup of coffee?"

"Thanks, no, but I'd like it if you could come into my office." I looked at the cup on her desk. "Bring your coffee in with you." I figured we might be a while.

Once we were settled, I shared what Matt had told me about the list of corporations on the Secretary of State's Web site. "I'd like you to check that out. If the corporation is doing business in this state, they have to be listed. Get all the information you can about it. If you come up with names or phone numbers, let me know right away."

She scribbled away on her notepad as I spoke and looked up, waiting for the next instruction.

"I don't want you to be viewed as a spy, but off the top of your head, is there anything I need to know about anything the employees are planning?" I didn't expect they were about to throw me a congratulatory party.

"As far as I know, everyone's at their desk working."

"Good, now one more thing. My mother is in the hospital. I could be called away at any time. I'll leave my cell number with you. If Bob agrees, I'll leave him in charge."

"But you are the CEO. We don't want this firm to close down because the terms of the sale weren't met." Her eyes grew large and round.

"As far as I'm concerned, I'm CEO in name only. I may not be upper management material, but I'm not stupid. We'll figure out a way around this."

When she finally left my office, closing the door behind her, I turned and gazed out my window. The sun already started its ascent, brilliant against the blue sky. Had it been a typical overcast gray day, I don't know if I could have held it all together.

As it was, my emotional tank sat on empty.

Lord, the past twenty-four hours nearly sank me. If You have anymore tests in mind for me, I'd appreciate it if you could hold off till I can regroup my defenses.

Somehow I knew He hadn't wanted to hear that, but mercy was what I felt I needed most right then.

I continued looking across the parking lot until my vision blurred. I shook it off, not daring to let myself cry in the office.

I reached into my bottom drawer and got a tissue. Where was all the moisture coming from? I blew my nose. Oh, this is just swell. My second day in charge and I'm sporting a red swollen face.

I tossed that tissue and grabbed another one. I put my head down in my cradled arms on the desk. If Jane were any kind of secretary, she'd announce any visitors and I'd have time to pull myself together. I would at least avoid being viewed as a bawl-baby.

I pulled in a deep breath. I couldn't avoid thinking about it any longer. Could I go through surgery and give up a kidney for a woman who so obviously despised me? I'd have to go through the rest of her life knowing my kidney rode around inside her.

But how could I not? My mother. In spite of everything, she'd given me life.

My intercom buzzed. Sitting up straight, I punched the button. "Yes?"

"Bob's here to see you."

I prayed he wouldn't bring bad news. "Send him on in." I knew I'd better learn to handle things without hesitating or flinching. That went for my personal decisions as well as my job.

"Sit down, Bob. I'm glad you stopped by."

"Oh?" His eyebrows rose.

"We'll talk about it in a moment. First, what is it you want to discuss?"

Bob lowered himself into the chair, so that he partially faced me across my desk. "I want to say . . . I mean, I apologize for yesterday. His brown eyes exuded sincerity.

"Apology accepted. I exhaled the breath I'd been holding since he sat down. Maybe I'd survive after all.

"I'm here to offer my assistance. I'm probably in a better position around here than anyone to help you learn the ropes."

"Why thank you." *OK Lord, this is beyond what I asked You for. Boy, are You ever fast.*

"I don't know where you'd like to start, but I could go over some of our major accounts with you."

"That won't be necessary." I watched him blanch and realized immediately I'd said the wrong thing.

"What I mean is, I have something else in mind for you."

Bob perked up a little, but still looked a little deflated.

"I suppose, as the new CEO, I have some latitude regarding personnel issues. I'd like to propose raising your pay, effective immediately. In return, I want you to take over running the firm. You were the logical choice for the job and should be rewarded. I'll keep the title, but not the pay or authority. In the meantime, I'm trying to contact the new owner to get this problem straightened out."

Bob silently chewed my suggestion over in his mind. I waited for his answer.

"I underestimated you. Anyone else would have leaped at the opportunity you've been handed."

I waved off his response. "I'll have Jane type up a memo to the employees right away. I think it's best if we keep the raise part between you and me, and the payroll supervisor for now. Continue at your current desk and title of general manager. Feel free to use the executive office and conference room whenever you need it. Oh, I didn't ask you if you agree with this plan."

Bob rose, reached across my desk and shook my hand.

Chapter Twenty-Six

"Daddy, I'm going to look into donating one of my kidneys to Mother. Since we're so closely related it shouldn't be a problem. I think you should convince her that this surgery is what she needs. I know she wouldn't listen to me, and I don't want to put this kind of burden on Cammie." I'd taken Thursday afternoon off work, leaving the office in Bob's capable hands. Since I didn't have anyone I had to report to there anymore, I wasn't faced with making any explanation for my absence.

My father looked long and hard at me, and then his face crumpled into overwhelming emotion. "Thank you. I'll go talk to her right away." He smiled through his tears.

"It might be better if she doesn't know it's from me."

Daddy composed himself. "I'm not sure she'll agree regardless of who the donor is. However, if her condition declines to the point she can't make her own decisions, I can do it for her. We had durable power of attorney papers drawn up when I retired."

"I'll leave her to you, then." I kissed him on the cheek. "I'm going to speak to her doctor now."

We left in opposite directions. As I rode the elevator to the floor I wanted, my hands shook so hard I had to jam them in my pockets. Was I doing the right thing? What if Cammie needed a kidney someday? I wouldn't be able to give it to her. I wouldn't very well be able to ask for mine back from Mother.

My nerves were shot by the time I arrived at the right office. *Lord, please give me strength to go through with this. You know I'd rather not. Couldn't you do one of your miracles and heal her instead?* I debated whether I should formalize my prayer by kneeling in the hospital chapel, but just then the elevator doors opened and I forced my feet down the hall to the nephrology department.

The doctor I spoke with did his best to reassure me. "However, donating a kidney is a major decision. There are many things you should know first."

I groaned under my breath. He was about to give me the bad news part. "How safe is it?"

"There won't be any long-term negatives for you. We can live very normal lives with only one kidney."

"How long would I be off work?"

"You'll have to stay in the hospital for a couple of days. When you go home, you'll have to take it easy and not lift anything heavier than twenty-five pounds for at least six weeks. You'll probably be tired the first few weeks. I wouldn't plan on returning to work until two weeks after your surgery, depending on the kind of work you do.

If I'd been a lumberjack or wrestler, I guessed I'd be out of a job for nearly two months. But I was merely a pretend CEO. "What happens next?"

"You'll need to get screened."

"But it's my mother. I assumed there would be no problem."

"It's a necessary precaution. We want to make sure you're a good match. Rejection of the new organ is one of the biggest problems in a procedure like this. We also want to make sure both your kidneys are functioning perfectly, and that you don't have any health issues that would make you ineligible for surgery."

"Let's get the testing done as quickly as we can." *Before I lose my resolve.*

"Usually it takes a while to screen a donor. First is the blood test. If your blood types are compatible, then we'll do the HLA tissue typing, or cross matching. These tests tell us the likelihood of your mother rejecting your kidney."

"If we're not a match?" I hadn't considered that.

"We stop everything. But if you're a match, then to determine your eligibility to donate, we'll do a series of laboratory and X-ray tests to screen for your kidney function, liver function, hepatitis and other viruses or infections. A urine collection shows if your kidneys are functioning normally. A chest X-ray and an electrocardiogram make sure your heart and lungs are normal. Other tests may be necessary depending on the results of these studies. If all looks well, at that point, then we'll do a CT scan and an IVP."

"Most of what you're saying is Chinese to me."

The doctor directed an understanding smile toward me. "You'll be assigned a counselor who will be with you every step of the way and answer any of your questions."

My head cramped up at the thought of rushing my decision. Would migraine headaches take me off the donor list? I felt for certain one was coming on.

"Would you like to begin the process?"

"I guess so." My voice sounded squeaky even for a coward like me.

"In your mother's case, we'll try to speed up the process as much as possible. We want your mother to be in as good a condition as we can get her. Unfortunately, end stage renal disease adversely affects other body organs as well."

"Will you keep me informed along the way?"

"Of course. I know how anxious you must be to see her on the road to recovery."

I left there and went to the lab for my blood draw, and then back to critical care to peek in on Mother. Her frail body rested under her the blanket, barely making a human-sized lump on the bed. Her breaths came in short shallow bursts. Daddy rested in the chair next to her, snoring softly. I backed out of the room so I wouldn't wake either of them.

I really needed someone to talk to about then. I'd decided not to tell Cammie what I was doing till all the tests had been run. She didn't need to worry about me. Her grandmother was enough for her to fret over. I noted the time, figuring it would be pointless to go back to the office. I had no confidant there anyway.

A little later, I pulled into my driveway and went straight across the lawn to Hildie's. She swung her front door open and pulled me in.

"You look troubled, child."

"I've made a decision, and have started the process to become a donor."

Hildie folded me into her arms. "Bless your heart. You won't be sorry you've done this." She stood back and quizzed me with her gaze. "You don't seem a hundred percent sure."

Leave it to Hildie to get right to the heart of the matter. "I'm committed now, but I'm not sure I'm doing this for the right reasons."

"Would you like some tea? My pot just started to whistle as you rang my bell."

"That would be great." I followed her into her kitchen. Gazing around, I noticed she'd put up new curtains and a matching wallpaper border. "I really like the red cherry theme you've got going in here."

Hildie came over to her little kitchen table carrying two mugs of steaming water and spoons. "The teabags are in that little crock on the table." She pushed the sweetener across the table toward me and sat down.

I dunked a bag of chamomile tea in my cup, and stirred it around absently, keeping my eyes pointed downward.

"We can talk about my decorating skills if you like, but you've got something else on your mind."

I looked up and tried to form my confused thoughts into words. "I'm wondering" I paused and took a shuddering breath, "if I'm only donating my kidney to get my mother to love me." My throat closed up as I forced the last few words out. The pain traveled to my jaw, which I kept clenched so I wouldn't cry.

257

Hildie's eyes filled with compassion. "I think what you really are worried about, is what if she doesn't respond in a loving way to your sacrifice?"

I nodded, not trusting myself to speak.

"Tell me. If you knew for sure your mother would never show you an ounce of love, would you still do it?"

The ache in my heart increased. I brought my fist to my mouth and closed my eyes. I knew what the proper response should be, but what did my heart tell me? "I know the choice would be easy if it were my daughter in the hospital. Or Daddy. Maybe even a friend."

"If you donate your kidney, and Maude continues to treat you the same as before, would you begin to resent her? Regret your decision?"

My head snapped to attention. She had dove into areas I didn't want to think about. "You're asking all the hard questions, Hildie. I hoped you'd be able to give me some advice. Tell me what the Bible says about this. I wouldn't begin to know where to look."

"Look to the Lord. Pray. Ask Him to give you peace in this matter. I can tell you, we are commanded to love others as ourselves. And to forgive." Hildie spoke with such conviction, I couldn't find fault with what she said.

"Do you think the Lord saved me so I would do this for Mother?"

"He saved you because He loves you. He loves Maude too. And I'm guessing He's extending her life because He's a loving God and is not willing that anyone perish." Hildie handed me a napkin and then sat sipping her tea.

I gulped mine down and stood. "I should go."

"Stay a few moments and I'll pray with you." She took my hand and led me to her living room where we knelt down on her carpet and prayed.

***

The next morning, I headed back to the office. "Anything going on I should know about?" I took the handful of messages Jane gave me.

"Everything's going pretty smoothly. " She followed me into my office and closed the door. "I looked up the CAD Corporation. It doesn't list the owner, but the registered agent is an attorney named B.A. Hood."

I laughed despite myself. "What kind of name is that for a lawyer?" It felt good to smile again. I'd slept soundly the night before, without any of the tension I'd carried around with me recently.

"I looked him up in the phone book. He doesn't handle criminal cases, so his clients maybe don't make the connection." Jane's grin matched mine, so she obviously felt more secure than she had earlier in the week. "He does mostly real estate, business law and corporate stuff."

"Well, at least now we're making some headway."

"Uh, not really. I called his office. They said they wouldn't give me the name of any of their clients."

"There must be a way to get to the bottom of this."

"Short of breaking into his office, I don't know what that would be."

I pictured Jan and I dressed in all black, carrying those tiny Maglites and a camera. Problem was, I couldn't get past the thought of shimmying up a drainpipe to find an unlocked window in a strange building.

"I guess we can count that idea out."

"How's your mother?"

Jane's question pulled me back to reality. "She's failing. I may have to take a couple of weeks off real soon."

Jane didn't ask me for any details and I didn't offer any. We took care of some office business and she returned to her desk. I headed to Bob's office.

"So you really don't know who bought the firm." Bob's tone reflected his doubt, but I could see he had come around one-eighty degrees from the day our former boss had walked out.

"I think we should give it a few more days to see if he reveals himself, and if he doesn't I think we should talk to

259

an attorney to see if he can legally force me to be the CEO. Doesn't it seem like blackmail to you?"

"The employees here can't afford to let you call his bluff, if that's what it is." He twirled his pencil between his fingers.

"I'm not suggesting that. That's not what I said at all." Was Bob deliberately being obtuse?

"It doesn't seem like closing a business you own would be illegal. Maybe he's hoping you'll fail, so he can use this place for a tax write-off."

"And put a couple of dozen people out of work? That's ugly beyond belief."

Bob put his hands out to his sides, palms up. "Things just as bad happens in the business world all the time."

"We've got to find a way to unmask this guy and find out his real motives."

"I agree." Bob raised an eyebrow. "When you figure out how to do it, let me know."

Our conversation reached a dead-end. I switched subjects. "I have a family matter which may require my absence for a couple of weeks. I'll try to keep in close contact. Is there anything which requires me to be here?"

Bob opened a folder and pushed it across his desk. "I have a couple of agreements that need your signature. Other than that kind of thing, I think we can manage."

I scribbled my name where he'd marked the X's. "I'll let you know my plans."

We discussed a few minor items, and I left his office knowing Bob would do his best to keep things running smoothly.

When I returned to my desk, I noticed Jane had left me a message from the nephrologists' office. I dialed and they put me right through to the doctor's assistant.

"I have good news for you, Ms. Hughes. It looks like you and your mother are a match."

I'd expected that, but hearing it made the surgery loom closer.

"We'll set you up with appointments for your exams. I should have that information for you on Monday."

"Thanks." I wondered where the counselor was they'd promised. It wasn't like I had someone else who could go along and hold my hand. The Doctor's assistant hung up before I had a chance to ask.

***

That evening Cammie and I cooked supper together. "It's been a while since we've had a Friday night home alone together."

"You sound wistful, Mom. Remember, if I'd gone off to the university, we wouldn't be doing this at all."

"I thought you wanted to stay here and go to the community college. Has that changed since you and Teddy broke up?"

"No. I like being here with you and my grandparents. I merely pointed it out because you were the one who wanted me to go off to school in Seattle."

"And I would have been living in Seattle too." Visions of the condominium I'd picked out flashed across my mind.

Cammie got all the green salad fixings out of the refrigerator. "Everything has changed."

"Yes. I guess life is like that. Constant change. We have to learn resiliency, like a willow, or we break in the wind." Was Cammie up for my news?

"I stopped and saw Gran after school today," Cammie said, providing me with an opening.

"Was your grandpa there?"

"Yes. He said Gran needs a transplant real soon."

"That's true." I braced myself. "There's a good chance I'll be able to donate a healthy kidney to her."

Cammie's face lit up like a five hundred watt bulb. "That's wonderful! I was going to offer, but figured you'd have a fit."

Relief washed over me. Better me doing the donating instead of Cammie. Plus it felt good that my daughter had enough grace not to point out what an unlikely donor I'd be

261

since Mother and I were less than close. "It's not final yet, but we're a match."

"I'll be praying for you, Mom. And of course, I've been praying for Gran all along."

Cammie and I had a cozy light supper together, of broiled cod, a salad, and store-bought rolls. Afterward, as we ate our way through a bunch of green seedless grapes, Cammie told me about her classes and shared a few anecdotes about the students there. She had no plans for the evening, which was quite unusual for a Friday night, so she settled down to get a head start on her homework.

I cleared the table and stacked everything in the dishwasher. As I wiped out the kitchen sink, the phone rang.

"Hey, how are you doing? I've been trying to reach you all week."

Charlie. The Lord must have known I couldn't tolerate him on top of everything else.

"I've been pretty busy."

"Not too busy for me, I hope."

When would Charlie get the hint? "My mother has been in the hospital for several days. She's not doing well."

"Oh, honey, I'm so sorry. I'll be right over there. You shouldn't be alone."

"No," I blurted, louder than I should have. "I'm not alone. Cammie is here, and Daddy is at the hospital with Mother."

"But you need a man around. What a week this must have been awful for you, what with your promotion and everything. It must have been hard to concentrate on your job or your family."

I froze. How did he know about my promotion? I hadn't told anyone except Matt. "Don't come over. I don't want company. And I definitely don't need a man." *Especially you.*

"Are you sure? I could be there in a few minutes."

"Yes. I'm sure. Now if you'll excuse me, I have to go."

262

I hung up. A creepy feeling took over where annoyance abounded before.

The phone rang again.

"Charlie, I told you I couldn't talk now."

"It's not Charlie, it's Matt." The soothing voice I'd longed for calmed me immediately.

"Matt! I'm so glad you called."

"You sound upset."

"There's so much going on. I'm going to donate a kidney to Mother. Charlie doesn't seem to know how to take no for an answer. We can't find the new owner at the office, and the employees are as nervous as all get out."

"Whoa. Let's take this one at a time. You're donating a kidney? When?"

"We don't know yet. I have to undergo a bunch of tests, but soon." I leaned my head against the wall. It felt so good to be talking to Matt again.

"And if Charlie's bothering you, tell him to back off, period. Do you want me to call him?"

"No. I can handle him. If he shows up tonight like he said he would, I won't answer the door. And here's the odd part. Somehow, Charlie found out about my promotion."

"From your mother?"

"No. You're the only one who knows. I wish he'd stop sticking his nose in my business all the time."

"Lock your doors and try to relax. I'm taking the next flight home."

Chapter Twenty-Seven

Saturday morning, I woke to the sound of a slamming car door. I peeked out my bedroom window to see Charlie getting out of his new vehicle. I glimpsed my digital alarm. Seven A.M.? What was he thinking? Even when we'd been getting along, he never showed up on my doorstep at such an inconvenient time.

I quickly tugged on a pair of jeans and pulled a sweatshirt over my head, so I could get to the front room before the doorbell woke Cammie. I didn't want her to hear what I had to say to her former employer. I sent up a quick prayer as I padded down the hall in my bare feet. *Lord, let me control my anger and not use any unbecoming language.*

I raced to the front door, released the chain, and threw it open. The sight before me caused my jaw to drop. Matt appeared from seemingly nowhere and sprinted across the street toward my house. He caught up with Charlie about halfway up the sidewalk. Charlie must have been surprised as I was, because he gasped when Matt grabbed him by the shoulder and spun him around.

"What do you think you're doing, coming here at this hour?" Matt demanded.

Charlie's back was toward me, but I heard him say, "I was invited. What's it to you?"

Matt stepped forward till his six-foot plus frame towered over him. "If Sandy invited you here, I'll eat my shoes and yours too."

Matt never acknowledged my presence behind the screen door, and I doubt Charlie had seen me. "You don't seem to understand, Sandy and I go way back. We have something special. You've known her less than a month."

"From what I understand, your friendship with Sandy has cooled off considerably. In fact, it's about to meet an untimely death." Matt never gave Charlie an inch of space.

264

Charlie drew himself up, but still the top of his head barely reached Matt's eyebrows. "That's where you're wrong. We've put up with you hanging around because Sandy needed your favor to get the job she wanted. But that's no longer necessary. She and I are going into business together. A partnership that will be as personal as two people can get, if you know what I mean." Charlie's tone spewed defiance.

What is he talking about?

"I detected a hint of a smirk on Matt's face. "Would you be talking about the business she already works for?"

"What do *you* know about that?"

A light brightened my brain. How could I have been so dense as to not guess Charlie had been behind the purchase of my firm?

"My guess is you've already put your little plan into motion. Isn't that right? Very clever, Dalan. You thought your behind the scenes shenanigans could make her stay here instead of moving to Seattle."

Charlie's chest puffed up. "That's right. I bought out her boss. And she's got reason to be pretty grateful, too."

Matt reached out and grabbed Charlie's upper arm. "OK. I'm done playing with you. Let me be abundantly clear. Sandy only has a reason to accuse you of harassment. I'm inviting you to leave here. Right now. If you don't, I'm going to make sure you're brought downtown to answer stalking or trespass charges."

Charlie shook him off. "You have no right—"

"He has *every* right." I stomped out the door and down the steps. "I don't want you here. I told Matt that last night."

Charlie whirled around. "Sandy! I'm glad you came out. I'm here to take you to breakfast."

"What part of *I'm not interested* don't you understand?"

Anger turned Charlie's face into a pathetic caricature of a rabid bulldog on speed. "What will you say when I give all your co-workers pink slips?"

265

"Do what you feel you have to do, Charlie, but I'm not changing my mind. You're not going to blackmail me into a relationship with you."

Charlie took a step toward me and Matt was on him like a cougar. He grabbed Charlie's arm and twisted it behind his back. Charlie struggled to free himself, but Matt put enough pressure on Charlie's bent wrist, that every time Charlie tried to wrench free, he yowled in pain.

"Let me help you to your car, Buddy." Matt steered him down the sidewalk and out to the street. Opening Charlie's car door with his left hand, he guided my former friend into the front seat, tucked him in, and shut the door.

Charlie started his expensive sedan and peeled away from the curb, leaving no doubt as to his feelings in the matter.

Matt waited till Charlie's vehicle disappeared, and then turn and bounded up the walk to where I stood waiting. He pulled me into a bear hug, holding me as close as a mother hen when she guards her chicks. I took a huge intake of air to absorb the fragrance of soap and aftershave on his skin. Staying in the cocoon of his arms suited me just fine, but half the neighborhood was probably wakened by the commotion at my house, and would be looking out their windows about then. I reluctantly moved away.

"Come on in. I'll put on a pot of coffee." I glanced down the street, just to make sure Charlie hadn't had a change of heart and decided to return, and then entered the house with Matt following.

"After starting the coffee, I said, "I need to go wash my face and run a comb through my hair. I just got out of bed."

"You look gorgeous, just the way you are. Not many women could pull off the natural look the way you do." Matt flashed a dimple, making my toes curl.

"I'll be right back." I trotted down the hall and came back the minute I'd completed my morning ritual. Matt stood with his back to me, looking out into my back yard. I

266

couldn't help admiring the broad shoulders, which I'd so recently rested my head against. He turned and pocketed his cell phone.

"That was fast.' He approached and mad a tiny circle on my cheek with his index finger. "You're even more beautiful than before."

I flushed with pleasure, sure that he noticed. But there was no use pretending I didn't enjoy his flattery. "Have a seat. Can I rustle you up some eggs or something?"

"Sounds good." He took a seat, turning the kitchen chair so he faced the area between the sink and stove where I worked.

"How did you happen to get here the same time as Charlie?"

"I've been here most of the night."

"What?" The shock must have shown on my face.

"I've been sitting in my car. I figured he might come around and bother you, and I wanted to be here if he did."

I melted. He cared that much? "I don't know what to say."

"Don't say anything. I intend to see that you are as safe and stress-free as possible."

Words failed me at that point. There was nothing for me to do but cook him the tastiest breakfast he ever had. I sneaked a look at him. What I really wanted was to kiss that handsome face of his. *Out of gratitude, of course.*

Cammie wandered in. "What's all the commotion?" She saw Matt. "Oh, hi." She headed straight for the fridge. "Do we have any orange juice?"

"It's right where it always is."

She poured her juice and looked over at the stove to see what I was fixing. "Do you want me to help?"

Fondness for my daughter rippled through me. All the Saturday mornings we'd cooked breakfast together would end one day. I wanted to savor every moment we had together. I glanced at Matt. *But priorities change sometimes.* I grinned when he winked at me.

267

"Everything's about ready. Why don't you sit down with Matt?"

Warmth spread throughout my being as I saw the two of them sitting at my kitchen table. Was this how other women felt when they served their families breakfast? I wanted it.

After I set everything on the table, Cammie offered to ask the blessing, getting me off the hook. Praying in front of company still made me a little nervous. We had a wonderful time together, and matt kept Cammie and I entertained with stories about the academy.

"When do you have to go back?"

"Sunday night."

I gulped. "You mean you flew all the way back here just for the weekend?"

"Don't act so surprised." Matt took another helping of scrambled eggs.

Cammie looked back and forth between us with a puzzled expression on her face.

"It's a long story, Cammie. I'll explain it to you later."

My daughter sighed. "Ok," she said, obviously disappointed she'd missed out on something, "but could you tell me more about the transplant? Will you have to be careful the rest of your life? I worried about you after we talked last night and prayed a long time."

"You must be very proud of your daughter."

Matt's compliment won over Cammie. She responded by directing a huge smile at him.

I spent the next half hour answering all of their questions that I could.

Cammie jumped up. "I'm going to head out to the hospital, but I'll do the dishes first."

Matt and I rose at the same time. "I need to run up to Seattle to shower and change, and pick up some stuff for next week's class." He took my hand. "Walk me to my car?"

"Let me slip something on my feet first." I reluctantly let go of his hand and trotted to my room and put on some flip-flops. Matt had waited for me at my front door and we walked out together.

"What are you going to do the rest of the day?" We arrived at Matt's car, but he kept hold of my hand.

"Go to the hospital. Clean house. The usual Saturday chores."

Matt reached for my other hand and we stood facing each other. "I don't think Charlie will come back, but if he does, call me right away. OK? I don't think he's operating on all his cylinders."

I gripped his hands. "Thank you, for coming to the rescue this morning."

He chuckled. "Gotta perpetuate my manly image."

I knew it was more than that. "Will you be coming down here for church in the morning?"

"I wouldn't miss it." He raised both my hands to his lips, kissing each one on the knuckles. "Now "I've got to run. Remember what I said about Charlie." He opened his driver's door and slid inside.

I longed for a different sort of kiss, but would settle for him being my hero for the short term. I waved as he drove off, and turned back toward my house.

***

Mother was asleep again when I got to the hospital, so Daddy and I stepped into the hall to talk. "How is she this morning?"

Daddy slowly shook his head from side to side, fatigue showing in his face and demeanor. "Not good at all. We can't get her to eat. She's hooked up to an IV to help keep her hydrated. They're coming in to check her every hour now."

I hugged him hard. "I'm so sorry. I hope the doctors can hurry my tests so they can get her to surgery."

"I've put the entire matter into the hands of God. That's where it rests anyway." He patted my back. "We need to trust Him for the outcome." He nodded to a nurse

269

who swept past us to go into Mother's room. "She'll be in there for a few moments. Let's go get something to eat."

"I ate at home, not too long ago, but I can have a cup of coffee while you eat something." We headed to the elevator. There weren't too many people around at that hour, so we got on and arrived at the cafeteria's floor in no time at all.

When we'd taken our selections we found a table near a window. The weather had been overcast when I left home, but had turned into a steady drizzle. I watched the drops of water slide down the glass doors to our left, and lamented the fact that summer had already gone. The gloomy outside seeped through the walls to where we sat. But Daddy was right. God was in control and we had to trust Him.

"Do you remember the man I told you about?"

"The cop, right?"

"He's a special agent with the FBI. He's in town for the weekend. I'd like you to meet him."

"Bring him around." Daddy buttered a slice of toast.

"I will. Probably tomorrow after church." I sipped my coffee and took in every detail of my father's face while he ate his breakfast. How many times over the years had I wished to sit across the table from him like this? Would I have appreciated this moment as much, if the miles and years hadn't separated us?

"Mr. Hughes, report to critical care. Mr. Hughes." A nasal voice came over the speaker just above our table.

Daddy jumped up, nearly upsetting his plate. "We have to go. They paged me." He rushed away without looking back to see if I followed.

A line had formed at the elevator, and a glance at the floor indicator above the doors told me we'd have to wait. "Do you want to take the stairs?"

He mumbled something and I trotted behind him as he careened around the corner to the stairwell.

"Don't go so fast You'll fall and break your neck."

Daddy kept going with me following close behind, our footsteps on the metal runners echoing behind us as we ran. By the time we reached the hallway to the critical care unit, my father's speed had increased to a level I couldn't match. I arrived at the nurses' station, panting and out of breath. I could barely overhear the doctor's words, but the grave expression on his face spoke volumes.

I lurched forward the last few steps and heard, "I'm afraid your wife is worsening. We're talking days, here. Or less. You need to prepare yourself. Is there anyone other family members we can call for you?"

"But the transplant," I blurted out. "I'm giving her a kidney."

The doctor's sad eyes turned toward me. "We don't even know if your kidneys are healthy. I'm afraid we may not have time to get through all your tests. Even if we could, I'm not sure her heart would handle the surgery."

"But there must be something to do while we wait," I pleaded.

Daddy shook his head and glanced toward me. "I'm going to go sit with her while I still can." He shuffled off to her room, his back bowed under the pressure of the news we'd received.

The doctor turned his attention to me. "You don't look too good. You'd better sit down."

"I can't sit down. Look. I know it's Saturday, but let's get my exams started." I could still feel my heart thudding from exerting myself, trying to catch up with my father. "There should be no reason it can't be done. You've got a hospital full of doctors and equipment."

"Even if we started now, we'd have to wait for the lab results to comeback."

"This is an emergency," I nearly screamed. "Are you in the business of saving lives or not?"

By then, several nurses had come running to see if they could help with the deranged woman who stood glaring at the doctor. One by one, they drifted off as more urgent matters rose.

The doctor waited for my tantrum to subside. "I can't believe God would put us through all this, and then hold out a little hope, only to let Mother die."

"God's ways are not our ways." Hildie's voice penetrated my frustration. Her arm slipped around my waist.

"What are you doing here?"

"I brought Cammie. Her car wouldn't start, and the hospital called her to come."

I looked over Hildie's shoulder and saw my daughter tiptoe into Mother's room. "I need some air," I whispered, turned on my heel and strode out of the unit, and out of the hospital. I found a concrete bench outside under the portico. Hildie joined me and we sat together, silently praying.

We remained there like that. Me, numb and in shock. Hildie, merely living her role as friend. "There's no chance at all now that Mother and I will ever mend the rift between us."

"I suppose that could be the case. But if you at least forgive her, you'll feel better."

"I've already done that," I said, realizing the truth of what I said.

"Good. Now I'm guessing your daughter needs you."

We entered the hospital again and walked back to where Daddy and Cammie were keeping vigil at Mother's bedside.

Lord, if she has to die, please at least let it be painless and peaceful.

Chapter Twenty-Eight

When Hildie and I arrived at Mother's room, we saw Cammie and Daddy standing outside the door. Noise from a commotion inside the room drifted into the hallway. I shot a quizzical look toward Daddy, but his eyes were on the activity inside. An orderly pushed past me, bumping my shoulder.

I clutched my throat, knowing the worst had happened. "Daddy, what's going on? Has Mother—?"

He looked at me blankly. "No. But pray. They've found a donor who's a perfect match."

"B-but I thought there was no chance of that. Who is it?" *It can't be Cammie, she's standing right here.*

"All I know is it's someone who sustained fatal head injuries in a car accident."

A cadaver donor? Mother's words came back to me. She didn't want that. But this could save her life.

"I made the decision for her." Daddy said, apparently reading my mind. "If she pulls through this, I'll take the blame. But at least my Maudie will be alive."

Suddenly the hospital staff emerged from Mother's room pushing a gurney. I couldn't see past them to my mother, and could only stand back and view their backs as they rushed her down the hall toward the elevators. I didn't get to wish her good luck or even touch her hand. I walked into the empty room. Nothing of Mother remained, not her spirit, or even the smallest personal possession.

A housekeeper came in, pulling a mop and bucket behind her. She parked them in a corner and began stripping the bed. Soon the room would revert back to a sterile lifeless place, waiting to be filled with a family and their loved one again. Would Mother ever come back there?

Someone came and spoke with Daddy. "You can go downstairs to the surgical waiting room. Someone there will keep you informed on your wife's condition."

The four of us found seats together. A mixture of fear and hope surrounded us. After a half-hour had passed, someone from the transplant unit came in to talk to us. Yet another unfamiliar face, which did little to comfort me.

"After the surgery, depending on a number of factors, your family member will go to either the transplant unit on this floor, or back to the intensive care unit.

She'll continue to be monitored closely, and will begin to receive medications to prevent rejection. During this time someone will talk to you about home care. This will include information about medications, activity, follow-up, diet, and any other specific instructions from your transplant team."

"How long will she be in the hospital?" Cammie asked.

"The hospital stay is typically one to two weeks." The woman looked at me. "Other questions?"

I thought about asking if the surgery involved a risk, but knowing she had no hope without it, any danger was a moot point. "How long will she be in the operating room?"

"The transplant will take from two to three hours."

She went on to explain the procedure they used to attach the new kidney. As informative as it was, I couldn't keep my mind on what she said. All I could think of was how God had answered our prayers.

The woman left after delivering her information. "She sounded so encouraging," Daddy enthused.

We all agreed. A positive outcome seemed very likely. We settled down to wait, knowing the next few hours would drag so slowly, we'd tire ourselves out if we tried to keep a conversation going. Hildie had brought her knitting again and sat working on her newest project. Cammie pulled out her cell phone and left a message for her former youth pastor to call her. Daddy stretched out on a sofa. Poor dear, it had been a while since he'd gotten a full night's sleep.

274

I eyed the other vacant couch and moved there to make myself comfortable. I took off my jacket, folded it up, and placed it on the arm as a cushion for my head.

"Why don't you lean on me?"

"Matt!" I took in his appearance. Khaki slacks and a crisp, perfectly pressed shirt. He should have been on the cover of a magazine. "You have a knack for showing up at the perfect moment. How did you know where to find me?"

"When I couldn't reach you, I took a chance and came down here." He sat on the couch and pulled me down with him. Guiding my head against his shoulder he cradled me against his chest. "The receptionist told me your Mom's in surgery. Are you scared?"

"Not now," I said, basking in his warmth. I closed my eyes. He still smelled of soap from his earlier shower. Was I smitten? Probably. I kicked my shoes off and tucked my feet up on the cushions.

Matt drew little circles in my hair with his fingertip. The hypnotic effect would have me sleepy in no time.

I heard loud whispering from across the room and snapped my eyelids open. Cammie and Hildie giggled, and then pretended they weren't watching us. I glanced toward Daddy, who looked as if he'd fallen asleep. When I moved my gaze back to my daughter, she gave me the two-fingered victory sign. I had a nearly irresistible urge to stick my tongue out. This kind of teasing was new to me.

"Looks as if we're providing some much needed entertainment." Matt chuckled against the top of my head.

"Yup. But just wait till Cammie starts dating again. I'll get even."

A group of a half dozen overweight bikers lumbered in. One, who wore a leather vest and pants, studded with metallic medallions of some sort, sprawled out in the chair next to us. Tattoos covered every inch of his exposed skin. Another identically dressed guy, except for a dirty bandana wrapped around his head, strolled over to the couch Matt

275

and I sat on, and looked meaningfully at the spot my feet occupied. I sat up and slapped my feet on the floor.

I waited for Matt to change places with me, or at least pull me closer. Instead he reached across me and shook the guy's hand.

"Dude," the guy said. He pulled a small New Testament out of his pocket. "We're here to pray with you folks."

Matt introduced me. "And these guys are with the Christian Motorcycle group at church."

I looked over to where Cammie and Hildie sat. One of the leather-clad men had already bowed his head to pray with them. Shifting my focus, I saw no one had bothered Daddy who still slept. I shook our prayer angel's hand and he led us in a short prayer for comfort and peace.

Little by little, other people from Cammie's church drifted in to sit with us, or offer prayer and well wishes. My heart overflowed with gratitude that all these people would take time from their day to minister to people they didn't even know. *I wish my mother could see this.* A cloud of well-being and love surrounded all of us.

Three hours passed and still we waited for word from the transplant unit. Matt squeezed my hand. "Don't worry," he said, after I'd looked at my watch for the millionth time.

At last somebody came out. "Hughes family?" A different person this time.

Cammie and I both jumped up. Hildie went over and woke Daddy. Every eye in the room turned in the direction of the speaker.

"Mrs. Hughes came through the surgery just fine. She's in the recovery room and as soon as the team feels she's ready, she'll be transferred to the transplant unit at the end of this hall." She gestured toward on of the four halls leading to the waiting room. "The doctor will be out to speak with you and fill you in on the details as soon as Mrs. Hughes is settled."

"Praise God."

276

"Amen."

"Thank You, Jesus."

People crowded around us, shaking our hands, patting our backs, and in general, loving on us. They left as quickly as they'd come in, leaving the room feeling empty. Cammie, Daddy and I hugged each other. Lastly, Matt hugged me and kissed my forehead. His hug cheered me the most.

We only had to wait another twenty minutes before the doctor appeared. "I'm sure you've been told that Mrs. Hughes came through the surgery with flying colors. We did a pancreas-kidney transplant. Because pancreas transplantation is currently the only treatment for diabetes that establishes consistent, normal blood-sugar levels, many times we choose to replace a failed kidney and a new pancreas simultaneously. What this means to her in the long run, barring rejection of the transplanted organs, is she will be able to live a normal life without the restrictions she's had before."

My mouth dropped open. I had no idea such a thing was possible.

"Because of the anti-rejection drugs she's getting, we're very careful about introducing any infection. I urge you to wash your hands before going in to see her, and if any of you have a cold or other illness, we ask that you postpone your visit with her till you're well."

Daddy rushed to the doctor and pumped his hand. "Thank you, doctor. Thank you for bringing my Maudie back to me."

I stepped forward. "Who was the donor? We want to thank the family for their wonderful sacrifice." The thought of someone having to lose their life to donate organs saddened me. I couldn't imagine losing someone and then having to make a decision whether to allow the hospital to harvest their organs.

"They've asked to be anonymous. But if you'd like to write them a letter, I'll see that it's forwarded to them."

Daddy asked, "How was it that Maude went to the top of the recipient list? We were told we'd have to find our own donor."

"I'm not altogether sure how that happened, other than it was a perfect match."

"A miracle, that's what." Hildie piped up. "God answered our prayers."

The doctor nodded his head. "I suppose you could call it that. At least there's no other explanation at this point. OK, if that's all your questions, I must get back to my patient. Wait for another hour or so and then check with the nurses' station at the transplant unit. They'll let you know when it's Ok to go back there for a visit."

As soon as the doctor strode out, we joined hands for a prayer of thanksgiving. Daddy prayed along with the rest of us.

***

Daddy went in to see Mother first, followed by Cammie, and then me. Our visits were limited to ten minutes each. We stuck around the hospital for a while, giving Daddy and Matt a chance to get to know each other. Hildie went on home, making us promise to call her if we needed to. Soon, they allowed Daddy to go in and sit, with the promise he wouldn't over tire her, so Matt took Cammie and I out to dinner.

After dinner, Cammie drove my car home and Matt and I went for a drive up on a hill overlooking the Puyallup Valley. Even through the misty rain, the lights below twinkled like stars on a clear night. Matt pulled over to a small outlook.

"Are we going to neck?" I joked.

"I suppose if you insist, I could be talked into it. But, I stopped so we could have a little quiet time together."

My face grew hot. Did he think I'd been too forward? "I was only kidding."

Matt chuckled. "I know." He tipped my chin up with his finger and planted a kiss full on my mouth.

278

Every nerve in my body tingled, and then screamed when he stopped the kiss. "Wow."

"My sentiments, exactly," Matt agreed. He shifted back to his side of the car. "I intend to experience many more "wows" with you in the future."

Nothing suited me better.

***

The next day, Mother improved hourly.

Matt and I sat with his sister and her family in church. Right afterward, he had to leave for the east coast again. "Remember, I'm only a flight away if you need me."

That afternoon, I unpacked some winter clothes and hung them in the closet. It didn't look as if I'd be moving anytime soon. That was OK. I enjoyed my little house, full of memories. The phone interrupted my unpacking.

"Sandy?"

"Charlie! Didn't I make it clear I didn't want to talk to you?" My hands shook. Matt's plane had probably already left.

"Don't hang up. I'm at the office. Your office. You haven't moved into the executive office yet. Why?"

I ground my teeth. "I don't want that job. I'm not even qualified for it. Bob is the one who should have taken over. And your threats to close the doors if we don't comply are nothing short of blackmail."

"But I did it for you. To give you security," he whined.

"I—don't—want—it." *Read my lips you fool.*

"I can't believe I wasted my time on such a stupid little—"

"I'm sorry too, Charlie. I'm sad for the loss of the friendship we used to have and can never have again because you ruined it."

"You ruined it, lady. You could have had it all and you've thrown it away."

"And you're a vindictive man." Fear ripped through me. Loss of my job. The impact on my coworkers. And it would be my fault.

279

"Lucky for you and your friends I can't afford to ruin my reputation in this community by letting my new firm slide into oblivion. As long as I'm stuck with it now, I might as well make some money off of it."

A ray of hope sliced through the gloom. "Does this mean everyone can keep their jobs?" *Including me? Not that I want to work for you.*

"Like I said. I want to make a profit. The firm has done quite well with its current staff. As long as that continues, everybody is safe. Does that satisfy you?"

Only if it's the truth. "Thank you, Charlie. You won't be sorry."

"Now, if you're through trying to bust my ego, I've got a certain secretary to call. I have a feeling she'd love to have dinner with the new owner." Charlie hung up with out any further threats.

I couldn't imagine who it was, but we'd had enough anti-harassment training at the office to warn off any potential victims. Charlie had better brace his feet for another letdown.

I went back to my room to finish hanging up my winter clothes. While going through the boxes, I spied the holiday decorations. I felt a smile overtake my face. This year the holidays would be full of love and family. I couldn't wait.

EPILOG

Maude's Journal
November 24, 2008

James and I move into our new home tomorrow. It's a new two-bedroom in an all-adult community. James took me to the community hall last week and we met some of the other residents. They seem really nice. I think I'll like it here. But I imagine I'll be way too busy to write my novel.

The best news is, I had another checkup today. The doctor told me there were still no signs of rejection. I couldn't wait to call Sandra and tell her. She doesn't know that James told me she'd offered to donate her own kidney. I'm not gonna tell her I know, either. Telling would only make us both uncomfortable. Now if she'd only quit hanging out with that G-man, she might prove she has a little sense.

Cammie is coming over in the morning before she leaves for the airport. Brian Chapman's parents sent her a plane ticket so she could go visit them. I guess Cammie at least deserves to know what half of her heritage is.

James has been going to church with Sandra every Sunday. Sometimes I go along. James doesn't nag me about it. I've waited for him to turn mean like my father was, but he just keeps on getting sweeter and sweeter.

Well, I must close now and turn out the light. James will be coming to bed soon.

###